ID0468320

6/12

# EVENTIDE

## BOOK ONE

TALES OF THE
DRAGON'S BARD

# EVENTIDE

TRACY & LAURA
HICKMAN

SHADOW
MOUNTAIN

© 2012 Tracy and Laura Hickman

All rights reserved. No part of this book may be reproduced in any form or by any means without permission in writing from the publisher, Shadow Mountain®. The views expressed herein are the responsibility of the authors and do not necessarily represent the position of Shadow Mountain.

Visit us at ShadowMountain.com

All characters in this book are fictitious, and any resemblance to actual persons, living or dead, is purely coincidental.

**Library of Congress Cataloging-in-Publication Data**

Hickman, Tracy, author.
   Eventide / Tracy and Laura Hickman.
      pages cm — (Tales of the dragon's bard ; book 1)
   Summary: When a traveling bard stumbles into a dragon's den, he is forced to tell it stories or be eaten. When he runs out of stories to tell, he makes a deal: if allowed to leave, he promises to return with more tales of adventure, romance, and bravery.
   ISBN 978-1-60908-897-2 (hardbound : alk. paper) 1. Dragons—Fiction. 2. Storytellers—Fiction. I. Hickman, Laura, 1956– author. II. Title. III. Series: Hickman, Tracy. Tales of the dragon's bard ; bk. 1.
   PS3558.I2297E94 2012
   813'.54—dc23                                         2012006217

Printed in the United States of America
Publishers Printing

10  9  8  7  6  5  4  3  2  1

*To the Unseen Citizens of Eventide:*
*Our Subscribers*

# Contents

# EVENTIDE

To Mordale

Mount Dervin

Fae Grotto

North Fields

To Welton

To Meade

To Blackshore

Boar's Island

To Butterfield

Wanderwine River

The Marshes

N

# The Dragon's Bard's
# Most Sincere Overture

I know what you're thinking! You've never seen a dragon at all—let alone any Dragonking named Khrag. You'd be right, friend, and it's my calling day and night to see to it that you *don't!* Now, you can discern with your own eyes that I'm no dragon slayer, but I keep old Khrag from burning down your door and savaging your town more surely than any knight who ever tilted a lance!

How? Why, good friend, I'm Edvard the Just! You've no doubt heard of me . . .

No?

But surely you've heard of the renowned Dragon's Bard, purveyor of peace—the Minstrel of Mystery who wanders the land in search of places, people, and their tales. The tales that save all innocents from the dragon's wrath.

That old and terrible monster Khrag, king of dragonkind, lies atop his hoard of inestimable wealth in a cavern deep among the roots of Mount Okalan, the accumulated treasure of a hundred wars beneath his deadly, ancient claws. It is as desirable a place as any dragon might long for all his long days, but dragons are creatures of adventure. Khrag lives for the stories told of the sunlit world so far above him and grows restless and angry when he is bored. But so long as his curiosity is satisfied, he'll rest at his ease in his dark home deep in the ground.

I chanced upon Khrag quite by odd circumstance. The humorless brothers of a discomfited young lady took umbrage at finding her name prominently featured in a fictional story of rejected love, and they unthinkingly threw me into the lair of the Dragonking. Khrag was then and remains an imposing creature who, upon my rushed acquaintance, was quite prepared to eat me at once. As he raised his razor-toothed head to strike, I said to him—for dragonkind all understand the language of men—I said:

"It is entirely too bad to come to so quick an ending, for this would have made an excellent story."

I stood humbly before the dragon, believing that I had told my final tale.

Yet the dragon—to my amazement and yours, too, I see—did *not* eat me! Instead he sat me down before him, surrounded by the gold of unnumbered kingdoms, and asked me, his great eyes gleaming, "You have stories? Perhaps I shall eat you later . . ."

Khrag hungered for stories, and I began immediately to tell him all the tales I knew. I told him all the great tales—those same epics and sagas you yourself have known since your youth. Tales of the House of Eldris—how Aubrey and his companions rallied the shattered and dispirited army of Duke Jonas the Unyielding in the Great Epic War and led them against the Nightmarch Warriors of Xander the Shadowmancer. Khrag became annoyed, and there is nothing more dangerous than an annoyed dragon. The tales were old to him. Indeed, Khrag had participated in many of these tales himself and was, I must tell you, frankly bored to dragon-tears with the same old legends of the great and powerful. So I switched at once to the tales from places of which no one has heard and of creatures whose stories are sung and praised only around small fires. Day and night were uncounted in the cavern, for my knowledge of stories is voluminous.

At last my tales ran dry. By this time I was haggard, thin, and quite worn out. I gazed up at the dragon with horrible expectation.

The dragon blew a puff of smoke from his left nostril, then spoke. "Good story—but now you have grown too gaunt, and eating you is no longer appealing to me. I think I shall find a nice village to terrorize with flame, burn to the ground, and utterly destroy."

Now, I did feel significant relief at not being eaten on the spot, and the inclination of any lesser man would have been to flee at once. I nearly gave in to such an impulse when a thought came to me: What of those villages, towns, ports, and cities? What of the women and children who lived their lives peacefully, not knowing that this Dragonking was planning to sweep all that they held dear away from them forever?

What a fine story *that* would make!

But, no! My great heart swelled within me and courage took hold in my breast.

"Mighty Khrag," I said, "there are many more stories across the land surrounding your lair. If you savage the countryside, they will be lost to you—to everyone. They are growing like unseen sweet truffles all around. All you need is someone to sniff them out for you. But if you go stomping about the world, you might ruin many quests and spoil their stories."

"I want more stories!" The dragon's great, greedy tongue flicked across his massive jowls as his eyes gleamed nearly as golden as his belly. Khrag reached forward, hooking one talon through my coat, and drew me closer as he growled, "You bag of bones! I'll leave your precious villages alone if only you come back every midsummer with your skinny carcass, a bag of truffles, and a head full of stories."

So it is that now I travel the face of our land, going from village to town, experiencing the lives, sights, and sounds of each place so that I might take them back to Khrag and . . .

I beg your pardon? Who? Oh, *that!* That is my apprentice, Abel. He is not terribly promising as a bard, but he is a faithful scribe— his ability to write and bind books is proving a somewhat useful addition to my already celebrated skills.

Oh, so you *read?* But of course you do! I knew at once that you were of that learned and educated class that has been trained in the art. Then perhaps I might interest you in this volume of mine, a true and accurate portrait of a village that might amuse you. You may have occasion to visit this charming locale, and such a book would serve you well, for it would acquaint you not only with the hamlet itself but with the inhabitants who live there. You would know where best to dine; where you might take your lodgings; the important eccentricities of the town's broken wishing well; the peculiar customs regarding gnomes, pixies, and haunts; and whom you might trust there, should occasion arise.

And the citizens of that village! This book will acquaint you well with them all: Tomas Melthalion and his tragic confrontation with the Highwayman Dirk Gallowglass over his daughter, Evangeline; the dwarven blacksmith Beulandreus Dudgeon, whose arts extend beyond iron and anvil; Jep Walters and the haunted adventures of the Black Guild Brotherhood; the gentle farmer Aren Bennis, whose past is a mystery; my good friend Jarod Klum, whose love will drive him to desperately glorious deeds; and, of course, Caprice Morgan, who keeps the wishing well supplied along with her two sisters. Indeed, Khrag himself said just before he fell into a satisfied sleep that he felt he knew them so well as to make the collection on the whole a treasure of inestimable worth.

And I have many such volumes now of different places where I have traveled, which may be made available to you at a price so trivial as to . . .

My pardon! The name of this town? But of course, you may read it plainly for yourself on the cover. Upside down? Really? Allow me, then . . .

It's called Eventide.

# CHASING ONE'S OWN TALE

*Wherein Jarod Klum meets unlikely
confederates who threaten to help him
win his true love . . . even if that means
turning him into a hero.*

## · CHAPTER 1 ·

# The Innkeeper's Glorious Service

Accounts apprentice Jarod Klum sat at his desk in the dim, chill confines of the countinghouse and dreamed up plans for his escape.

It was not just from the countinghouse itself that he wished for his release, although he did think it appropriate that the countinghouse doubled as Eventide's village lockup. Jarod considered himself a prisoner of his circumstances, held in the shackles of his trade, bound by the chains of his family traditions, and enslaved by fate. Here at this wooden desk and tall stool he spent his days learning the trade of counting other people's wealth, sitting among scrolls and ledgers as dusty and quiet as his own life.

Whenever possible, Jarod gazed out beyond the wavy glass panes of the window next to him and saw himself leaping over the snow-encrusted Cursed Sundial just across the Wanderwine River to the center of Charter Square. He would be brandishing a sword or a yardstick or whatever weapon was at hand. Caprice Morgan, the beautiful, green-eyed daughter of Meryl Morgan, would happen to be standing in the square, petrified with fear. A terrible monster with seven heads—or maybe nine—would be attacking the village up the frozen river as he took her protectively in the crook of his arm . . .

Or sometimes he imagined swinging from a rope out of Bolly's Mill just at the north end of Trader's Square, sweeping up the vivacious form of Caprice Morgan out of the clutches of marauding pirates who would somehow have gotten lost and wandered up the length of the Wanderwine River's frost-coated shoreline from the Blackshore Coast . . .

Or occasionally he would be at the head of a triumphant parade, with the enemies of the town in chains behind him as he rode a warhorse up Cobblestone Street. His crimson cape would billow in the winter wind as all the townsfolk turned out to cheer him—especially Caprice Morgan, who would look up admiringly through her grateful, tear-filled green eyes. He would reach down easily despite his brilliantly polished armor, grasping her waist and lifting her to sit in front of him as he . . .

The bell above the door jangled into life, jarring the young accountant back to his dreary world. A man with a narrow jaw and high cheekbones entered with a pronounced flourish of his very real if somewhat threadbare velvet cape. The chill winter air rushed past him into the room, billowing snow around his slight figure. His black mustache and beard, carefully trimmed to a point, only accentuated the general angularity of his appearance. His manner was far too flamboyant, but it was obvious to Jarod that excess in performance was not likely to be considered a bad thing by this man. His hat was an outrageous leather affair with a too-wide brim, in its band a feather from a roc that came nearly to the center of his back. He wore a thick, padded coat, kid gloves, and tall boots—the latter two items exceedingly fashionable and completely unsuitable for the weather. A bright doublet of red occasionally flashed through the open front of the coat with each gesture as he spoke. "I am Edvard the Just!" he cried, as though the counting room were filled with an appreciative audience instead of the one miserable accounts apprentice. "I am . . . the *Dragon's Bard!*"

Jarod stared at him and said, "Close the door."

"Surely you've heard of me," the outrageously costumed man said through a beaming smile.

"Nope," Jarod answered simply.

Instead of disappointment, Edvard bestowed upon Jarod a look of genuine if misguided pity.

The biting wind swirled icy snow into the room through the open doorway. The Dragon's Bard was followed into the room almost at once by a short, slightly underweight young man who was nearly overwhelmed by a shouldered pack. Behind him came Xander Lamplighter, Eventide's Constable Pro Tempore for the last eight years. The large constable with the intimidating scowl was known as one of the gentlest men in all of Windriftshire and one who also had an uncanny knack for catching pixies—a very troublesome local menace.

"Morning, Xander," Jarod said with as much warmth as the room would allow.

"'Tain't nothing good about it," Xander replied as he pushed the door forcefully closed against the wind behind him. "Where's Ward?"

"Gone over to the Widow Kolyan's bakery," Jarod said, though his eyes were on the pair of strangers and the growing pool of melting snow on the floor at their feet.

"Again?" Xander said, pulling off his thick gloves. "What's her problem this time?"

"She claims that pixies keep magically changing her account balances no matter how many times Father goes over them with her. He could be quite a while." Jarod shrugged, then reached over for an enormous leather-bound journal on his father's desk next to his own. He opened the book and pulled a fresh quill from a collection he kept in a mug on his desk. Sharpening quills often took his mind off Caprice on long winter afternoons. It was becoming difficult to find an unsharpened quill anywhere in the office. "You here for the lockup?"

"It's not necessary at all, I assure you," Edvard said quickly before anyone else's thought might intrude on his own. "I am Edvard, and this is Abel, my apprentice. We are mere travelers passing through this charming village . . ."

"Vagrancy . . ." Jarod muttered half to himself as he carefully dipped the quill in the inkwell.

"No, good sir! I assure you we are but storytellers . . ."

"Liars," Jarod said to himself.

"We go from town to town spreading cheer and wonder . . ."

"Ah, rogues," Jarod noted on a parchment he had pulled from his desk, not wanting to risk the vellum of the arrest ledger until he had all the particulars.

"Never! We are honest men who take it upon ourselves to gather stories from everywhere we go . . ."

"Thieves," Jarod commented. He was writing as quickly as possible on the parchment, trying to catch up on the litany of evils he was concocting for the official record.

"Begging your pardon, Jarod, but that ain't why I arrested 'em," Xander spoke up.

Jarod looked up, relieved he had not inked any of this onto the precious vellum just yet. He had intended to make a more careful copy in the book so that his father would not have any further excuse to criticize his work. "Oh, of course, Xander—sorry. Constable, of what are these men accused?"

Xander straightened up and squared his wide shoulders. "These men were arrested by me—Constable Pro Tempore Xander Lamplighter—on charges of suspicious activities and annoying behavior."

Jarod looked up from his scratch parchment sheet. "Is that a crime, Xander?"

"'Tis so far as I'm concerned," Xander said with the conviction of a man who had no idea that he was wrong. "The complaint were lodged by the Widow Merryweather and several other ladies of Cobblestone Street at the insistence of Ariela Soliandrus."

"The Gossip Fairy?" Jarod smiled. "She's the one who's behind this?"

Xander blushed. "Well, this-here gentleman—" the constable gestured at the Dragon's Bard—"he were asking the ladies all sort of questions 'bout they personal lives and pasts and such."

"Which," Edvard interrupted, "they provided most graciously and freely, I might add."

"Free or no," Xander continued with a cold glance in the Bard's direction, "when Miss Ariela arrived and heard what were happening, she flew straight away to each lady's ear and told 'em that this-here stranger were a bounder and were using his wiles and magic and such to ruin them all and most likely murder them in their beds this very night and steal they best clothes!"

Jarod had stopped writing. "The Gossip Fairy told them this man would murder them in their beds?"

"Aye," Xander nodded, then blushed again. "That or—well, you know—ravish them mercilessly."

Now it was Jarod's turn to blush. "You mean . . ."

"Well, that were what the Gossip Fairy said," Xander sputtered. "It were a good thing, too, or I might not have gotten these two free of them women without them doing some harm to 'em. Widow Merryweather were ready to do 'em in with her hatpin right there in the street, and Missus Taylor swore if someone would point her to a cutlass she'd run 'em through on the spot. But then the ladies fell to arguing about which among them were most likely to be ravished, and that gave me time to get these gents here to the lockup whilst they were still debating among themselves."

Jarod closed the arrest ledger. He thought briefly of the strangely dressed man in front of him carrying off Caprice Morgan and how he, Jarod, might rescue her. In that moment, he knew he could not possibly write any of this in the ledger. Better to leave it to his father, who, he considered wisely, might be able to keep a steadier hand about such things than he could. "This is a matter for my father to consider," Jarod said, sounding as official as he could. "You'll just have to wait until he returns."

Xander groaned.

"Is that a problem?" Jarod asked.

"Well, look here, Jarod," the constable whined. "I've got to see ol' Dudgeon about that new banded-iron door for the lockup in the basement, see. That's where I were going when all this started, and you know how he gets about folks what's late. Look here, these two are considered prisoners now, ain't they?"

"Aye," Jarod nodded. "You arrested them, so I don't see why they wouldn't be."

"Well, it be coming up on noon as it is," Xander said. "These prisoners are under the care of the village, so they need to be fed."

"I don't see what . . ."

"Well, you could take 'em over to the Inn while I see the blacksmith . . . get 'em both some lunch and a bit for yourself as well," Xander's voice seemed to gather speed as the idea took form in his head. "You can tell the Squire I said to put it on the village accounts."

Jarod grinned. He would do about anything to get out of the countinghouse, stretch his legs, and let some time pass with a more pleasant speed. "Why, that would be our duty, wouldn't it, Xander? I'd be glad to help."

The assistant to the Dragon's Bard had said nothing, but he rolled his eyes as the conversation came to its mutually beneficial conclusion.

"Yes, I think that should just about solve everyone's problems." Xander smiled back as he reached for the door. A cold blast of wind, snow, and bright light burst into the room, and Xander was gone, the door closing firmly behind him.

Jarod hopped off the stool and walked across the fitted floorboards to a row of pegs arranged with careful and equal spacing on the wall. He plucked a heavy, hooded cloak from a peg. Jarod was all arms and legs, tall and muscular but not yet grown into his grace. He had a handsome face that was still a little soft, with no real beard to speak of. A few stray hairs along the ridges of his jawline made a valiant if lonely effort at a beard, but their population was not yet sufficient for a reasonable quorum to convene. He was a man striving to break out of being a youth. He was not quite free of his chrysalis—a butterfly who did not know that his wings were still wet.

Jarod pulled the cloak about his body, turned to his two charges, and said, "Well, come on. Let's get . . . oh, bosh! I almost forgot!"

Jarod rushed past his prisoners to the desk next to his own. There, hanging from a hook at the side of the desk, was a set of keys on a looped steel ring. Jarod snatched the ring from the hook a little too quickly, pulling the desk slightly across the floor with a grating sound. The young man gave a quick look of exasperation, stepped back to the desk, and carefully pushed it back into its accustomed alignment.

"My dad is very particular," Jarod said with a quick, nervous smile. "Come on."

"Indeed we shall," Edvard chimed in with his usual overwarm grace and exaggerated charm. "Show us the way, my good friend Jarod, and we shall follow in your steps as boon companions!"

"What?" Jarod was not sure what the man was talking about, but he ushered both the Bard and his companion, who obviously suffered in silence, through the door.

The bright sun shone down through a clear winter sky, its light reflecting off the snow that still covered areas of the square. A bitter wind cut through the town out of the north, blowing stinging snow—ice crystals formed from the previous partial thaw—that caused Edvard to grip the brim of his hat against the moaning gale and Jarod to hold the edge of his hood down so that he might protect his eyes. That was of little help, since any moisture had been frozen out of the air and Jarod was forced to blink anyway just to keep his eyes moist. The apprentice gently pushed the Bard and his servant out of his way as he turned to the door of the countinghouse and, using one of the keys on the enormous ring, locked it behind him.

"So, my good man, tell me," Edvard began, pitching his voice to carry over the wind. "Have you lived in this charming town all your life?"

"Yeah, that's about right." Jarod glanced at the Bard and then started walking northward across the large square.

Edvard quickly fell into step next to him, leaving Abel, with his weighty and overstuffed backpack, struggling to keep up. "Then perhaps you might acquaint me with your village. This square, for instance: what is its history and what deeds have been played out upon its surface?"

Jarod shrugged as he walked, his head turning slightly toward the Bard as they walked. "Well, this is Trader's Square. There's a lot of selling that goes on here during the spring and through fall harvest. It's not actually a market because the village elders don't want to become a township, so they just call it Trader's Square rather than an actual market, see?"

Edvard nodded and smiled, but he clearly had no idea what the young man was saying to him. "What's that large building over there?"

"That?" Jarod glanced up at the long architectural hodgepodge that lined the northwest side of the square. "That's the Guild Hall. That road beyond it goes to Meade, maybe five leagues to the west. South, back there," Jarod pointed behind them, "that's Cobblestone Street and Chestnut Court—but then you were arrested there, so I guess you know all about those. Up there," he pointed ahead of them this time, "is Bolly's Mill. It's just above Bolly Falls there on the Wanderwine."

They came to the northeast edge of the square, which was defined by the steep banks of the Wanderwine River. A low wall of fitted stone ran from the mill all along the riverbank on both sides, with a stone bridge crossing just before the falls and connecting

Trader's Square to another square lined with buildings on the far side of the river.

Edvard stopped on the bridge for a moment, gazing at the wide waterfall just to his north. "So that is the famed Bolly Falls!"

Jarod looked back at him. "No."

"But you just said . . ."

"We call it Bolly Falls, but that's not its name," Jarod replied.

"Ah," Edvard replied, but Jarod continued walking over the bridge, and the Bard and his companion were again forced to catch up.

"This is Charter Square," Jarod continued. "Cooper Walters is there on the right. Across the square are a lot of smaller shops— Charon's Goods is nice and Mordechai will treat you right. King's Road is there just left of the shops . . . that way takes you to the smithy if you need something repaired. There in the middle of the square is the Cursed Sundial, and over here on the left is the Griffon's Tale Inn, where . . ."

"A cursed sundial?" Edvard exclaimed as he quickly strode over to the pedestal, gazing at the charred and cracked surface peeking out from beneath the snow. "What deep mystery is there here, my good friends! How came this place to become cursed? What tragic story unfolded at this very spot where time itself was assaulted by . . ."

"Come on," Jarod urged as he crossed the square to the north where a building nearly three stories tall looked down over the street. A large ornamental sign swung noisily from the iron bracket: a crest with a griffon emblazoned on it with a long tail winding around its body. The lettering proclaimed it the *Griffon's Tale Inn*. "Let's get inside."

Jarod opened the door, and Edvard, seeing another chance to

make an entrance, rushed into the opening and flourished his cape as he bowed deeply.

"Good day and good morrow to one and all," Edvard proclaimed, his voice carrying past the great room in which they stood and probably well past the kitchen beyond. "Let no fear enter your hearts, for I have come to ward off the evil that is nigh upon you. I am . . . *the Dragon's Bard!*"

There were two humans in the great room and a gnome in one far corner. Each looked up at the interruption in mild curiosity. A third human near the large fireplace in the far wall did not even move.

Harv Oakman squinted for a moment. "What was that again?"

"'Tis I," Edvard crowed once more. "The Dragon's Bard!"

Harv shook his head. "Sorry, don't know it."

Squire Tomas Melthalion broke the awkward moment as he hurried into the room from the kitchen, slamming the door shut behind Jarod and his charges with his shoulder even as he wiped his wide hands on an already filthy apron. "Friends of yours, eh, Master Klum? Well, welcome to the Griffon's Tale Inn, which—as the proprietor of this-here establishment I can tell you—has been in this location since even before the founding of the village itself."

"Thank you, good Squire Tomas," Edvard replied in sudden earnest. "But I come on a matter of great urgency, which . . ." Edvard stopped and pointed at a dark, hunched figure seated by the great fireplace.

"Oh . . . him! Do not concern yourself with Lord Gallivant over there—no one knows his real name—he just sits in the corner talking to his own memories. But as you'll no doubt be needing a place to lodge, have you heard the story of the great service that I, myself, did for the King when he passed by the village not far from this very spot?"

"Ah, and you touch on my very point at last," the Dragon's Bard began. "This beautiful village of Ever-tide . . ."

"Eventide," Jarod corrected.

"Of course . . . Eventide . . . this very selfsame beautiful village is in the gravest of danger. The great and terrible Khrag—King of Dragons—has sent me here to collect stories for his amusement, and unless . . ."

"Stories! Oh, I've a story for you!" Tomas exclaimed.

Jarod groaned. Tomas pressed the stranger down into a chair.

"Here, sit you down next to our resident Lord Gallivant and let this Squire tell you about it! Of course, he was not the King then, and some might have said that the service done was nothing of any real importance, but when you hear how . . ."

"Squire," Jarod spoke up, "these men are hungry—please bring them dinner."

"Now?" Tomas sputtered. "But I was just about to tell these travelers . . ."

"Yes, but they have both been arrested by the Constable Pro Tempore, and I must get these dangerous men back under lock and key soon," Jarod explained. "Of course, if you don't want the village's coins for their dinners, then I can take them right back and . . ."

"No bother! No bother," Tomas replied as he hurried off.

"Are you getting all of this?" Edvard said sotto voce to Abel.

Abel only nodded, not quite keeping up.

As Abel scribbled furiously on a large parchment scroll, Edvard inquired why Jarod had stopped the innkeeper from telling him the story.

"Look, Mister Dragon's Beard . . ."

"Bard," Edvard said through a tight smile. "Dragon's *Bard*."

"Well, if you're really interested in hearing the Squire's story," Jarod continued, "then I'm sure that the Squire would be more than happy to tell it while dinner is served . . . then refresh your memory of the telling by telling it again while you're leaving the Inn . . . and again anytime, for that matter, that you come within earshot of the Squire. Believe me, there's practically no avoiding it, as anyone in the town can pretty well attest, including me."

"And this fellow here—this Lord Gallivant?" Edvard asked, gesturing toward the gaunt and grizzled man who sat muttering to himself near the fire. His clothing was faded and nearly threadbare; he wore a military cape that looked older than the Epic War itself.

Jarod shrugged. "Don't know . . . nobody knows. He's been here as long as I can remember."

"So what about your story, eh?" the Dragon's Bard asked.

"Don't have one," Jarod answered with a deep-felt sigh.

Abel stopped scribbling at once, glancing up questioningly.

"Then we shall write you one," the Dragon's Bard offered cheerfully. "No! Better still, we shall help you to live one! Tell me, are there any women in your life?"

Jarod eyed him with suspicion. "Why do you ask?"

The Dragon's Bard smiled. "Because every young man's great story begins with a woman!"

# CHAPTER 2

# Wishers of the Well

aprice Morgan leaned her seventeen-year-old face over the edge of the wishing well, her elbows resting on the cool stone edge and her elegant hands, embarrassingly calloused, cupping her small chin and smooth—if smudged—cheeks. Her carefully combed auburn hair fell around her face. Her wide green eyes gazed down the circular shaft of the well, trying to see something of her own future, though she knew that even if the well *were* working properly, it was not a scrying pool and could not possibly know her future. Still, she leaned against the edge and peered into it.

Her future, if the well were to be believed, was dark.

The village had been founded largely around the Inn, but the Inn had come into existence to serve the travelers who for ages untold had come to the wishing well. The well, in use since the time of legends, sat in the woods northwest of the town, snugly surrounded by the Norest Forest near the foot of Mount Dervin, the highest point in three counties. For centuries the well had been tended by the wish-women—heiresses to enchantment, blessed with knowledge of wishcraft—who kept the well supplied from the magic of the surrounding woods. Dwarves, elves, humans, and others of all ranks and classes would make their way to the well from their distant homes to make wishes come true. The Griffon's Tale Inn was built to serve those pilgrims, and the town grew up around the Inn.

This great, long, and profitable tradition kept the town safe and secure—until a wizard came one day with a wish that was too big for the well to grant. Brenna Morgan, the High Wish-Woman at the time, failed to please the wizard or fulfill his terrible wish. In dreadful anger, the wizard broke the wishes of the well with a curse that would last until the sundial in Charter Square heralded both sunrise and sunset at the same time.

It was a blow to the economy of the village but a disastrous tragedy for Meryl Morgan and his three daughters. The breaking of the well also broke Brenna's magical ability and her health. She faded away, this wish-woman who had tended the well since long before her wedding to Meryl, and he was left with his three daughters to struggle on without her. Their girls—Sobrina, Caprice, and Melodi—were natural talents at gathering wishes, as their mother had been, but none of them had the opportunity or the wealth to be properly trained in wishcraft at the Enchanting Academy in Mordale. So each gathered what meager wishes she could to keep the well going.

But the wishes that were now granted from the well always had something peculiarly wrong with them. That they would grant the desires of the wisher was true, but the boon from the well always came in unpredictable and occasionally disastrous ways. One man wished for untold wealth—only to have a sum appear that was too small to mention. A woman asked for renowned beauty—only to find herself the talk of all the Ogre lands. One very unfortunate young lady presumptuously wished that her boyfriend would "grow up." He thereafter could only find employment as the "tall boy" in Captain Kobold's Carnival of Freaks.

Although the pilgrims quit coming for the broken wishes of the well, the sisters were able—if barely—to make a living by supplying smaller wishes to the villagers nearby. But such wishes came hard for the wisher-women of the well, and it seemed as though they never had any wishes of their own left over.

"Caprice!"

The sound of her name echoing through the surrounding woods drew the wisher-woman back from her dark reflections at the well.

"Capriiiiice!" came the distant sound.

"Coming, Sobrina," she called back.

Caprice turned from the well and stepped out of the gazebo that enclosed it. It once had been a beautifully maintained lattice structure that rose gracefully to a point exactly above the well. Now the paint that had protected it from the elements was badly weathered, and pieces of the ornamental carvings had fallen into such decay that some of them were no longer recognizable. Short pieces of the latticework had also fallen down and lay kicked to one side or the other. The ground about the well was covered in glittering white where ice crystals had formed on the crest of the snowfall. There were paths trodden down through the snow that led from the wintry glade down the slope from the well to Wishing Lane and more narrow paths that led into the surrounding forest of trees in their winter sleep. Caprice knew them all because she and her sisters had made them in their continuous work at keeping wishes in their well.

She paused by the rusting iron box next to the gazebo. The lock had long since broken and there had never been enough coin to have it fixed. She raised the lid on the box quickly, half out of habit and half out of hope. The hinges squealed terribly into the silence of the woods around her.

The box was empty.

Caprice slammed the lid shut with a clang and pulled her thick shawl closer around her shoulders. It had been an impulse to look in the box, and now she felt both angry and foolish for having done so. She knew that there had been times in the past—her father's past—when that box had had to be emptied morning and afternoon because of the grateful donations that had been left in it by wishers at the well. There had been more wealth than even the wish-women could have wished for, which, Caprice reminded herself, would never have worked anyway because wish-women wishing their own wishes from the wishes they collected formed a complete circle, which was forbidden by the basic rules of wishcraft—or so her mother had told them when they were young.

Not that she or any of her sisters actually knew much of anything about the craft, she thought darkly as she plodded down the path to the lane below. Her mother had taught them the basics at home. It was part of their family life—especially after her mother had delivered a third daughter into the household. Her mother told each of them that when the time was right they would be sent to the Enchanting Academy in Mordale and learn proper wishcraft. But that was before the well was cursed, the wishes were broken, and her mother passed away.

Caprice reached the lane. Left would take her farther down to the banks of the Wanderwine River and the footbridge that eventually crossed the river to the Mordale road and Eventide. She turned to the right instead and followed the more narrow lane around a low hill and into Wisher's Hollow.

Her home was in the shadow of a grand edifice only partly

realized. The foundations had been laid for a palatial structure with grand turrets at the corners and cone-peaked roofs. A quarter of the intended building had been fully finished by Meryl Morgan at the insistence of his wife, Brenna, so that they might live there while the rest of the house was completed. Thus the kitchen, pantries, and what would have been servants' quarters were finished, with the archways to the imagined rooms beyond boarded over. The stone for the walls, the tools, the hods, piles of timber, and frayed bags of sand lay stacked under the blanketing snow. They had seen many such snowfalls down the long and painful years, hiding the memory of their abandoned hopes.

Thin smoke rose from the chimney, curling over with the chill northern breeze falling down the side of Mount Dervin beyond. A tall, thin figure stood on the porch still calling out her name.

"Capriiiiiiiiice!"

"Here!" she replied as loudly as she could, risking the release of one side of her shawl to wave her gloved hand.

Sobrina, standing on the step, looked in her direction and then turned, reentering the house. Caprice knew that it was all the acknowledgement she would get. She continued down the lane to the finished portion of the house, carefully climbed the short steps onto the porch, opened the door, and stepped inside.

She stopped momentarily in the mudroom, pulling her shawl from her shoulders and hanging it on a wall peg. She tugged at the shoes on her feet, impatient about unlacing them, and finally managed to get them off. Then she slid her feet into her slippers and donned an apron. She didn't much care for the apron and would have eschewed wearing it if possible. Her elder sister's presence nearby made such a choice impossible.

Caprice entered the kitchen and was struck by a flood of

sensations: the wet warmth of cooking and the smell of boiling on-ions and cabbage. She heard the hiss of the stew as it boiled over the edges of the iron pot suspended above the fire and the faint humming of her sister Melodi as she sat completely lost in the book she was reading in the corner. A long wooden spoon stirred the pot seemingly on its own while Sobrina leaned over the table in the center of the kitchen, her left index finger running down the lines of a recipe in the narrow book while her right hand twisted behind her in the air as without thought she projected her magic to move the spoon in the pot. Everything in the kitchen seemed timed to the gentle, rhythmic creaking of the rocking chair in the inglenook next to the fireplace, where their father sat staring into the flames that never seemed to warm him.

"How is the well?" Sobrina asked, her eyes never leaving the recipe in the book. Sobrina was thin and taller than her sisters. She had a narrow chin like Caprice's that her father said favored their mother. Her hair was flaxen and long. It may have been her one vanity, for she combed it faithfully every night, and Caprice knew that it extended well past her narrow waist. But during the day, and on those occasions when she visited the town, she always wore her hair tightly wound into a bun at the nape of her neck, pulled back in such a way that it seemed to pull at her face as well, making it impossible to tell if her stiff smile was genuine. She affected a cold distance with the townspeople, a fortress of ice that kept her inner pain secure and the world at a distance.

"I've stocked it in case anyone happens by in the night," Caprice answered as she reached back to bind her long, auburn hair. "It was thin wish-gathering in the woods today. I found a fairy nest, though, and that provided enough wishes to supply the well for the night." She called across the room, "Good evening, Father!"

Meryl looked up, blinking as though he were returning from a far place. "Oh, good evening, Caprice."

"How was your day?"

"Better, I think," Meryl answered. "I think tomorrow I might just get out and do something about the foundation walls on the expansion. It's the next step, you know. I think tomorrow would be a good day to take it up again, don't you?"

"Of course, Father," Caprice replied. Meryl had vowed to take up some aspect of finishing the home every day since their mother had died, but somehow each day had gone by without him being able to pick up a hammer or chisel.

"Melodi, would you get the bowls?" Sobrina asked, though it was not spoken as a question.

"Oh, gladly," Melodi answered, glancing up from behind her book. She flicked her wrists four times and, with a whump sound, four ornate bowls appeared on the table, clattering as they settled abruptly onto the surface. The sound made Sobrina jump.

"Melodi! Pay attention!" Sobrina said as she straightened up. The forgotten spoon, no longer enchanted, slowed with the stew in the pot. "What is that book your nose has been in so long?"

"This?" Melodi looked up. Melodi would have been considered pretty were she not constantly eclipsed by her sisters. As it was, she had a voluptuous form, an upturned nose and an easy, seemingly perpetual, mischievous smile. The only feature she had inherited from her mother was her raven black hair, which she often coaxed into tight curls.

It was rare that Sobrina took any interest in her reading, and Melodi delighted in the chance to talk about it. She stood at once and leaned over the table. "It's absolutely wonderful! It's called *Drakeskeep*—the tale of a fortress near a dragon's lair. There's this wonderful story about this Lady of the Keep who falls for this ne'er-do-well Bard and her three brothers find out about them and—"

Sobrina rolled her dark eyes. "Melodi, you know we can't afford—"

"Oh, I didn't buy it!" Melodi countered.

"I should hope not!" Sobrina sniffed.

"I found it."

Sobrina's eyes narrowed as she looked at her sister. "Found it?"

"Yes," Melodi said as she sat down on one of the four mismatched stools surrounding the table. "I was gathering wishes around the Fae Grotto and went a little too far south through the woods. I found an abandoned camp off the Meade road, and the book was just lying there."

"Melodi, nobody just abandons a camp," Sobrina said in her sternest voice. "That book belongs to someone, and you'll take it back first thing in the morning."

"Very well." Melodi frowned slightly but there was still a twinkle in her eyes. "I'll have finished it by then anyway."

Caprice took the spoon out of the pot, her enchantment twisting it into a ladle. "How long will the bowls last, Mel?"

"Half an hour, I think," she answered, turning the bowl in her hands as she examined it. "I patterned them after a description from the book. Do you like them?"

"They're lovely," Caprice replied as she ladled stew into each of the bowls.

Melodi beamed.

Caprice helped their father to the table, then took her place. The bowls would vanish after dinner; anything remaining of their meal would fall into the bucket into which the bowls had been placed. The ladle, too, would disappear, as would the shining forks and knives

Melodi had provided. She was the most talented of the three, it was true, but, as Caprice reflected, in the end it would not matter. The enchantments always ended, their small magics were but temporary, and their lives remained as broken as the wishing well they tended.

The Morgans took hands around the table and bowed their heads to thank the gods for the wishes of the day.

Caprice opened her eyes. Looking into the bowl of stew, all she saw was an empty well of wishes.

"Caprice?" the Dragon's Bard repeated. "That's her name, then?"

Jarod had once jumped off a cart as a boy. It had been going too fast, and no matter how fast he ran, his feet could not catch up with his body and he finally crashed, sliding across the ground. He had known he was going to fall but he had kept desperately running anyway.

The rush of words coming out of him gave him the same feeling.

"Yes! She's the most beautiful . . . I mean . . . if you could just see her . . . not that you should see her . . . but if you *did* see her you'd know . . . there are other girls . . . women, I mean . . . or girls . . . who I know and they're fine . . . some of them more than fine . . . but not all . . . but they're nothing compared to . . . well, just her green eyes alone . . . and her hair, and . . . well, you know . . . well, you don't *know* . . . and if you ever laid a hand on her . . . which you *wouldn't* because I'd . . ."

Edvard put his hand on the boy's shoulder, which somehow managed to make his mouth come to an abrupt halt. The Dragon's Bard gazed into Jarod's eyes with all the earnest intensity he could muster. "So, I take it that you've explained your feelings to her in just these words, then?" he intoned.

Jarod and the Bard were sitting facing each other from high-backed benches on opposite sides of a table near the stained-glass window of the Inn. Abel sat behind them, enjoying the company of his pack while he continued to listen to the conversation and write.

"It's hopeless," Jarod said. "I try to talk to her, but every time I do, my mouth opens and no sound comes out. My jaw works up and down, and for all the world I must look like a fish that's just been pulled out of the river and is flopping around on the stones."

"And what does she do?" Edvard asked.

"She just looks at me with those wonderful, big green eyes and then takes pity on me, I guess, and goes away to relieve me of my suffering," Jarod moaned. He leaned forward. "I tried writing sonnets, but then I wasn't sure whether she could read or not. I thought of trying to get someone else to read them to her, but I would be too embarrassed to ask another girl to read them out loud, and if I asked another fellow to do it, she might mistake my sonnets as coming from him, and that would be awful. Then, what if she *could* read and thought that my sonnets were crude or stupid? I composed a ballad, but how could I possibly sing to her when I can't even speak two words in her direction?"

Jarod dropped his head heavily down on the table.

"She is so wonderful," Jarod mumbled into the table. "And I'm only Jarod Klum."

Jarod felt the jarring of boots swinging up onto the table. He looked up. The Dragon's Bard was leaning back on his bench with a broad smile on his face.

"Perhaps I can help," Edvard said with a twinkle in his eye. "Have you ever considered becoming someone *else?*"

## · CHAPTER 3 ·

# Farmer Bennis

H ow can I be someone else?" Jarod asked, his warm breath billowing out in front of him in the chill air. He glanced at the charred sundial as they passed it in the middle of the square and wondered if its curse were about to extend to him personally.

"We're all trying to be someone else," Edvard mused as they walked back across the bridge to Trader's Square. "That, my friend, is the very essence of the theatrical experience! The ability to enlarge oneself above the mundane and the ordinary and to become the ideal . . . the stuff of true heroes! I have no small experience in this, Master Jarod. I should be delighted to be of service to you in your conquest of the fair Caprice."

Jarod was not altogether sure he understood what the Dragon's Bard was saying—and what he thought he understood he did not like hearing. "If you lay one finger on her, I swear I'll—"

The Dragon's Bard gripped Jarod by his shoulders, stopping him in mid-stride and turning him around so as to face him. "No! It is for *you* that we shall create such an air of mystery, such a cloud of desire, such a glorious haze of allurement that your fair Caprice shall be powerless to resist you! You shall woo her as I have said, and win her with both heart and head. Then to her you shall soon be wed . . . and take her to your warm soft bed!"

Jarod flushed in the bright winter afternoon.

Abel struggled along behind them, trying to write; his orders apparently included capturing in print every immortal word that fell from the lips of his master. The pack filled with his belongings occasionally slipped off his shoulders, making his writing as awkward as his master's rhyme.

Trader's Square was starting to come to life. There were only a few cart stalls, which their vendors had wheeled across the fitted cobblestones and in which they were now setting up their wares in the bitter cold of the winter afternoon. They would be there with their wares for the warmest hours of the chill day before carting them back home at night. Even now a few of them were issuing half-hearted calls out to those few villagers who were passing through the square. Unbidden, Jarod imagined the highwayman—the dreaded Dirk Gallowglass—riding suddenly into the square with the fearful Caprice Morgan slung across the back of his midnight-colored horse. Jarod would spring to Shaun Slaughter's cart and turn to confront the rogue, holding a butcher knife firmly in one hand while swinging a string of linked sausage menacingly in the other.

"Master Jarod?" Edvard again put a restraining arm on the young man's shoulder.

Jarod was so preoccupied with his envisioned heroics that he had nearly run into a lamppost in the square. He turned quickly to face the Dragon's Bard. "All right! I *do* need your help. What do I do?"

"I should be delighted, as I said, to assist you in winning the heart of your fairest of all damsels." Edvard's voice had that lyrical quality that so often endears one to the foolish and irritates those who have been taken in by it before. His carefully trimmed beard quivered with excitement before his countenance fell into sorrow and despair. "Alas, as you so well know, I am a prisoner of this good village—under the warrantless charge brought against me by the otherwise good ladies of this same Cobblestone Street on which we stand. How can I possibly help you if I am locked up in the depths of your most secure and punishingly chill dungeons? I do not mind for myself, you understand, but what of my poor assistant?"

Abel looked up with a skeptical eye. Of the two of them, he was by far the more suitably dressed for the weather.

"Fine!" Jarod said as they reached the northern wall of the countinghouse. "I'll talk to my father. He's on the village council and . . . well, maybe we can work something out . . . but you keep your promise!"

Jarod and the Dragon's Bard turned the corner of the building together in such earnest conversation that they did not see the enormous creature standing in front of the countinghouse door before running squarely into its blanketed flanks.

"Begging your pardon, Master Jarod, but you should pay more attention to where we are—by the heavens!" Edvard exclaimed as he backed hastily away several steps.

Edvard's upward gaze was met by the deep-set stare of an enormous centaur that more than filled the Bard's vision. The beast was large even among others of his kind—more like a draft horse or warhorse in size as compared to the much lighter thoroughbreds or show hunters. His arms were larger than Jarod's thighs. He wore a padded coat over his doublet and a thick but well-worn caparison that extended from the base of his torso back over his flanks. His wide head was topped by a beaten leather hat with a brim whose original color and shape could only be guessed.

His hair was long, as most centaurs wore it, but it had gone grey, and even under his hat it was evident that his hairline had receded so far as to leave his forehead a wide beach at low tide. His face was broad and strong, but wrinkles had disturbed and softened the original angular lines. His chin was covered in pronounced grey stubble.

The centaur had been engaged in conversation with a thin, haggard-looking man, but the latter was both literally and figuratively overshadowed by the gigantic being.

"Our apologies, Farmer Bennis," Jarod called up, his breath forming momentary clouds in the frosty, still air.

"Good day, Master Jarod," the centaur replied in a deep, resonant voice, though his eyes remained on the Dragon's Bard. "I don't believe that I am acquainted with your companions . . ."

"I *know* you." Edvard blinked. "I'm just sure of it."

Jarod glanced at the Dragon's Bard and shrugged. "This is Edvard the Just. He's some kind of bard and that's . . . uh . . . well, that's his apprentice. Xander asked me to take them over to the Inn for lunch before locking them up, since he had to go . . ."

"They're prisoners, Jarod?" The haggard-looking man was Ward Klum. He wore a round cap with a silver tassel that signified his office as a Master in the Counting Guild. The elder Klum made a habit of holding his head in such a way that the brim of his cap remained completely level with the ground. He wore a long black coat that uncomfortably reminded Jarod of a shroud. A tall man with a hooked nose, he looked out from beneath his thick, bushy eyebrows at the accounts apprentice with all the painful wariness that only a father can bestow upon his son. "Did you enter their names in the arrest ledger?"

"No, sir, you see, I—"

"But that's the very first thing you should do when they're presented for arrest!"

"Yes, sir, but—"

"And then you just took them over to the Squire's for lunch?"

"Well, Xander said that I should . . ."

Ward Klum shook his head. "Until their names are entered into the arrest ledger, they aren't officially under the protection of the town, Jarod. There's a proper order to things here in Eventide that must be followed, especially in our office."

A dark chuckle rumbled from the centaur, cutting under the squawk of a gaggle of geese being herded into Trader's Square.

"Don't be so hard on the boy, Ward," Bennis said with a deep, warm laugh. "Jarod, if Xander arrested them, then where is he? They're supposed to be under his charge."

The Dragon's Bard had closed one eye and was peering at the farmer with the other.

Jarod was relieved to have the questions asked about anyone other than himself. He had never thought much about Farmer Bennis. He knew that the centaur worked his own farm north of town on the Mordale road past Wishing Lane, but the apprentice had never been out so far as to see it. Aren Bennis occasionally had dealings with his father, but they always made a point of speaking out of his hearing or taking their business elsewhere. Otherwise "the old half-horse"—as some in the town called him—kept mostly to his farm and himself.

"The Constable Pro Tempore said that he had an appointment with Beulandreus about a new door for the lockup," Jarod said. "I was trying to get the charges from him to write them in the arrest ledger—just like you told me to, Father—but the charges were complicated, and I thought it best if you—"

"YOU!" the Dragon's Bard exclaimed. "I should have known!"

Bennis's eyes narrowed, his face falling into a frown.

"Can it possibly be?" Edvard's face was filled with wonder as he stared at the centaur. "After all these years . . ."

"No, you must be mistaken," Bennis said after drawing in a deep breath.

Edvard's smile beamed. "In all my travels, I've never dreamed that one day I would be standing here and—"

Xander Lamplighter was rushing toward them from the stone bridge, calling out as he came, his voice all out of breath. "Master Klum! Beggin' your pardon, but I need to be having a word with you, sir . . ."

The Dragon's Bard took no notice of the rapidly approaching Constable Pro Tempore, reaching out with both his hands. "May I say . . . it is such an honor . . ."

"Just a minute, Xander," Ward Klum said, holding up a narrow hand in a useless attempt to deflect the sound of the Constable Pro Tempore's voice. He squinted with the effort of trying to pluck meaning through the noise. "I can't hear what the jester is saying . . ."

"He's not a jester, Dad," Jarod offered over the conversation. "He's a bard."

"A what?"

"A *dragon's* bard, Dad."

"A dragon ward? But *my* name's Ward . . ."

"HAR! HAR! HAR!"

The laugh of Farmer Bennis rolled like thunder across Trader's Square, causing everyone to stop speaking at once. All the merchants setting up their stalls in the square looked up in amazement. Even the gaggle of geese seemed to hold still.

Bennis had reached forward in the confusion, grabbing both of Edvard's hands in his right grip and dragging the Dragon's Bard forcefully toward him. Now the centaur held the flailing minstrel in what appeared to be an affectionate hug with his massive left arm, except that Edvard's face was pressed so firmly into the centaur's padded coat that only muffled sounds were coming out.

"Well, now," Bennis said, looking down at the distressed minstrel, "if it isn't my old friend Edmund."

"Edvard," Jarod corrected.

"My old friend Edvard," Bennis repeated with a broad, gap-toothed smile, "come to pay me a visit after all this time."

The centaur gripped Edvard's doublet at the back of the neck. Edvard hung suspended about hand's breadth above the frost-coated cobblestones as Farmer Bennis held him out for his friends to see.

Edvard gasped for air.

"We've got a lot of catching up to do, Edvard," Farmer Bennis said cheerfully to the still sputtering bard. "But we won't be boring our friends with old stories about the past, will we?"

Edvard dragged in a painful breath. "But, surely, I—"

The centaur's friendly shaking of the bard was playfully rough. "No, I think it's best we keep those embarrassing tales just between us, don't you?"

"But I—"

"Well, *don't* you?"

Edvard nodded and managed a thin smile. "Indeed. We've . . . got a great deal of catching up to do . . . old friend . . . just between you and me."

"Indeed," Bennis's mouth opened into a wide though cheerless grin. "Just between you and me."

"I were just coming to tell you 'bout—oh!" Xander, his breath puffing out in great chuffs from his exertions, saw the centaur holding the Dragon's Bard for the first time. The Constable Pro Tempore bent forward and placed his hands on his knees. "I see you've done already met the prisoners, then."

"Just now, it seems," Ward Klum replied, his eyebrows rising. "Although there also appears to be some disagreement among the assemblage here as to whether they are suspected rogues or guests."

"Beggin' your pardon, sire?" Xander tended to blink when he was confused or uncertain. In the view of the scribe, Xander seemed to blink quite often.

"Farmer Bennis has avowed that they are friends of his who have come—why have they come, Farmer Bennis?"

"Catching up on old times," the centaur replied, though the prospect sounded more threatening than inviting.

"Well, be they friends of Farmer Bennis or no," Xander said, his face reddening in the chill, "I've a complaint lodged against that one by the Widow Merryweather and Missus Taylor, and you know how *they* can be! They'd like to have my head if I was to let him go. I thought they might have given Jarod the slip whiles they was off to lunch, but seeing as he's still here . . ."

"Yes, yes," Ward responded with an impatient nod. "Well, I'm sorry to inconvenience you, Xander, but as they did not escape from my son, as you had evidently hoped, we had better arrest them properly. Bring them inside. I take it that Beulandreus hasn't finished the door for the lockup yet, so there's every chance that they may escape later on and save either of us the trouble of having to answer on the matter to either Marchant Merryweather or Winifred Taylor . . ."

"I'll take them," Farmer Bennis said.

Everyone, including Edvard, looked at the centaur in complete surprise.

"You'll what?" Xander gaped.

"I'll take them. Release them into my charge, Xander, and I'll keep an eye on this Dragon's Beard for you."

"Bard," Edvard managed to correct before once again being silenced by a vigorous shake from the centaur.

"I don't know," Ward frowned. "It's highly irregular . . ."

"Now, Ward, you know I've been a member of the village militia longer than our Constable Pro Tempore has been constable," Bennis said, his enormous hand still gripping the Bard's shoulder so tightly that the Bard was forced to grimace, much to the enjoyment of his scribe. "If that's not enough, you can make it official if you like: swear me in as . . . oh, Adjutant Pro Tempore if that will help. They would still be under arrest, and all you have to worry about is keeping the ledgers straight."

Xander smiled. Ward bit at his lower lip.

"And that would get those hens on Cobblestone Street satisfied, wouldn't it?" Bennis added with a wink.

Ward chuckled once. "Very well, Aren, these two are now in your charge. Should they escape your watchful eye while they're on your farm—"

"I'll be sure to report it to you at once," Bennis said, curling his right fetlock back beneath him as he bowed slightly. "But this Bard and I have a great deal to discuss—and I don't think he'll be leaving anytime soon."

"Wherever did it go?" Edvard spoke his thoughts aloud for the benefit of those who might be paying attention to him. He stood upright, taking off his flamboyant hat so that his magnificent brain might cool as he scratched his head.

"What is it now?" Aren Bennis grumbled as he knelt down on his forelegs, quickly rolling up the painted canvas tent. They were not more than a quarter of a mile beyond the town just off the western road to Meade. The Dragon's Bard had set up camp just north of the road up a gentle rise. The crest of Mount Dervin could just be seen above the dense line of trees farther to the north.

"My book, I've lost my book," Edvard answered with a distracted air.

"What book?" Aren was losing patience with the Bard.

"*The* book! *My* book!" Edvard answered hotly. "The one Abel gave me so that I could learn how to re . . . the one I was reviewing for a second publication! It was here when we left this morning."

"Well, find it or leave it," Bennis said with a dismissive sigh. "We're going to lose daylight soon, and I've got cows that need caring for yet."

"Now, see here, my good man . . ."

The centaur scowled at the Bard.

"I mean, my good fellow," Edvard corrected at once. "Can we not come to an understanding between us? This road to Meade runs well beyond that town and, might I add, far from any concerns of yours. I could be persuaded to start such a journey even now . . ."

"And be telling your tales along every measure of its length," Bennis added.

"That *is* my greatest calling!"

Bennis turned toward the Dragon's Bard, folding his enormous arms across his chest. "But there are *some* tales best left untold.

Tales, I believe, that are best forgotten on behalf of all concerned. So until I feel that those tales are safely forgotten—I'll keep you right here within reach to see that they don't get told."

Edvard's face rose to meet the centaur's gaze. "And just how long might that be?"

"As long as it takes me to trust you."

"That long, eh?" Edvard said without much hope.

Jarod's father had allowed him to come with Farmer Bennis to help strike the camp of the prisoners. He smiled as he gathered Edvard's odd belongings from where the Bard had evidently tossed them haphazardly about. Vials—some still filled but the majority mostly empty—lay around the firepit. Odd brass spheres and copper tubing wound in coils lay in strange and wondrous array, as did a variety of pouches filled with strange-smelling herbs. Jarod was beginning to feel almost content to be out under the cold winter sun and away from the ledgers for an afternoon.

"One thing I don't understand," Jarod said. "Are you *the* Dragon's Bard or *a* dragon's bard?"

"Well, both, actually," Edvard answered absently as he searched around the logs surrounding the firepit. "I am a dragon's bard—it is a description of what I do. At the same time, as I am the one who serves stories to the Dragonking Khrag, I have a title—like king or queen or village farmer idiot—and that is why I am called *the* Dragon's Bard."

Jarod thought for a moment. "I don't see it."

"Well, if I had that *book*," Edvard exclaimed in exasperation, "I could show you pictures that would clarify the point so that you *could* see it!"

"What you don't see could fill a dozen of your books," Bennis said, clomping carefully over to where the Dragon's Bard was searching. The centaur pointed toward the snow. "Look. Those tracks through the snow come down from those woods and lead back into them again. They're too big for pixies—who would be my first thought for your thief—and too small for a human male. Female of your kind, I should think."

"And this woman stole my book?" Edvard huffed.

The centaur chuckled. "Considering where you placed your camp, it wouldn't take Dirk Gallowglass to find and pillage it. With the painting on that canvas tent of yours, it's a marvel thieves don't rob you daily and take more than a book." Jarod had gaped at the tent when they had first arrived: It was covered with intricate illustrations of noble kings, sword-wielding knights wearing impossibly complex armor, damsels in assorted forms of distress, and an epic battle panorama filled with creatures—some of which Jarod could not even name. The largest illustration featured two figures towering over the rest: a bard—who bore some passing resemblance to Edvard—defending himself against an enormous, fire-breathing dragon armed only with a quill. It was vibrant, garish, poorly rendered, and calculated to call attention to itself.

"What's in this book that's so important anyway?" Jarod asked as he pushed the Bard's provisions haphazardly down into a pack.

"Important?" The Bard's eyes flashed. Edvard evidently sensed the opportunity for performance and had never been known to let such opportunities pass. "Why, the book contains the essence of life itself! It holds a *quest!*"

"A quest?" Jarod asked with a hint of his father's skepticism.

"Oh, yes, my boy." Edvard warmed to his performance despite the chill in the air. "A quest is everything! It is the embodiment of our dreams and the vision of our better selves. The quest brings us to a place where we are tested not just for who we are but for who we are to become! It takes us beyond our safe home, past the portals of our horizon, and into the realms of power and magic, desire and nobility, passion and humility. It tries us to our core as we travel strange roads and overcome the forces of evil that oppose our rightful desire. It tempts us down paths that would steal not just the breath from our breast but the soul from our heart. And always in the end it brings us to a prize of inestimable wealth!"

"That would be Caprice, right?" Jarod offered, trying to follow the chain of thought.

"Well, no," Edvard blinked, his rhythm momentarily stumbling over the question. "The actual prize may be many things, depending upon the quest. It may be knowledge from the gods or spiritual understanding or power or wealth untold . . ."

"And if I bring this prize back, then *that's* what impresses Caprice?" Jarod asked again.

The centaur's great laugh shook the frosted ground.

"I'll have you know that there is no higher form of love's expression than that of the great quest," the Dragon's Bard sniffed. "If Jarod is to win his fair Caprice, then a quest is the surest path by which he may secure her affections. All the best books tell us so."

"Caprice." Farmer Bennis stopped, looking up into the darkening sky for a moment. "You mean Caprice Morgan—Meryl's daughter of the wishing well? Is that what all this is about?"

Jarod flushed, his voice daring the centaur to contradict him. "I'd do anything for her."

Farmer Bennis glanced at the young man who was barely tall enough to meet his flanks. He tied off the rolled canvas tent and laid it across his own back. "I dare say you would, son . . . and don't mistake me; she's a worthy woman to pursue."

"Then I guess I need to fulfill a quest," Jarod said with more certainty than he felt. "What kinds of quests are there? I mean . . . can I choose a quest?"

The centaur spoke as much to himself as to anyone else. "You don't choose quests, boy—they choose you."

The Dragon's Bard thought for a moment before he answered. "There are so many tales of legendary deeds, each so difficult to quantify in its respective genre . . . give me a moment's leave to recall . . . ah! There was the quest for the Godly Prize—the greatest gift ever given to the king."

Bennis chuckled. "Ah, give her an impressive present."

The Dragon's Bard continued, "There was the quest for the Shield of Glory given by the gods to a hero who distinguished himself by his—"

The farmer laughed. "He means you should impress her with your charm!"

"What about the Quest of the Heart?" the Dragon's Bard countered. "The Quest of Riches . . . the Quest of Power . . . the Quest of Valiance . . ."

"All fine enough," Bennis chuckled, "so long as you peel back the fancy talk and get down to the roots. Buy her with money, impress her with the strength of your arm or fancy words: it's all the same story for the lords and the peasants alike."

"Well, they all sound like fine quests," Jarod said, "and . . . well, it's grand to be talking about slaying dragons and griffons and demons . . . but I'm an apprentice in my father's countinghouse and I've got chores at home and . . . this whole quest business sounds pretty far away."

Farmer Bennis stopped packing and turned to the young man. He leaned down closer to Jarod and laid both his massive hands as gently as he could on the youth's shoulders. "Master Klum, you don't have to go to the ends of the world to fulfill your quest. The best quests are those here, close to your heart. The quests in all those distant lands of story seem more important somehow because they are far away—but the quests that make a difference are the smaller ones in the places of power, glory, wealth, and magic that lie just around the corner from your own home."

"Not from *my* home," Jarod said with a glum expression.

"Yes," Bennis insisted. "Your home . . . I'll show you."

Bennis turned Jarod so that he was looking back down the Meade road toward Eventide. The evening rays cast a pink color across the landscape and the buildings around the center of the town.

"There's your quest, boy," Farmer Bennis said in a rough whisper. "A place of treasure, adventure, honor, and glory."

"It's just the village," Jarod said, puzzled.

"Look through better eyes, boy," Bennis insisted. "It won't be the same town we'll be going back to, Master Jarod. It will be a different land altogether by the time we're done. I'll help you, boy, to win your woman and to do it proper, too."

"*You?*" the Dragon's Bard scoffed. "What know you of romance and the wooing of a gentle lady?"

"I'll thank you not to ask that question again," Bennis growled. "Take my help or not, boy . . . but you'll need all the help offered, I'm thinking."

"And I shall aid you as well, chronicling your every adventure," Edvard said, trying to regain his audience. "I came in search of these very quests of which our friend Farmer Bennis speaks. Neighborhood heroes . . . princesses down the lane. Perhaps you don't need to slay some distant dragon; all you need is to slay a more manageable one right here."

"Slay a dragon?" Jarod's voice broke with panic.

"I speak metaphorically, of course," Edvard said dismissively. "Perhaps the Treasure Quest may be just the thing for you. You must find some gift of inestimable worth and with it capture your true love's heart. Come! The evening is deepening quickly. Let us to Farmer Bennis's homestead, where we shall set in motion the tale of Jarod's Quest for the Greatest Prize of All!"

Jarod started walking back toward Eventide between the laden Farmer Bennis and the continually chattering Dragon's Bard, his mind struggling to imagine a treasure of inestimable worth that might be had for the wages of an apprentice bookkeeper and found within the confines of the village he had known since birth. Were there places he had missed where a manageable quest might be undertaken? How would he present such a rare prize to Caprice if he could not say two words together to her?

So filled was Jarod's head with puzzled thoughts that he did not notice the Bard's scribe standing at the edge of the cold campfire in the deepening twilight, staring off into the line of trees where the tracks of the book's thief led.

# FEET OF PROWESS

❖

*Wherein Jarod tries to find
a gift for Caprice in the town
but discovers the heart of a poet
in the most unlikely of places.*

## · CHAPTER 4 ·

# The Milliner and the Pixies

Merinda Oakman sat leaning against her ornately carved workbench, staring with weary eyes at the hat on the wooden form in front of her. The wind howled fiercely against the windows that nearly spanned the end of her workroom, sending whirling flashes of white snow in great whirlpools across the panes, illuminated for a moment in the glow of her lamplight before they vanished into the darkness of the alley beyond. She sat perched atop a tall chair, its back carefully and lovingly formed to fit the curve of her own back though at the moment she found no comfort in it.

"A quest hat," she muttered to herself. "What a notion!"

Merinda gazed up at the storage shelves that rose from floor to ceiling on either side of her workbench. She looked to the ranks of carefully organized ribbons, thread spools, patches, buttons, stays, feathers, dried flowers, bundles of rye straw, leathers, pelts, wools, felt, and bolts of cloth. She searched among them for inspiration in the textures and colors. It was hidden there, she thought, among the bits and pieces of her trade: that special form of this hat that was yet to be discovered. From among the chosen bits and pieces the hat would emerge under her careful and talented hands; all she had to do was pluck them out and put them together. The pieces of her puzzle did not leap into her hands and make themselves evident, no matter how hard she willed it.

It was certainly not a question of *having* hats, she mused, turning back to the conical felt shape she had placed on the hat form and twisted this way and that without satisfaction. Indeed, the workroom had an overabundance of hats from her more recent labors. What else was she to do while Harv was away?

Her husband, Harvest Oakman, had gone to Butterfield not yet a week ago with his wagon filled with his magnificently crafted tables, chairs, and sideboards. He had a great inventory of pieces he had crafted in the autumn stored under the large shed bordering the yard behind the store. During the winter months he would make the rounds of the local towns, each at its prescribed time, with his large wagon piled with goods and come back with his wagon empty and his purse filled with what he considered a fair price for his craft.

Merinda wrinkled her nose at the thought. She was a short, comfortably round, sparkling woman with large, wide-set eyes and a button nose that everyone mistook as a predisposition to joviality. But the longer she stared at the hat on the form, the deeper her bowed lips settled into a frown.

Harv was better than the price he asked for his carpentry. He was truly a gifted craftsman, in Merinda's opinion, but he never seemed to value his own work highly enough when it came to the coin of the realm. He thought of himself as a poor country carpenter, and, in the words Merinda found herself swallowing daily, that was why everyone else thought of him that way too. She knew he was better than that, but the prices he settled on for his work would keep them—keep her—in this little shop in the country forever without the recognition that her husband so rightly deserved.

Harv loved her as dearly as she loved him. He had built the shop for her so that she could contribute to their income through her own considerable skills as a milliner. So it was that each winter he would make his trips to the neighboring towns and she would spend her lonely hours in the shop making hat after hat after hat in an ever-increasing inventory of haberdashery that anticipated the Spring Revels and her own high selling season.

Queen Nance herself had ordained the Spring Revels throughout the kingdom as a celebration of the end of winter and the return of the growing season in the country. It was, perhaps, the one time of year when all the highborn folks of the larger cities like Mordale suddenly found the country in vogue. Mordale would become desolate as the wealthy, the powerful, and the fashionable would flee the city walls and inundate the countryside, making great pretense of "getting back to the old and simpler ways." Playing at farming became the order of the day, and, Merinda reminded herself with every drop of glue and needle stitch, the purchasing and wearing of country hats was a practice led by the Princess Aerthia herself.

It was with this object in mind that Merinda, as late in the fall as she dared, made her annual journey to Mordale. There she would stay at an inn whose reputation was tolerable and whose rates were within her careful budget. She then would spend her preciously counted days not in seeing the great castle there, or the cathedrals, or the tournament lists, but in visiting every hat and clothing shop possible in the city. She would come away with precious few purchases but a wealth of information regarding fashion trends and which designs would be most desired in the spring to come. Then she would make her way back to Eventide, draw up her order for materials from Charon's Goods, and settle in for a winter filled with furious hat making—dreaming all the while that someday she would be presented at the great castle, be invited to the cathedrals, and be a popular figure in whose company others wished to be seen in the tournament lists.

Her local trade was dedicated but few in numbers and consisted primarily of the ladies of Cobblestone Street, who came by with more of an object to talk and less to purchase hats. The men of the town found Merinda's shop such a warren of femininity that they would cross its threshold only under the direst of circumstances—usually at the insistence of a young woman on their arm. Men of the town purchased their hats from the more sensible establishment of Charon's Goods next door, even though when they ordered their hats from Mordechai Charon they fully knew that he would simply have his wife, Alicia, order them in turn to be made next door by Merinda Oakman.

So it was a mystery that morning, as Merinda was working on a hat in her storefront, that she had spied three odd men and a centaur passing back and forth in front of her shop.

They would pause for a time facing each other in front of the leaded glass panes of the display window and wildly gesture in animated conversation as the snow fell in a great blanket of large flakes about them. The youngest of the men—Jarod Klum, by the looks of him—would stare straight at Merinda through the window and then bolt off in one direction or another, followed closely by the two other men, who were strangers to her, and an enormous creature that could only be Farmer Bennis.

This curious scene was reenacted with slight variation several times before Jarod Klum took a determined stance, set his jaw, and marched determinedly through Merinda's shop door, his companions at his heels.

Merinda's storefront was a wonder to behold, for her husband had lovingly carved every pillar, arch, and beam to his wife's delight. The columns featured reliefs of intertwining ivy runners weaving their way up an otherwise smooth and polished surface. Pixies and fairies could be found carved among the leaves. These columns rose to a wooden lattice carved from a single piece of wood detailed with intricate reproductions of branches and leaves filled with doves, pheasants, and small dragonettes playing with one another. The lattice curved to form the top of a heart shape over the ornate counter. The bases of each corner of the counter were carved into unhappy trolls—each an individual with a different comical expression—holding up a frieze depicting Eventide from the Blackshore road in breathtaking detail.

Jarod passed it all by with a fixed stare as he marched directly toward Merinda at the counter.

"I would like to order a hat!" Jarod announced in a voice that was entirely too loud and too high-pitched.

Merinda smiled slightly at the unexpected sound and looked from face to face at the four beings suddenly filling her storefront. She succeeded in speaking on her second attempt. "Well, all right then, Master Klum. I'll be happy to help you with that. What kind of a hat would you like?"

Jarod blinked uncertainly.

"A quest hat!" said the angular man with the pointy beard who was leaning on the counter next to Jarod.

"A . . . what kind of hat?"

"Jarod here is on a quest," Farmer Bennis said in a warm, soft voice. The centaur was holding his great leather hat by its brim respectfully in front of him with both hands. "He needs a special hat for a special woman."

"Oh! A lady's hat, then . . . well, you've come to the right place, Master Klum." Merinda pulled out a small slip of parchment and one of the pencils Harv was always making for her.

"But it can't be just any hat," the centaur concluded.

Merinda looked up from her parchment. "Oh?"

Jarod had found a piece of string in his pocket and was winding and unwinding it repeatedly around his finger as he bit at his lower lip.

"Forgive me, my dear Missus Oakman," the thin man said, removing his own enormous hat with a flourish that almost avoided hitting his writing companion squarely in the face. "I am Edvard—the Dragon's Bard—the author of this noble—"

Merinda set down her pencil and folded her arms across her chest. "Ah, yes. I have heard of you."

Edvard beamed. "No doubt you are an avid follower of my tales!"

"No," Merinda said, her eyes narrowing slightly. "The Widow Merryweather was in here not two days ago with Miss Ariela telling me about you and your dangerous writing companion." In truth, the Widow Merryweather had given a chilling account of what might have happened to her at the hands of this charming, mystical, and dangerous stranger had he not been apprehended by the Constable Pro Tempore before any mischief could be done. By the time Miss Ariela had added her own embellishments, it was clear that the Widow had narrowly escaped the very worst and most interesting of fates. "And I suppose that fellow scribbling behind you goes by the name of Abel?"

The scribe glanced up in surprise at hearing his name mentioned, which caused him to make an unsightly mark on his page.

"Yes, he does, but that's not important right now," Edvard continued, his smile forced into an even brighter countenance.

"That's all right, Missus Oakman," Jarod said nervously. "Sorry to have troubled you . . . I think maybe we should just go."

Both the Dragon's Bard and the centaur farmer put restraining hands on the youth's shoulders.

"Courage, lad!" Edvard said to Jarod. "We've crossed the threshold into uncharted realms where lesser mortal men fear to tread! That is the very nature of a quest!"

"Perhaps," Merinda asked, "if you could describe this hat that you wish to order?"

"Well," Jarod said, obviously gathering up every ounce of courage he hoped to possess, "it's . . . it has to look like a quest hat."

"A quest hat," Merinda coaxed, picking up her pencil once more. "And just what does a quest hat look like?"

"It has to look like the greatest prize in the world!"

"Greatest prize in the world," Merinda repeated as she scribbled on the parchment scrap. "What shape would the greatest prize have? Loaf? Conical? Pie?"

"Well . . . it needs to be perfect."

Merinda was feeling her frustration mount. The one time men came into her shop and her husband had just left town. Who could possibly translate for her now? She decided to try herself. "Wide? Narrow? Short? Tall? Feathered? Wrap? Train? Brim?"

"Those all sound fine . . ."

"Pelt? Felt? Straw? Wool? Cloth?" Merinda continued,

hoping that something she said would make sense to the boy. "Knit? Bonnet? Cap?"

"Anything . . . so long as it's perfect."

Jarod had answered her with such an expression of earnest desire that a single laugh escaped Merinda Oakman's tightly drawn lips before she could stifle it. "Of course, Master Klum," Merinda nodded. "A perfect hat."

"A perfect *quest* hat," Edvard added.

Merinda paused, drew a line through her last note, and added, "One perfect *quest* hat."

Merinda hopped down off her chair in frustration. She had negotiated a price for the quest hat that was nearly double her usual rate—"no one wants a cheap quest hat"—which should have pleased her. Now, however, in the night, with the wind howling outside her window, and faced with the prospect of having to create the perfect quest hat for a woman whose identity Jarod refused to divulge, she was beginning to feel she may have gotten the worst part of the deal.

She gazed again out the window at the raging storm without. Harv was supposed to have come home sometime in these last two days, and now she was worried. She hated to be away from her dear husband for any period of time; it was not like him to be late. No doubt the storm was delaying his return to her. She offered a short, heartfelt prayer to Plania, the god of travelers, that Harv would have the good sense to wait out the storm and not try to foolishly push through its dangerous fury.

Something beyond the glass, in the swirling eddies of blowing snow, caught her eye. She was not sure she had seen it at first, but—there it was again, a streak of bright light falling outside her window. She considered for a moment that it might be a trick of her flaring lamp reflected in the glass, so she turned and, with a quick puff, extinguished the flame.

The workroom fell into instant darkness, and it took Merinda a moment for her eyes to get accustomed to it. The alley beyond slowly emerged in the window, lit with a faint blue light that she could not recall seeing before. She leaned closer to the window, trying to see the source of the strange, dim light.

A third brilliant streak fell almost against the glass. Merinda leaped backward with a yelp, pushing over her chair. As her breath came quickly, three more streaks of light plunged downward beyond the glass in the alley, and then a cascade of light falling like a sudden, driving rain filled the glass for a moment. She heard the soft impacts in the snow piled up in the alley, dull thuds that came at her through the shop wall.

Just as suddenly, the falling lights stopped and a deep winter silence filled the workroom.

Merinda reached for her lamp, consciously steadying her hand as she took it from the workbench. She held still for a moment, holding the unlit lamp, and listened.

No sound at all.

She drew in a deep breath.

BAM! BAM! BAM! BAM! BAM!

The milliner blinked, uncertain as to what to do.

BAM! BAM! BAM! BAM! BAM!

It was the door—the back door to her kitchen off the alley.

Someone was banging at her door.

Merinda turned from the workbench, wishing fervently that she had not quenched the lamp. The glow from the alley window had brightened and she could make out the stairs at the far end of her workspace, one set leading up to the rooms where she and Harv lived above the shop and the other set leading down to the storeroom in the cellar space beneath. The right-hand door led to the storefront, but the door to the left would take her into the kitchen and closer to the banging on the door.

She could make out the bright, cheerful outline of the door that led into the kitchen, illuminated by the hearth fire still burning there. Merinda knew that she needed to light the lamp and that the hearth was now the most ready means of doing so.

"It's your kitchen, Merinda," she muttered to herself; then she took another deep breath and pushed through the door.

BAM! BAM! BAM!

"I'm coming!" Merinda shouted as she pushed a stalk of dried goldenrod into the fire and relit her lamp. The kitchen hearth was burning low in the evening. Merinda had intended to bank it before going to bed but was now glad she had not. The flame sprang to life on the lamp's wick, illuminating the cheerful kitchen and making it feel comfortably familiar. The long, beautiful table in the center of the room and the carefully built, oversized hearth dominated the space. The three windows set in the wall across from the hearth normally afforded a view of Harv's work yard and sheds—now completely obscured by the night and its storm. Her china cabinet stood next to the alley door with all of her best plates—such few as she had managed to collect—carefully cleaned and stacked. Her kitchen was her joy, the place where she and Harv filled most of their evenings together.

BAM! BAM! BAM!

"Just a moment!" Merinda glanced around the room, wondering what kind of company she would be entertaining on a night like this. She frowned at the far corner of the room. With her husband away, Merinda liked to keep busy, and she had spent part of the day cleaning out a few pieces of trash from the cellar. She had not gotten as far as taking it all to the yard, however, and it remained an unsightly stack in the corner. She decided that there was no help for it now—whoever was in need at her door would have to put up with her house as it stood.

Merinda gripped the lamp, wished again that her husband were home, and opened the door.

The gale nearly doused her lamp, but the dim glow of the hearth fire gave enough light to see.

On the stoop before her, standing up to its neck in a drift of snow, was a pixie, its wings stiff and coated with ice. It stood shivering uncontrollably, its arms folded across its chest. Its normally brilliant shine was replaced now by a blue glow that illuminated the surrounding snow.

Merinda slammed shut the door.

Merinda had no love for pixies and no patience with their antics. They were a notorious public nuisance in Eventide and the perpetual bane of Xander Lamplighter, the Constable Pro Tempore, whose knack for capturing these small, flying hoodlums was a serious relief to the townsfolk and ensured him of his job. It was Xander's suggestion, in fact, that pixies caught in their nefarious acts be incarcerated in the streetlamps lining Trader's Square and Charter Square during summer evenings, allowing the public areas to be well lit by their glow while punishing them at the same time. Ariela Soliandrus, the Gossip Fairy, had let everyone in town know just how terrible pixies were and that they were never to be trusted in civilized communities. The fact that fairies and pixies were distantly related only seemed to lend credence to Ariela's assertions.

Pixies wore next to nothing, being naturally warm beings to begin with and not caring for the weight that clothing added when they flew on their diaphanous wings. They had a humor all their own and a penchant for theft. Everyone knew that to invite a pixie into your house was to open your door wide to trouble.

BAM! BAM! BAM! BAM! BAM!

Merinda knew that she should just walk away from the door.

But . . .

The image of the little creature, blue from the cold and shivering on her porch step, kept returning to her thoughts. Little crystals had formed in its hair, and its pointed ears had quivered as it stood before her. She could not shake off the image of its large, violet eyes staring up at her.

Merinda considered herself a good woman. She visited the Pantheon Church weekly and had promised the Lady of the Sky that she would help those in need.

She wondered if that included pixies.

"Merinda," she said to herself, "what a notion!"

She turned back to the alley door and opened it.

"You promise to behave yourselves," Merinda said, shaking her finger at the pixie named Glix.

"Whenever have we not?" answered Glix with a sly grin.

"Promise me!" Merinda warned.

"That we do, ma'am! We promise to behave yourselves," Glix nodded in the affirmative as he turned to his fellow pixies. "Don't we, boys?"

Merinda had plucked more than a dozen pixies out of the banks of snow in the alleyway. They had not been particularly difficult to find, since they glowed in the snow, but all of them were literally frozen stiff into little pixie statues, which she had brought into her kitchen and, not knowing what else to do, lined up on her mantel above the hearth. She had then enlivened the fire with a pair of well-placed logs and, within a very short time, the pixies had all begun to come around.

The other pixies on the mantel, who had now lost their blue chill to a more healthy red-brown color and were looking far too animated for Merinda's liking, all answered Glix in the affirmative.

"Behaving yourselves we will," said Dix.

"We've never behaved like yourself before," piped in Plix, "but we'll be doin' it fer you!"

"Just how long would you be liking us to behave like yourself?" Snix wanted to know.

"I don't think you understand," Merinda said nervously. "You're all feeling better, I see, so perhaps if I just saw you back out the door . . ."

"Back into that ice?" Glix whined. "We fell out of the sky on account of that! You wouldn't be doin' that to us now, would you? Us being poor little creatures on a night such as this and all!"

"No, I suppose not," Merinda answered wearily.

"Don't you worry, love," Glix said with another wide grin. "It's be a party you'll not soon forget!"

In the first hour of the night, Merinda tried to organize a dinner for the pixies. Finding it not to their peculiar tastes, the pixies threw the food in the general direction of the cleaning basins and set out to make dinner for their hostess instead as Merinda worked furiously to clean up the meal she had just made.

By the second hour, the pixies had spilled cornmeal onto Merinda's floor as they were in the process of mixing up their cakes. This led to the almost immediate discovery that the combination of cornmeal and pixie feet allowed for a tremendous ability to slide across Merinda's floor. Pixies being what they were, they immediately established rules and contests for one another regarding sliding across the floor on cornmeal, a distraction that kept them from getting their cakes baked for quite some time. Merinda grabbed her broom almost at once and began sweeping up both cornmeal and pixies in an effort to once more establish the cleanliness of her kitchen. Unfortunately, the pixies considered this a considerable challenge to their game and added new rules incorporating the broom into their play.

By the third hour, Merinda had managed to put her kitchen back in order just as Plix discovered Merinda's workroom. All of the pixies were astonished at the idea of how hats were made, and Merinda, grateful for something to distract the pixies from the kitchen, began telling them about the millinery craft. The pixies saw an immediate possibility for improvement in the craft and began reorganizing Merinda's workspace as an expression of their appreciation for her help. This reorganization was entirely along the thinking lines of pixies—which generally categorized all of Merinda's notions, cloths, pelts, felts, and supplies according to the third letter of the object's name and in order of time required to manufacture it. By the fourth hour, every scrap of material owned by Merinda once more had a place, but everything was out of place and impossible for Merinda to find.

By the fifth hour, Merinda had gratefully discovered that singing to the pixies seemed to quiet them and prevent either further damage by them or their discovery of other as-yet undamaged areas of her shop and home. Merinda was rapidly running out of songs to sing—and it was still not yet dawn.

Merinda's voice was hoarse but she sang on. The pixies were all sitting comfortably in pots, pans, large spoons, ladles, and anything else Merinda could find that could not easily be broken. These she had scattered across the table in the kitchen.

Merinda knew that the song was coming to an end. She had sung the chorus four times already, and though the pixies did not seem to either notice or mind that, her voice simply could not go on.

> *. . . we'll sing to the wind and the heroes,*
> *Of willows in field far away, dear lass,*
> *Of willows in field far away.*

Merinda fell silent.

Glix stood up on the table and pounded it with his foot, joined immediately by all his fellow pixies, their wings flicking in added appreciation. The racket their feet made jarred Merinda, who had momentarily fallen asleep, back to wakefulness.

"That were grand!" Glix shouted. "Now it's our turn."

Merinda sat up warily. "Your turn to . . . to what?"

"Sing, ma'am!" Glix shouted. "Pixies are famed in every corner of the land for their gifts in the lyrical arts."

> *There was a lad of the name Tat*
> *Who came to the bawdy house and sat—*

Merinda leaped up from her chair. "Stop!"

Glix looked up at Merinda, upset that his song had been interrupted.

Merinda glanced around the kitchen. She had managed to keep it in order despite the pixies but her strength was waning and she knew it was only a matter of time before her guests utterly destroyed her perfect, sensible life. She had to do something to end her terrible ordeal. Her eye settled gratefully on the one object in the room that suddenly gave her hope.

"Your song, Glix, is . . . um . . . most amusing and diverting," Merinda said quickly. "But I have a gift for you."

"But what about my song?" Glix asked insistently.

"It's a gift . . . *for* your song," Merinda replied.

Glix's brows arched up with interest above his violet eyes.

"You've never really heard a song properly until you've heard it . . . inside a pickle barrel!"

The following morning, with the storm abated and the sun not quite yet over the horizon, a bleary-eyed Merinda Oakman rolled a pickle barrel out the alley door of her kitchen. The lid she held firmly in place, and the faint sound of singing could be heard coming from within its staves.

Merinda looked both ways down the alley, making sure that no one was watching. Then, in a rush, she snatched the top off the pickle barrel, dashed into her home, and slammed shut the kitchen door behind her. It took her the remainder of the day to put her house back in some semblance of order, and the shop itself did not open for two more days. Harv Oakman returned on the third day, and as they greeted each other warmly, Merinda could not find the words to explain what had happened. She was too embarrassed by her foolishness in letting the pixies in and decided not to mention what had happened.

Out in the alley, Glix, Plix, Dix, Snix, and the rest of the pixies climbed out of the pickle barrel and into the daylight.

It is a little-known fact that some pixies actually prefer the interior of an empty pickle barrel to other spots—especially when it is sitting next to a warm fire with its lid held down by a large iron pot on a cold winter night.

"That Merinda is a right woman," Plix said happily. "She knows how to show a pixie a good time."

"Right that!" Snix agreed. "She sure were right about singing our songs in that pickle barrel. Never better!"

"Took us in, she did," Dix nodded, slapping Glix on the back. "Saved our lives and all when she didn't have to lift a wing. Wish we could do something for her."

"We own her a debt, we do," Glix agreed. "Don't you worry, lads. Pixies never forget them who they owe. Ever she needs us in the future, you can be sure that every pixie among us will be there to help."

## · CHAPTER 5 ·

# Treasure Box

W ould you remind me once again why we are here?" the
Dragon's Bard sniffed.

Jarod did not hear the boredom that permeated the Bard's
words. "Just wait . . . you'll see. I come here every day for this."

Edvard looked around the interior of Beulandreus Dudgeon's
blacksmith shop with a critical eye. There was a large stone hearth
at the back of the shop with two smaller forges to the left. An enormous overhead bellows hung from the ceiling, its handle uncomfortably low to the ground for the use of a human. An anvil stood
mounted firmly on a wide stone platform within easy reach of where
the bellows handle extended. A spot in the stone under the handle
had a perceptible wear to it—a slight hollow announcing the spot
where the smith so often stood. Near this was a large, carved-stone
water bath where forged metals could be tempered into their intended strength. The fires in the hearth and the forges blazed hot,
making conflicting eddies in the air of heat and chill. Everywhere
there was ironmongery. Heaps of metal—both those finished and

those yet to be shaped—were scattered about the area in a chaos of plows, war axes, horseshoes, rapiers, kettles, helmets, scythes, pikes, breastplates, cleavers, and hammers. All this metallic chaos was housed under a pitched slate roof supported by large, rough-cut wooden posts. Two sides were completely open to Hammer Court.

"All I am seeing is that brute Aren Bennis talking horseshoes with a dwarf," Edvard said through a yawn. "It is a gripping encounter and, no doubt, normally the prime source of amusement in Even-dyed, though I honestly do not see why this should fascinate you when you've got *me* to entertain—"

"No, not that . . . I come for *that*," Jarod said, pointing outward across the court. The open sides of the blacksmith's shop not only allowed easy entrance to Beulandreus's establishment but afforded a panoramic view of all Hammer Court and down the length of King's Road beyond. The streets were busy with both town and country folk, as a break in the winter weather had afforded a more pleasant day and an opportunity for trade before another storm settled on the town.

"You mean that fat woman pulling the cart?" Edvard said, perplexed. "I'll admit she looks amusing, but—"

"No, not Missus Conway," Jarod said. "More to the right!"

"My right or her—oh!" the Dragon's Bard exclaimed.

Walking from Charter Square down the length of King's Road and seemingly directly toward them was a beautiful young woman, her auburn hair and heart-shaped face framed perfectly beneath the wide brim of her straw hat. A cloak was clasped about her neck, but in the unexpected warming of the changeable winter afternoon, she had pushed it back behind her shoulders. Her dress fit her perfectly, hinting at her exquisite figure, though the once rich cloth of the panels was faded and the hem showed signs of wear and permanent stain. Across the crook of her arm she carried a large, covered basket with careless ease despite its apparent weight, her chin held high as she took in the sights of the people moving through town about her.

"Here then, I take it," Edvard asked knowingly, "is the fair Caprice?"

"Caprice," Jarod sighed as he nodded and moved to be slightly more hidden by the shop's post. "I wanted you to see her . . . you know, the reason for this great quest of yours."

"It's *your* quest, Jarod," Edvard corrected, "not mine."

"That's what I said," Jarod replied, confused.

"Never mind." Edvard shook his head, then turned to his scribe. "Strike out that last part and be sure to fix it later so that I make sense."

The scribe, sitting on an uncomfortable iron bench nearby, pretended to make the notation. Abel had been so consumed by the arduous task of knowing which of the Bard's unending utterances were worthy of being immortalized on the page that he had had far too little time to consider the mystery of the vanished book and the woman who had come from the woods to steal it. When occasion permitted—which was rare indeed—he would ask the Dragon's Bard about it, but Edvard was entirely too wrapped up in the manufacturing of Jarod's quest to be bothered with actual criminal doings or the question of why, of all their belongings, a woman should wish to steal a book. Still, even the scribe had to admit that Caprice Morgan looked like a woman who deserved a champion, even if he were of the local variety.

Caprice entered the square and then turned, crossing the cobblestones of Hammer Court southward, nodding to acquaintances as she passed the blacksmith's and entering the shop just beyond.

"Madeline Muffin?" Edvard asked as he read the sign above the shop.

"It's Madeline Muffe's bakery," Jarod answered, relaxing slightly now that Caprice was no longer in view. "Her husband gave the shop its name, but Madeline hates it, or so I've been told. Caprice comes into the shop every Four-day to bake her bread in the ovens."

Edvard looked sideways at the young man. "Every Four-day?"

"Yeah," Jarod sighed.

"And, I take it, you find some reason to be here in the noble if somewhat cluttered shop of Beulandreus Dudgeon on that same Four-day each week as well?" Edvard chuckled. Seeing the pained look on Jarod's face, he hastily continued, "Why, that is perfect, young man! You have already anticipated my plan! You must present yourself everywhere before your beautiful and thus far oblivious Caprice. Have you spoken to her?"

"Well, of course I have!" Jarod replied at once, his face taking on a ruddy color.

"When?" Edvard pressed.

"Why . . . I try to talk to her every Four-day when she comes out of the shop!"

"How endearingly bold of you!" Edvard said with what passed for encouragement. "And have you learned much about her in your conversations each Four-day?"

"Of course I have!" Jarod protested. "All sorts of things."

"Such as . . ." Edvard prompted.

"Well, I've learned that her father prefers brown bread," Jarod said, swallowing hard. "I learned it's harder to come by the finer flours now than it used to be and that Madeline has to be cautious about taking wishes in exchange for baking since one of her ovens started being critical of which kinds of dough it bakes."

The Dragon's Bard stared at the young man for a moment.

"Do you even *know* this woman?" Edvard asked at last. "Outside of the types of bread her father likes, I mean?"

"Of course I do!" Jarod protested. "I've known her all my life. We used to play in the Norest Forest together growing up. She could read long before I could, and she would tell me all the stories of the Elder Times before the Epic War—the stories of the heroes and the monsters and the gods all being jealous of each other and fighting between them over mortals. We would sit at the top of Mount Dervin and find those legends in the clouds that passed so close overhead and talk of lands past the horizon and what it might be like for the people who lived there. We told each other secrets there and swore we would find our own adventures one day."

"I am impressed," the Dragon's Bard nodded. "And just how long ago was that?"

Jarod turned away, looking back toward the bakery. "I was fourteen years when we last did that."

"Long ago, then?" Edvard coaxed.

"Too long."

"Long, perhaps, but not too long," Edvard said, slapping the boy on the back. "You are, indeed, on a quest, friend Jarod . . . and we have an infallible plan! You have obtained a token of your feelings for your beloved Caprice in the haberdashery styling of your local expert milliner. But the token alone is not enough; it must be presented in a memorable and dramatic fashion, filled with the words of your heart and the demonstration of your devotion."

"Oh, and just how am I supposed to do that?" Jarod snapped.

"By remembering the plan!" Edvard replied heatedly, his frustrations mounting with the young man. "First, obtain a great gift—this you have already begun. Second, present your gift as an undeniable invitation to attend the Spring Revels with you as her escort. Third, accompany her to the Spring Revels with her magnificent gift on display for the entire town. And—finally—win her heart through your attentions! It's classic romantic quest fundamentals!"

Jarod looked pained. "I don't know . . ."

"Listen, how do you plan on presenting your gift?" Edvard asked.

"What do you mean?"

"How were you going to ask your amazing Caprice to go with you to the Spring Revels?" the Dragon's Bard urged.

"Well, I was going to just, you know, give her the hat and ask her."

"You were not!"

"I wasn't?"

"Look," Edvard said, his voice carrying above the hiss of the forge around them. "I'll be Caprice."

Jarod squinted with one eye. "What do you mean?"

"I am going to pretend to be Caprice, and you be you."

"I *am* me," Jarod answered.

"Of course you are you!" Edvard roared. "But I'm going to pretend to be Caprice. *You* pretend that I am Caprice and that you are going to present your amazing gift to me and ask me to accompany you to the Spring Revels."

"Oh!" Jarod nodded. "You mean, like practice?"

"Yes!" Edvard said with infinite relief. "We are just practicing. Now, I'm pretending to be Caprice. You pretend that you are asking Caprice to the Spring Revels. You've got your treasure with you to present to her. Now, what do you say?"

"You're Caprice?" Jarod said with uncertainty.

"Yes," Edvard nodded.

"And I'm asking you to the Spring Revels?"

"Yes," the Dragon's Bard urged. "What do you say?"

Jarod bit at his lip. For a moment he fidgeted with an imaginary hat in his hands and then thrust it out toward the Dragon's Bard.

"I got you this hat, Caprice . . . I don't suppose you want to go to Spring Revels with me?"

"NO!" Edvard bellowed.

"You don't?" Jarod blinked.

"You don't just shove a hat at a woman like that!" Edvard shouted. "You have to do it with style and grace! A treasure has to be discovered gradually . . ."

"You need Treasure Box," came a gruff voice behind the Bard.

Both Jarod and Edvard turned in surprise.

The ladies of Cobblestone Street all believed Beulandreus Dudgeon to be the ugliest dwarf in the world—although, in truth, none of those same ladies of Eventide had ever seen any other dwarf for comparison. He was barely four feet tall and seemed nearly as wide, with a great barrel chest and massive arms and legs. He kept his head shaved bald. Mordechai Charon believed it was because he was a smith and worked around open fires all day; none of them suspected the real reason and he wouldn't have told them even if they had asked. No one ever asked Beulandreus anything about himself, and the smith never bothered anyone else. He retained his dwarf beard and had been seen on his rare trade excursions in town to let it splay out in a long, frizzy bush from his face. While in his shop, however, he kept it carefully braided and secured beneath his wide belt. His apron and clothing may once have had a color but now mostly resembled soot. His hands and face were so blackened with the iron that he worked with constantly that Marchant Merryweather claimed he would rust if he were ever to take a bath.

He had bright, grey eyes that shone out from either side of his bulbous nose and, according to Aren Bennis, a beaming, gap-toothed smile when the humor struck him.

"Uh," Jarod grimaced, "I guess you overheard that."

"At that volume," Aren Bennis chuckled as he clomped up behind the dwarf to join them, "I would have been surprised if the folks in Meade didn't overhear you."

"You need Treasure Box," the dwarf asserted, wiping his hands on a cloth nearly as dirty as himself.

Jarod had been largely raised in or around his father's counting-house. It was filled with massive, locked, iron boxes, many of them made by Beulandreus. "Thank you, Master Dudgeon . . . but I don't think one of your strongboxes will do for a—"

"*Treasure* Box," the dwarf asserted. "No strongbox. Different. Special."

The centaur, towering over the dwarf, looked down in surprise. "You have a Treasure Box, Beulandreus?"

The old dwarf only snorted loudly, then trundled over to the back wall. He snatched a huge iron key from its peg and opened a door in the back wall of the shop, grumbling to himself, "Idiot humans . . ."

"You have one here?" Edvard exclaimed in surprise.

"Secret!" Beulandreus exclaimed. "Wait!"

The dwarf returned a few moments later, gripping the iron key in one hand and a small object in the other. Returning the key to its peg, Beulandreus walked up to Jarod and held out his hand.

It was the most delicately carved, magnificent box that Jarod had ever seen. Beulandreus set it in Jarod's hands. It was remarkably light, and the relief carving on the lid was so intricate that Jarod was afraid to touch it.

"It's beautiful, Master Dudgeon," Jarod whispered. "But, I'm afraid it's too small. I need something that can hold a lady's hat and—"

"Humans!" the dwarf snorted. "See everything . . . understand nothing."

"I don't understand," Jarod said, shaking his head.

"It's a Treasure Box," the dwarf stated emphatically.

The young man glanced over at the Dragon's Bard, who only shrugged. Jarod looked back at the dwarf, not comprehending.

The dwarf took the box back and explained. "Something special to hold the love that is bigger than anything can contain." Beulandreus pushed in hidden catches on either side of the small box and, with a click, the box began to unfold into larger and larger sizes. When the box reached the size of a hat, the dwarf pressed a second set of hidden catches on the other sides of the box. The box stopped unfolding at once.

"These set the size of the treasure box," the dwarf explained. "When you push these other catches, yon box folds back as small as it ever was. Push the same again, and the box unfolds to this same size. You want a different size . . . push the second catches again when it is open and box resizes till you push second catches again. Simple . . . even for human. Look inside!"

The dwarf opened the box, and Jarod was astonished. It was larger inside than it was on the outside.

"Treasure Box," the dwarf said matter-of-factly.

"I think that the box," Jarod said in wonder, "is perhaps a greater treasure than the hat I hope to put in it."

Beulandreus reached out and took the box from Jarod. He pressed a set of catches and the box folded itself down to its original, palm size.

"Box unimportant," the dwarf huffed. "What you put in it what counts. You not win true heart with an empty box."

"There!" Edvard exclaimed. "Now you have the perfect container for the most precious gift you can give your beloved! All you need now is the means of presenting it!"

Jarod groaned. "I suppose by that you mean something better than, 'Hey, Caprice, here's a box with a hat in it.' How am I going to make some great, romantic speech when I can barely speak to her as it is?"

"The plan, my boy!" the Bard insisted.

"What plan?" Aren Bennis asked suspiciously.

"Consider it! You get tongue-tied whenever you face her, yes?"

"Maybe," Jarod fumed.

"Then all you have to do is present your gift and tell her your feelings without looking at her." Edvard threw his arms out in triumph. "I have devised a stratagem whereby you will be able to convey your true feelings to your beloved without ever having to look into her eyes!"

Aren Bennis frowned. "What nonsense is this?"

"I have already spoken with Father Patrion Trantus of your local church, who has offered his services to arrange—"

"Father Pantheon?" Aren roared. "He cannot even seem to pick a god to worship. You cannot seriously consider asking that addle-brained—"

"Hey!" Jarod shouted. "This is my quest! I'll take care of this myself and without any help from—"

"Jarod? Is that you?"

The young man turned quickly at the sound of the familiar voice.

"Caprice!"

"I thought that was you! I was beginning to wonder if I would run into you at all today." Caprice smiled beneath her large green eyes.

Even the blacksmith shop brightened in that moment, as though the sun had risen in Jarod's heart.

"Did you make brown bread today?" Jarod stammered as he reached back behind him.

He felt the dwarf press the Treasure Box into his hands.

## · CHAPTER 6 ·

# Father Pantheon

Eventide was set on both sides of the Wanderwine River, the main waterway through Beauford County in Windriftshire and, as such, an ancient trade route between the sea and the plains cities to the north. There, beneath the falls next to Bolly's Mill, the Wanderwine split at Prow Rock into the West Wanderwine and the East Wanderwine Rivers, the West Wanderwine being six feet longer than the East Wanderwine. This was measured twice by Jep Walters after he had lost a bet with Squire Tomas Melthalion. From the tip of Prow Rock to the end of the sand spit at the rivers' confluence just south of Lucius Tanner's tannery, the river measured exactly one thousand forty-four feet and five or seven inches. The rivers diverged in the north and converged in the south, surrounding a piece of land known locally as Boar's Island—although no one remembered ever seeing a boar there. It was a matter of local pride that the course of both the West Wanderwine and the East Wanderwine resided entirely within the charter limits of the town.

Reaching skyward just above Prow Rock on Boar's Island, the

Pantheon Church stood nestled among the trees, its four corner spires towering more than eighty feet above the town, no more accurate measure being available, as Jep Walters was unwilling to take that bet. The church was blessed with a surrounding and densely foliated copse of trees that insulated its holy place from the more mortal town around it. An elevated rectangular platform of polished stones formed its floor. This was reached by wide stairs on each of its four sides. Ornately carved columns set between the towering corner spires supported the tiled roof overhead, leaving the interior space majestically open. It was not the grandest structure, but the setting was perfect for showing its beauty, and it graced the town above the diverging rivers like a polished gem.

For Father Pantheon, however, it was a depressing sight.

His name was actually Father Patrion Trantus of the Order of the Lady of the Sky, or so he would tell anyone who asked, though no one ever did. He had begun his sojourn through mortality as Patric Fielder, son of Morina and Ned Fielder of Springtown in the farthest reaches of distant Notheringshire. Springtown had a small church with a most charismatic Sister Priestess Estra, whose amazing brown eyes and deeply dimpled cheeks may have led to Patric's early religious stirrings. Too soon, the Sister Priestess Estra was recalled to the Cloisters in Mordale, replaced by a Father Mendacious who, despite his gruff demeanor, took an interest in Patric. He taught the young man how to read holy script as well as the common letters and instructed him in the ways of the Lady of the Sky and the infallibility of the clerical leadership. When the time came, it was Father Mendacious himself who recommended Patric for admittance to the Lyceum in Mordale—the religious school within the Cloisters. There he proved adept and remarkably attentive— especially to classes led by Sister Priestess Estra, who by that time was an instructor in Spiritual Interpretations. His ordination was complete when, after finishing the coursework, Patric took the name of Father Patrion Trantus and eagerly awaited his first task from the Lady of the Sky.

It was a remarkably short wait. The ink was barely dry on his patents before he was summoned before the Lord Masterpriest and the Council of the Sky. A town's congregation was calling for a priest to conduct the ancient rites in a newly built church. By the command of the council—and presumably the direct wishes of the Lady of the Sky—Patrion set off at once to minister to the spiritual needs of the congregation, filled with all the fervor of his faith and a determined conviction.

Except that when he arrived there was no congregation.

It was true that there was a new church, but no one in the town had heard of his goddess, the Lady of the Sky, nor did they particularly care to learn about her. Of those who claimed worship of a deity, there seemed to be as many different gods and means of worshiping them as there were followers. The application of elemental magic forces—such as the wishers of the well employed—seemed to be of far more interest and devotion in Eventide than blessings or curses from a distant spiritual power.

However, the parish council for the village was most anxious to have someone of religious training conduct services in the new church they had just completed. The matrons of the town believed that religion—at least as a general concept—would help civilize Eventide, and the patrons who led the town knew that they could never be considered more than a hamlet until they had some sort of church. As they could not agree among the citizens on the parish council which particular god the temple should honor, they determined—after a committee recommended it—that they would build a pantheon temple to include all the gods that anyone might care to worship. They did so at once; all that was wanting was an authoritative figure with an open-minded view of worship to administer it.

Father Patrion may have gotten his religion from Sister Priestess Estra and Father Mendacious, but he had gotten practical and pragmatic wariness from his father. He was sure that his Lord Masterpriest had made a mistake in sending him here but was also a man who devoutly believed divine inspiration never made a mistake. If he were to go back to the council of Masterpriests claiming that one of their inspired leaders had made a mistake, he would be dismissed—and he most desperately needed to succeed here.

After all, he told himself, his assignment was for only one year. Then he would be recalled to the Cloisters and be reassigned by the Masterpriests, and his replacement could deal with the moral and ethical issues of being mistakenly assigned.

Since then, more than twenty years had passed.

It seems that an unprecedented *second* error had been perpetrated in not recording his assignment to the church in Eventide. Yearly, then monthly, then weekly he began writing the Masterpriests at the Cloisters in Mordale, each letter an exquisitely crafted prose offering that would gently remind them that he was in the wrong place and for the wrong period of time without ever once even implying any fallibility on the part of the Council. Their responses were equal to the task, thanking him in each case for his work on behalf of the Lady of the Sky and avoiding mention of anything remotely related to a mistake ever having been made or, for that matter, any action that might possibly either rectify or remedy his status.

Year revolved upon year, and his handsome young lines softened over time. He grew a belly on the offered meals by the fine ladies of the town and occasionally at the Griffon's Tale Inn. His hairline receded as his bald spot grew until they met, forming a small island of hair struggling to survive at the top of his forehead. He wore the robes of his calling less often than perhaps he should, choosing a felt-brimmed hat more often in winter than the knitted cap of his office. Graying stubble covered his cheeks more often than not. Yet still he hoped that perhaps through his influence over time he could convince these people of the error of their various ways and bring them into the true fold of his Lady's gaze.

Instead, he found himself conducting every kind of worship service imaginable for any number of different gods, goddesses, natural forces, and spirits. He had to be all faiths to all people, and it was beginning to wear on his own soul. Despite his insistence, the people of the town had quickly begun to refer to Father Patrion as Father Pantheon. It was an endearment to them while also somehow defining his place in their very small circle of community. As an outsider, it meant that he was, if not entirely accepted, then at least recognized as having a connection to them and the land. They never acquired much use for his "Lady of the Sky" goddess, and his hope of converting any of his patronage to his religion faded over time. Still, he had come to love the many different citizens of Eventide and believed that in his own way he served them to his Lady's approval.

Perhaps it was inevitable that this strain between conscience and pragmatism would eventually lead to problems.

"Just one moment . . . I am coming!"

The banging continued insistently on the heavy front door.

Patrion tugged with one hand at the mantle vesture that he had hastily thrown over his nightshirt while gripping the precariously swaying candleholder in the other. The feeble light from the candle flickered dangerously as he hurried down the small arcade of his home, his bare feet slapping against the cold stones.

"Why is it that trouble always comes in the dark?" he muttered to himself. In the moment, however, the answer came to him unbidden from a lecture in Masterpriest Duffetus's Scribner Class: *Night is when our Lady is at rest and trouble awakens in the world.* Still, he wished people could just keep their problems to themselves until a more reasonable hour of the morning—or, better still, early afternoon.

Father Patrion set his candleholder down on the small table next to the door, clasped his vesture unevenly, and then spoke loudly through the door. "Who is there?"

"Percival!" came the muffled voice. "Percival Taylor."

Father Patrion reached for the door catch and then hesitated. The priest knew the young man all too well. Percival Taylor was the son of Joaquim and Winifred Taylor. His parents were "locals," meaning that their family had been in Eventide for many generations and had not merely moved in due to some arbitrary convenience. They were well respected, hard-working, and considerate of others . . . in short, they were everything that their son was not.

Percival was a handsome lad who knew it and ensured that everyone else knew it too. He had a strong, cleft chin that was always closely shaven and flaxen hair that was always perfectly coifed. His flashing grey eyes could spot a skirt from a quarter mile, and, truth be told, odds were that it would be moving in his direction as iron to a lodestone. He was always impeccably dressed for any oc-casion that did not include manual labor and never present at any that required it. He was constantly busy but had never worked an honest hour in his life so far as anyone could recall. Those who were younger than he admired him. Those who were older suspected him. Those who were about his own age fell into two camps: those who were attracted to him . . . and everybody else. He was like a perfectly formed peach on the tree, desirable to look at and tempt-ing, but not anywhere near ripe.

Father Patrion shook his head. A young man in the middle of the night knocking at his door was never joyful news. Their prob-lems invariably revolved around the courting arts, an area where Father Pantheon had no experience whatsoever on which to draw. Worse, Patrion mused, why was it that young lovers always seem inclined to involve the clergy in elaborate, dramatic, and often problem-filled romantic schemes?

Father Patrion drew in a deep breath and opened the door.

Percival rushed in and then flattened himself against the arcade wall, doing his best impression of hiding in the shadows—only there were few shadows in which to hide since he was still within full illumination of the candle.

He was dressed for the occasion, Father Patrion noted with a thin smile. Percival wore a rakish felt cap with a long feather in it that, Patrion realized, looked remarkably similar to the hat worn by that fool Dragon's Bard who had been parading about the town this last month or so. Percival was wearing hose—a rather odd choice, given the bitter winter night—and stylish brushed-leather boots with soft soles. His tunic and doublet were made of matching deep plum fabric, and the grey great cape that Percival wore over the en-tire ensemble was held up with his left arm so as to cover the lower half of his face. The entire outfit looked as though it had been made specifically for the well-dressed skulker. No doubt his doting mother had made a point of producing it especially for the occasion.

"Brother Percival," Father Patrion said, suddenly aware that the hairs on the sides of his head were most likely sticking out at the oddest-appearing angles, "It is late and I must soon to bed."

Percival nodded, his golden curls bouncing slightly around the sides of his cap. "Yes, but I just have to see you, Father Pantheon—it's a matter of life and death!"

*Such an easy phrase,* Father Patrion thought sadly to himself. *How easily the young use it when they have so little knowledge of either.*

"Very well," Father Patrion said, motioning the youth out into the atrium. His home had been built by the town after the Mordale style popular with the country estates a few years ago. It was actually a small structure but it did feature an atrium garden surrounded by a small arcade. It reminded him strongly of the Cloisters and often made him feel better just to see it and work in its central garden. There was a path that led into the center of the atrium, where a pair of stone benches allowed for conference. "Please sit down."

"Oh, I just can't, Father Pantheon," Percival continued in a rush. "This is one of the most important nights ever—maybe of my whole life!"

"Then I'll sit," Father Patrion replied, sitting down as slowly as his aching back would allow. "What do you need, Brother?"

"You've got to help me, Father Pantheon," Percival moaned. He placed one foot on the stone bench and leaned toward the priest. "It's about a woman."

Father Patrion sighed, and then, seeing that Percival had come to a full stop, urged him on. "Of course, go on."

"I need to invite this woman to the Couples' Dance of Spring Revels," Percival replied.

Father Patrion rolled his eyes. Spring Revels! What person in the town *wasn't* concerned with Spring Revels? All the inhabitants were stuck in their homes, the fields all covered under snow or frost and asleep until spring. There was nothing to do *but* talk of Spring Revels. In a flash, however, Father Patrion thought he might see a way out of this discussion. "Then you have my blessing, my brother, to go and ask this woman to the Revels. I trust that the blessings of—"

"No!" Percival continued, "I can't just ask her like anyone else. It needs to be special, romantic and memorable, so that she'll see how great I really am. My mother told me the other day—"

"Your mother?" Father Patrion asked.

"Yes, she told me this great story she heard the other day about a man who met a woman in a romantic secret rendezvous—that was the very word she said, *rendezvous*—and how the man asked the woman in secret and she was so overcome by his romantic-ness that she swooned in his arms. That was the very word—*swooned*."

"That's fine, Percival, but what has all this got to do with—"

"You'll arrange it for me!" Percival crowed, poking his finger firmly into the priest's chest for emphasis. "You, the honest, trusted cleric of our community, will convey my invitation to this secret rendezvous."

"But that's over a month away," Father Patrion exclaimed.

"Sure, but you've got to get this message to her right away," Percival said earnestly. "I mean, what if some other man arranged for you to deliver this message before I did?"

"Percival, I really don't think this is anything that I—"

"What was that!" Percival leaped back with less the grace of a cat than the stumble of a startled puppy.

There was a banging once again against Father Patrion's front door.

The priest frowned.

"Quick! Hide me!" Percival said to the priest.

"Hide you? Whatever for?"

"I don't want anyone to know I'm here," Percival said sourly. "Someone might think I'm having trouble asking her out myself!"

The banging on the door resumed.

"It's going to be all right." Father Pantheon held up both his hands, then pointed toward the east side of the atrium. "You see that doorway there? Go in, close the door behind you, and wait for me."

"But it's dark in there," Percival whined.

"That's because it's night," Father Patrion answered, shoving the young man toward the doorway. When he was sure Percival was properly out of sight, the priest threw open the latch to the door once more.

"Good evening, Father, may I see you a moment?"

Before the astonished Father Patrion could answer, the Dragon's Bard had slipped past him and into the atrium.

"You!" the Father exclaimed.

"Indeed, it is I, the Dragon's Bard, in your very atrium, good Father Pantheon," the Bard replied with a flourish of his hat.

"That's Father *Patrion,*" the priest corrected, "and what are you doing here at this time of night?"

"I have come on behalf of a young man in need of your assistance," the Bard intoned in his most serious, resonant voice. "It's about . . . a *woman!*"

Father Patrion felt the blood coming into this face. "If you have had a dalliance with any of our good women, the town council will—"

"It is not for *me* that I come!" Edvard drew himself up with as much dignity as he could muster. "I am but a servant in this matter of one of your own good men who needs the help of his friends in order to secure the woman he loves!"

Father Patrion slowly drew his hand down the features of his face. "My good man, I am in no position—"

"Ah, but you are in the *perfect* position, and that is the point of my coming here," Edvard exclaimed. "Only you are in such a position of trust that your message may be believed without question and—"

"Hold!" Father Patrion thought he could hear some moaning from the eastern room. "Edvard . . . isn't it?"

"At your service, good Father Priest!"

"Edvard, do you see that doorway?"

"The one to the west, you mean?"

"Yes, the one that I'm pointing at—await me there and I will be with you directly."

"With heartfelt assurance," the Bard replied.

Father Patrion smiled and waited until the Bard had closed the door behind him. Then he turned quickly and padded to the east room door, his candle in hand.

Percival looked enormously relieved as the light entered the room. The room itself was Father Patrion's study, and Percival was rather out of place in his newly tailored sneaking clothes. One of the chairs had been knocked over as the youth had moved about in the dark, but gratefully nothing more had been disarranged by his blind stumbling.

"I appear to have a very busy evening, so if you do not mind—"

"It's very simple; I've worked everything out," Percival said. He turned and started rearranging the items on the top of Father Patrion's desk. "This book thing . . . what is it?"

"That's my Psalter of Morning Reflections!"

"Right. This psalter is the Pantheon Church, see? This plate over here is Chestnut Court, and this . . . what is this ribbon?"

Father Patrion shook his head in despair. "The Sash of Prayer."

"Well, now it's the West Wanderwine," Percival continued without pause. "This inkwell is the Cursed Sundial, and that blotter is Jep Walters's place on the south side of Charter Square. Here's all you have to do—"

"All I *have* to do?"

"It couldn't be more perfect," Percival went on. "You go to Vestia Walters—that's Jep's daughter—and deliver a message to her. She's to meet me in the deep shadows of the Pantheon Church right after the Ladies' Dance. There in the darkness I will deliver to her the feelings of my heart—along with one really expensive present my mother picked out—and then, HUZZAH! We're off to the Couples' Dance, with Vestia completely smitten with my charm and grace."

Father Patrion shook his head. "Tell me, Percival, just where did you get an idea so—"

"From my mother," Percival answered quickly.

"Your . . . your mother?"

"Absolutely!" Percival beamed. "She heard this story the other day from the Dragon's Bard about a young princess who desperately wanted to be loved but her beauty was so great that no one in the town could speak with her but there was this handsome prince who really wanted to court her but couldn't figure out a way to do it and so the young woman was told by the local priest to console herself by the light of the moon under the shadow of a gigantic oak tree that—"

"Percival, I don't need the whole story," Father Patrion said, holding up a staying hand.

"Of course, I've adapted it myself," Percival basked in his own cleverness. "I mean, I figured out to substitute your church for the oak, which is much better suited for lurking and skulking, and, of course, I'm not actually a prince but then Vestia is no princess either—"

"Well, that may depend on who you ask," Patrion muttered to himself, but then he spoke up again. "So, all you want is for me to tell Vestia Walters to meet you after the Ladies' Dance in the church."

"No!" Percival said, slamming his hand down hard on the desk and scattering the map of the town he had just built. "You cannot tell her it's me! That's the *mystery* part that will draw her heart into the church!"

"And presumably the rest of her with it," Father Patrion chuckled.

"Huh?"

"Don't you worry," Father Patrion answered through a yawn. "I'll deliver your message for you. Now, go home before your father figures out you're running about in the night looking like Dirk Gallowglass."

Percival grinned as Father Patrion took his candle in hand. They both left the room and entered the arcade around the atrium. Father Patrion watched with a weary smile as Percival moved with exaggerated stealth among the columns before letting himself out the massive front doors.

Father Patrion chuckled into the darkness of the atrium and was about to turn back toward his bedchamber at the back of the house when he suddenly remembered that he still had company. His eyes were stinging and longed to close for the night, but he could hardly leave such a rogue cooling his boots inside his own house. The priest stepped across the atrium and opened the door.

This room was a guest room set aside for any visiting Masterpriests who may happen to call upon him from Mordale. That there had never been any visiting Masterpriests had not deterred Father Patrion's hope, so the room was always kept ready for visitors who never came.

The Dragon's Bard was lying on the bed, and it galled Father Patrion that the first person to lie there had been this cad. "What do you want?"

The Bard leaped to his feet at once. "I come on most earnest behalf of a most earnest suitor—who begs your assistance in a matter of the heart."

"Oh, no," Father Patrion said, shaking his tired head.

"Oh, yes!" Edvard exclaimed. "I come on behalf of Jarod Klum. He begs your most august self to convey a message to a woman of honor for whom he has all the most honorable intentions. If you were to undertake this task for him, he would be grateful beyond his ability to convey."

Father Patrion realized that he was about to repeat the same conversation he had just had with the earnest young Percival—but apparently taking a great deal longer in the words. He wondered if he might shorten the process and finally get to bed. "You mean like the story."

"'Beauty and the Silent'?" Edvard's face broke into an appreciative grin. "You have *heard* my story, then? Well, I am flattered indeed!"

"I suppose your Jarod wishes to remain anonymous?"

"It is essential!"

"And he wants this woman to meet him after the Ladies' Dance?"

Edvard was astonished. "You *are* a man of the gods indeed if you possess such a gift of prophecy! That would be the perfect time!"

"And you want this delivered to Vestia Walters to be met in my Pantheon Church?"

Edvard was about to answer, but his mouth just hung open for a moment before he spoke. "Ah . . . no."

"No, you don't want the message delivered?" Father Patrion rubbed his eyes.

"I *do* want a message delivered—but it is intended for Caprice Morgan," Edvard said. "And it isn't in your silly church—she's to meet him in Chestnut Court under the great tree there!"

"Why in Chestnut Court?"

"Because there was no suitable oak available!"

Father Patrion growled from deep in his throat. "I'm not sure I understand."

"It's very simple," Edvard said. "Let's go over it again . . ."

By the time Edvard left his company, Father Patrion felt sure he had the whole thing straight and promised himself to write it all down first thing after he awoke in the rapidly approaching morning. Suddenly aware that there was a flaw in that plan, Father Patrion took a quill and ink in hand, his eyes barely open slits as he wrote down both messages, fell into bed, and let his troubles melt into comforting darkness of sleep.

When he awoke, the notes were there still by his bedside, and he was relieved that he had written them down. He remembered his mother having once told him that the dullest quill is better than the sharpest memory, and he took comfort in the barely legible words scratched onto the two parchment pages.

He rolled up both messages and sighed in relief. His memory might be bad and, he had to admit, he vaguely remembered the instructions differently . . .

. . . But certainly he would not have *written* the details down wrong.

# · CHAPTER 7 ·

# Pixie Hats

Pixies are a fearsome menace.

That knowledge comes both from experience and with the sure authority of Xander Lamplighter, the Constable Pro Tempore of Eventide, who will explain the dire threat to any who mentions a pixie in his presence. They look innocent enough, he will readily concede, with their tiny stature and their opalescent, translucent wings. Their lithe forms have a ready grace that larger folk envy, and they seem to have perpetual smiles on their eternally young faces.

But if you were to look closer behind that smile—and Xander cautions you fervently to never get that close—you would see mischievous, wanton, and malicious thoughts brewing constantly in their miniature brains.

Xander's arrival in Eventide was—as Ariela Soliandrus, the town's Gossip Fairy, often put it—the most fortuitous of events. Eventide, having never before in its history had a problem with a pixie infestation, had been suddenly overrun by the malicious creatures, who were causing havoc all about the town at the close of each day. Pigs' bladders filled with the most horrific-smelling solutions, stolen from Lucius's tannery south of town, rained down on unsuspecting ladies on Cobblestone Street, bursting against their heads and drenching them in smells that no amount of applied powders or perfumes would eradicate for several days. Jep Walters was stuck in one of his own barrels while a nasty group of pixies made a game of chasing Livinia—one of the town's most distinguished ladies—about her husband's cooper shop and tallying scores over which of them could get her to screech the loudest. Joaquim Taylor's entire stock of linens was ruined when the pixies painted patterns on each bolt with paint stolen from Mordechai Charon's stockroom. Deniva Kolyan's bakery was completely covered in a sticky paste of wheat flour. Town councils were held, speeches were made, and plans were agreed upon, but nothing, it seemed, would abate the escalating spree of the pixies. There was even talk of trying a broken wish from the wishing well, but no one was certain how a broken wish would react with a pixie. Sunset became a time of fear, for it heralded the coming of the pixies once more.

No one questioned their good fortune when Xander happened to arrive five days into the plague, walking down the road from Meade with the intention of plying his lamplighting skills in Eventide. He inquired as to why the townsfolk were so upset and, upon being informed of the infestation, humbly offered his services as an expert pixie catcher, should the town be willing to provide him with a bounty of fifty gold pieces, discounted from sixty-five. Xander was a large, somewhat overweight man, and there were many at the time who questioned how such an individual might catch the spry and elusive pixies. However, as Ward Klum offered to keep the fee in trust until Xander proved himself, the bargain was struck. The exhausted and discouraged citizens of Eventide managed to collect the bounty and lock it safely in the charge of the countinghouse. That night the townspeople gathered in trepidation at their doors, the flame of hope flickering feebly in their hearts.

Xander did not disappoint. As the pixies swept into town from the road to Meade, Xander stood his ground in Trader's Square, his knapsack at his feet. He reached down and pulled out what appeared to be the long horn of a steer that had been polished, its large end stopped with a bright brass plug. A fipple notch was cut at the back, wide end, with holes made down the length of the horn. Ariela flitted about, informing everyone that it was called a gemshorn even as Xander raised the instrument to his lips.

Xander blew softly into the flibble of the gemshorn, his thick fingers dancing along the length of the instrument. A soft, haunting tone came out, forming a simple, repeating melody with its rising and falling notes.

To the astonishment of the townspeople, the pixies flew directly at him and then settled into an undulating circle drifting above his head. As more pixies joined the circle, it grew larger and split into two, then three smaller circles of pixies all dancing about Xander's head.

Xander slowly moved toward one of the streetlamps that stood at the edge of Trader's Square. Iron frames forged by Beulandreus Dudgeon each held a thick storm lantern glass with an oil reservoir base and a wick. One side of the glass was hinged and held closed with a catch. Xander, still playing the gemshorn with one hand, reached up to the first lamp, opened the catch, and pointed inside.

To everyone's amazement, several of the pixies flew directly into the lamp housing, whereupon Xander flipped closed the glass and secured the latch. The trapped pixies suddenly blazed with a light far brighter than the oil flame the lantern normally contained.

Xander continued from lamp to lamp around Trader's Square and then crossed the bridge to Charter Square, the remaining pixies circling his head until he had put the last four of them together in a lamp housing and latched it shut.

In the bright, pixie-illuminated square, the townsfolk cheered for Xander and his marvelous ability to deal with the pixie menace. As their previous constable had gone in search of the highwayman Dirk Gallowglass and had never returned, Xander was offered the job of Constable Pro Tempore—a temporary appointment until the missing constable was found. He could take the pay for both the constable and the lamplighter position at the same time, since the town was grateful to him for ending the menace and everyone very much liked the brighter lights the now-secure pixies provided each night.

Xander accepted at once and, as a result, had been the temporary constable in the town for the last eight years.

As to the shining light of the trapped pixies, Ariela explained to all the ladies of Cobblestone Street that it was no doubt a result of their anger at having been tricked themselves. Everyone who lived in Eventide knew that pixies were thieves, scoundrels, and liars who could not be believed even if you were to deign speak with them.

But a visitor to the town who might not be immediately familiar with this history might, late at night and alone, find himself in conversation with a lamppost in a remote corner of the square. If such a person were to engage the pixies in the lamp, he might be told that pixies actually *prefer* being in the lamps. The pixies might tell a person that from their protected glass perches in the lamps, they find watching and listening to the townspeople below them better than any other entertainment. They might inform such an unsuspecting individual that no one ever thinks that a lamppost might be watching or listening to everything near it or that one can learn a lot by being a lamppost.

But, as most everyone in Eventide knows, pixies are liars.

"Merinda?" Livinia Walters called out. "Helloo! Merinda?"

Merinda Oakman managed somehow to lift her heavy head. It was well after dark. She longed for the day to be over but somehow just could not imagine it ever coming to a conclusion. She eyed the door to her shop with longing. She had been so close with her burden of cloth and ribbons she had just bartered from Charon's Goods next door. A few more steps and she would have safely been inside and not have to face Livinia or the prospect of conversation. Yet it could not be avoided now.

"Good evening, Livinia," Merinda said, taking another step toward the door.

"Have you heard the news?" Livinia said, stepping deliberately in front of Merinda and blocking her escape.

Merinda sighed, looking up through bleary eyes. She asked the question less out of curiosity than out of a desire to move things along. "What news?"

"Duke Hareld, third cousin once removed to the king himself, will be celebrating his Spring Revels right here in Eventide!" Livinia was a tall woman, which allowed her the luxury of looking down on every other woman in the town. As the wife of Jep Walters—town cooper and guildmaster—she considered herself the patroness and first lady of the town. She had fine high cheekbones and arched eyebrows over brown eyes. Her mouth was small, with perpetually pursed lips. Her nose was upturned, although Merinda often wondered if this should be attributed to nature or demeanor. She wore an elegant, fox-trimmed coat and a tall fur hat against the chill night air. The snows had largely vanished in the warming days, but the evenings remained cold.

"The third cousin to the king?" Merinda was having trouble understanding as she shifted the cumbersome fabric in her arms.

"Once removed," Livinia corrected. "He is the descendant of the king's great-great-grandfather on his father's mother's mother's father's side through Dora of Ethandria . . . she married that brother of the despot . . . oh, why can I never remember his name! You know the one. Anyway, he'll be here for Revels tomorrow and that can only mean he'll bring ever so many more people into our town!"

Merinda only nodded. She had heard the same rumor from the Gossip Fairy earlier in the day and had immediately discounted it. Ariela was always exaggerating, and even if this duke-once-removed somehow miraculously showed up, it would not change her problem. "That is good news! Now, if you'll excuse me—"

"It is more than good news!" Livinia insisted, still blocking Merinda's escape. "We've been preparing for months for these Revels! Much of our town's future depends upon this occasion, and with the blessing of someone in the royal house—"

"Livinia, Duke Hareld is not even allowed at court," Merinda said tiredly. "The only reason we even know who he is is because he's had to move from town to town ahead of any number of debts or women to whom he owes more than a debt. If he shows up, it can hardly be to the town's credit."

Livinia affected a shocked look. "Why, Merinda! That's not like you one bit! I thought you were excited for the Revels to begin!"

Merinda wished she could get away. "I am. It's just . . ."

"Just what, dear?"

"Harv's not back," Merinda answered in a rush. Maybe if she got it all out it would give Livinia enough to think about that she could end the conversation. "He was supposed to return from Welston with all my finishing supplies—ribbons, lace, and those fashionable small feathers from the East. The basic hats are made, but he hasn't come with the new trims. I've got piles of old stuff in the storeroom, but I'd just die if I had to show outdated notions to the fashionable women from town. Harv should have been here a week ago. He's never missed Revels before. I've been so upset. I haven't been able to trim my hats, and now the Revels are starting tomorrow and I just don't have enough fashionable findings to finish. I'm in real trouble, Liv."

"Oh, I'm sorry, Meri," Livinia said with the smile of someone who can appreciate trouble when it is not her own. "But I'm sure it will all work out for the best."

"I only wish Harv were back," Merinda said, tears welling up unbidden in her eyes. "I could really use some help—"

"Oh, look how late it has gotten," Livinia said at once, suddenly rushing past the milliner and launching across Charter Square toward her home above the cooperage. "My Jep will be wondering where I have been. Best of luck to you, Merinda, and I hope we'll be seeing you at the Revels Dance tomorrow night!"

Merinda stared at the back of the rapidly retreating Livinia. "Thanks, Liv, for all your help," she said meekly. She turned and took her final steps to the door of her shop, wiped a tear from her eye, and turned the key in the lock.

As Merinda entered her shop, three pixies stared down from the lamppost above her.

"Have you been hearing that, Glix?" said one of the pixies.

"I have indeed, Snix," the pixie replied. "Merinda's asking for help, and who is there about to give it to her?"

"Who indeed?" Plix smiled. "But she's a bit twitchy, friend Merinda. You figure she'll let us in?"

"Actually, I was thinking this would be better as a surprise than an actual association. Dix! You got any of that magic snooze booze about?"

Dix closed one eye as he thought. "That I have, Glix! You ciphering a plan?"

"Gather the clan, boys," Glix grinned. "We're paying a debt tonight!"

BANG! BANG! BANG!

Merinda tossed the hat in her hands down at her worktable.

"Who is it?" she called out.

BANG! BANG! BANG! BANG! BANG!

Exhausted, Merinda got up slowly from her chair and walked into the kitchen. Who could possibly be at her door at this time of night? It could only be bad news. She grabbed a poker iron from the hearth as a precaution. She did not really know what she would do with it if there were some highwayman at the door, but holding it made her feel better. "I'm coming!"

She drew back the poker and opened the door.

Standing on her stoop was a single small pixie, its hands folded behind its back.

It was the last thing she remembered that night.

Merinda was staring at the ceiling of her kitchen.

She could not remember how she had gotten there or why she should be sleeping on the hard floor. She was still wearing yesterday's dress. Merinda lay still for a few moments, wondering why there was a knocking at her kitchen door and why would it be so insistent.

Knocking? At this time of the—

Bright sunlight was streaming through her kitchen windows.

Merinda sat up at once and immediately regretted it. Her head was throbbing with a sudden and terrible headache that seemed to center behind both her eyes, a pain that pulsed to the banging on her door.

"Missus Oakman?" came the muffled voice beyond the door.

Merinda held one hand against her forehead while she staggered carefully to her feet. "Who is it?"

"Jarod, ma'am," came the youthful voice. "Jarod Klum."

Merinda opened the door. The morning sun shone through a bright blue sky as it crested just above the storage sheds and buildings east across her husband's work yard. A gaggle of grey geese were honking in the yard but there was another, rushing sound that filled the air from west down the alley. Most of her vision, however, was filled with the lanky frame of Ward Klum's apprentice son.

"Jarod, of course," the milliner said as she blinked at the brilliance behind the young man. "What brings you here so early?"

"Early?" Jarod puzzled. "Missus Oakman, it's past midmorning now."

"What?" Merinda squawked.

"I came to get my hat—the one I ordered?" Jarod suggested, eyeing the milliner with concern. "Oh, please tell me you remembered! If you didn't, I just don't know what I'll do!"

"It's all right, Jarod." The morning air was helping to clear her head. She was beginning to feel as though she might recover her faculties. "Of course, I remembered your hat—your quest hat, as I recall. Come on in and I'll get it for you."

Jarod followed Merinda into the kitchen. "I'm sorry to bother you, Missus Oakman, but I tried the front door and it was still locked. There's quite a crowd out there right now waiting for you to open your shop, so I thought I might try your kitchen door. I hope that's all right."

Merinda gripped the edge of the table for a moment to steady herself. When the room stopped moving she continued through the door into her workroom space, waving for Jarod to follow. "Come. Your hat is out front."

Merinda stepped through the second door and into her shop.

What happened next remains a matter of lengthy and unsettled debate among the people of Eventide. Some say that Merinda's scream was heard only as far south as the tannery, while others maintain, by careful time calculations and accounts of witnesses, that it was heard as far as the docks of Blackshore. A few assert that it was Jarod who screamed, but these statements were largely accredited to those who were jealous of his having been on hand for the event. Some added that Merinda fainted at the sight that greeted her as she stepped into the shop. Still others—Jarod Klum among them—maintain that Merinda did not faint but after uttering her unnatural shriek stood shaking violently for several moments before Jarod could get her to respond.

"Missus Oakman!" Jarod was shouting. "What is it?"

Her mind, knotted at the sight that greeted her, suddenly unraveled into a torrent of words that were indistinguishable until they collapsed into a stuttering series of "My hats! My hats! I didn't . . . I mean, who could have possibly . . ."

Her eyes widened.

"Those pixies . . . they've ruined me! Ruined my life! My hopes! Everything!"

Her shop was filled with hats, floor to ceiling, of the most hideous, gaudy, and downright frightening design. It was as though the contents of her entire inventory of out-of-date and out-of-fashion materials, along with quite a few of her husband's woodcraft hardware pieces and many of her kitchen tools, had been emptied into the room and then arranged on her hats in the most unimaginable forms. Hats shaped like boats, complete with sails and full rigging, plying green tulle seas that rocked back and forth at the crown. Hats shaped into tall willows with fronds hanging past the brim, each one filled with bells. Hats with cartwheels attached to rotate at the crown with flowers dangling from their rims. Bonnets with blue-linen waterfalls shaped down the back. Hats with a great hole in the crown and a brim of enormous yellow petals forming a sunflower out of the wearers' head. Hats with shaped glass casting rainbows in the sunlight. Hats formed with wired buckram into the shape of her own shop, complete with a miniature sign hanging off the front. Hats—every one—mixing colors and forms that had no reason for being together.

Jarod, whose fashion sense about hats had already been demonstrably lacking, said, "Shall I open the door?"

"NO!" Merinda screeched.

"But they're all waiting," Jarod said.

Merinda looked through the glass in the front of her shop. A sea of faces stared expectantly back at her.

"I can't! I just . . . I'll explain that there's been an accident in the shop and that we . . . we regret that we cannot open today." Merinda stepped to the door, unlocking it. "I'm sure they'll understand if I—"

She never got to open the door. The crowd took the sound of the latch to be permission and pushed open the door, pressing Merinda and Jarod both to seek refuge behind the counter.

"Please, everyone, may I have your attention . . ."

The throng was unwilling to give her any attention, being distracted by the ridiculous hats.

Merinda tried again. "Please! I have something to say!"

Unexpectedly, the crowd filling her showroom parted. A woman wearing a deep blue velvet dress fitted with diamonds walked into the shop.

Merinda gasped. She recognized the woman immediately, though she had only ever seen her once from a distance during one of her fall trips to Mordale. She knew her as the Lady of Lorem Street—that avenue in Mordale where all the finest milliners plied their trade. She was a legendary beauty, with bards falling over themselves to compose tunes to her praise. Her attendance at court was never questioned. She was the confidante of Princess Aerthia and Queen Nance. Hats were all the rage in Mordale among the women, and every woman in the King's City—including the Queen—looked to the Lady of Lorem Street to know what they should wear.

Merinda stood frozen in her own nightmare as the Lady of Lorem Street walked directly through the crowd toward her.

"Are you the proprietress of this shop?" said the Lady in a deep, soft voice.

"I am, dear Lady," Merinda heard herself saying.

The Lady of Lorem Street smiled. "May I see that hat?"

Merinda reached back behind her, taking one of the bizarre creations off the shelf and handing to the Lady.

"Is this a teapot used for the crown?" the Lady asked.

"Yes, dear Lady," Merinda answered, her hands gripped together in front of her so tightly that the color was forced out of them. It had been her best teapot, a blue and white china piece that Harv had bought for her three years ago on a trip to Blackshore.

"And these long feathers sticking out from the spout," the Lady continued. "They look like a stream of colorful pouring tea. Tell me, do you wear it with the feathers facing front or down the back?"

Merinda considered answering truthfully for a moment by saying it would look ridiculous either way, but instead answered, "As you wish, dear Lady."

The Lady of Lorem Street pursed her lips in thought, then gestured with her hand to another hat. "And what of that one there?"

Merinda braced herself and turned. It was a conical hat on first impression, but then she noticed the cone was made up entirely of ribbons hanging from a central wooden dowel and spaced around a circular block. The ribbons hung down even farther beyond the block, ending with tassels and small pipes like chimes. The skullcap itself underneath had long ribbons to tie the entire assembly to the head. It made no sense to her when she picked it up, but as she turned to hand it to the Lady, the circular block rotated, winding the ribbons around the dowel as it spun.

The Lady gasped in delight. "It's a ribbon dance! How delightful! It winds the ribbons around the pole and then unwinds them the other way."

Merinda smiled. It defied all the rules of hats, but it was somehow charming.

"I'll take them both," said the Lady of Lorem Street.

Merinda blinked.

The Lady dropped a velvet purse on the counter, which landed with a heavy ringing sound. It was more gold coin than Merinda had ever seen in an entire season of hats.

The Lady turned with a smile. She removed her fine blue-silk-brimmed hat and placed the ribbon dance hat on her head at a rakish angle. The ribbons spun and danced about her head.

"What a charming shop," said the Lady of Lorem Street as she walked out holding her teapot hat in her hands. "I shall have to visit it again."

The rush to Merinda's counter was immediate.

The shadow on the Cursed Sundial had not yet reached noon when Merinda was forced to close her doors for good. Every hat in her shop had been sold, and each for more gold coins than she would have dared dream possible.

As she locked the door, she turned and saw Jarod standing behind the counter looking rather glum. "I guess there's nothing left, is there?"

Merinda gave Jarod a tired smile. "No, there's one left."

Jarod looked up.

"I didn't forget you, Master Klum," Merinda said, walking behind the counter. She reached down and pulled out the last remaining hat. It was a flat-brimmed hat with a felt-covered dragon wrapped around the crown. It appeared to be sleeping, with smoke puffing out of its snout. Its wings were folded up like the brim of the hat, and its tail hung down long over the side.

Jarod took the hat in his hands. "I don't think I can afford it now. Your hats have gotten pretty expensive."

Merinda laughed. "It's yours, Jarod. You've earned it. You said it was supposed to be a quest hat. What better quest than a dragon?"

Jarod smiled.

"I'll let you out the back," Merinda said. "If I open the front door again, there's no telling what will happen."

As Jarod passed through the kitchen door, Merinda saw her beloved husband, Harvest, jumping down from his wagon.

"I'm sorry, love," he said. "I lost a wheel outside of Welston going out and coming back. I'd have come sooner but—"

Merinda rushed across the work yard and threw her arms around her husband.

"Say, what's happened?" he smiled.

"I'll tell you later," she said, the twinkle back in her eyes. "Take me to the dance?"

That summer, teapots and colorful feathers became all the rage in Mordale. For many years afterward, Merinda Oakman would make her way to that castle city in the late fall, though not so late as before. She would visit the shops of Lorem Street, but now in the company of the Lady, with whom she grew a great friendship. She was presented to court at the great castle, introduced to Queen Nance and Princess Aerthia, invited to the cathedrals—and she always turned heads whenever she deigned to attend the tournament lists.

But she always returned to Eventide, to her little shop and to her beloved Harv Oakman. On wintry nights, it was said by her neighbors, the strange sounds of loud songs and raucous laughter were heard coming from her kitchen when Harv was away on his deliveries.

And she always kept a pickle barrel by her kitchen door.

Jarod stepped down the alley toward the crowded square. He reached into his pouch and pulled out the Treasure Box. It unfolded to just the right size in his hand. He slipped the hat into the box and folded it back up, slipping it back into the pouch.

"It's all going according to plan," he said to himself as he stepped into the crowded Charter Square. Revelers—many of them in Merinda's hats—were moving from cart to cart among the vendors or singing with the musicians performing in the square.

He was so distracted by his own success that he did not hear his name being called at first.

"Master Klum! Master Klum! Hold a moment, please!"

Jarod turned and was astonished to see Father Pantheon pushing his way toward him through the throng.

"Father?"

The priest grasped him by both shoulders. "Thank the Lady I've found you. I've made a terrible mistake!"

· CHAPTER 8 ·

# Mumbles and Bumbles

You've had a terrible brisket?" Jarod responded dubiously.
Charter Square was packed with people, turning the usually
quiet town into a teeming sea of noisy strangers largely capped with
very strange hats.

"No!" Father Patrion shouted at him. "A mistake! I've made a
mistake!"

"What are you talking about?" Jarod yelled back. It was impossible to hear over the jubilant crowd and the approaching bleating
of the Flag Four Troubadours, a traveling group of musicians out
of Butterfield who had been hired by Livinia Walters to perform
throughout the day of Spring Revels and especially for the dance that
night. The troubadours were professional musicians, strictly speaking, in that they were being paid by Livinia to perform, though they
were more often recognized in the neighboring community as the
local butcher, baker, chandler, and farrier. Their particularly spirited
version of "My Lady Still Standing in the Tavern," performed with

panpipe, krummhorn, rebec, and tambourine, was getting louder as they made their way across the square.

"Last night I had a vision," the priest said.

"You had a lesion?" Jarod squinted in concentration beneath the noon sun. "Is it painful?"

"A *vision!*" Father Patrion yelled. "A dream that was more than a dream! I saw her . . . she spoke to me."

"Who spoke to you, Father?" Jarod was having trouble following the priest's words, let alone his meaning.

"It was the Lady of the Sky!"

"What baby? What sty?"

The troubadours' song reached its rousing conclusion and the crowd erupted into applause and cheers.

"No! The *Lady* of the . . . it doesn't matter," Father Patrion went on quickly. The troubadours were speaking to the crowd, preparing to announce their next number, and the priest knew he had only a few moments before it would be impossible for Jarod to understand him again. "I told your lady the wrong place to meet you."

Jarod went suddenly pale in the late winter light. "You did what?"

"The Lady came to me in the night—"

"Listen, Father, that's really none of my business if—hey, *what* lady came to you in the night? If you so much as touched Caprice, I'll—"

"Listen to me!" Father Patrion could hear the troubadours hastily and unsuccessfully tuning for their next song. "Where is Caprice supposed to meet you?"

"In Chestnut Court beneath the great tree right after the Ladies' Dance," Jarod said. "I've arranged it with Xander Lamplighter so that—"

"She won't be there," Father Patrion said quickly. "She'll be at Pantheon Church . . . and that's where you have to be, too."

"Pantheon Church?" Jarod repeated.

"Right after the Ladies' Dance," Father Patrion nodded firmly. "You meet your lady at Pantheon Church! Now, have you seen Percival?"

The troubadours suddenly struck up their next number. It was the crowd favorite "The Sea Does Not Want Me Again," which elicited a great cheer. The noise was deafening.

"Percival? You mean Percival Taylor?"

"Yes!" The racket from the troubadours and the crowd had become a nearly impenetrable wall of noise. "Have you seen him?"

"No," Jarod yelled at the top of his lungs. "Why, Father?"

But the priest had already disappeared in the crowd.

Percival Taylor knew himself to be an expert at improvising. For many years now, he had improvised his way out of chores, improvised his way out of responsibilities, improvised his way out of debts, and, in more recent years, improvised his way out of awkward relationships that had—due to no fault of his own—gotten entirely too serious or too complicated for his improvised life. Whenever change had come, he had known to change with it—and to do so with a brilliant smile and a sense of panache. He knew with all his soul that he was destined for something great and did not particularly care what that greatness would be. His destiny would find him without all the planning, fretting, and, worst of all, pointless labor that his father seemed to feel—in his obviously limited vision—was required. He was beautiful, and he was profoundly aware of that fact and that the world owed something to the beautiful.

One of those beautiful things the world owed him was a beautiful woman at his side to balance his own glorious and gorgeous countenance. Admittedly, the selection in such an insignificant place as Eventide was limited, but in this he believed that fate had been kind. Having placed him in this small town, it would have been unjust not to have put an equal splendor here to balance the world.

His original plan had been completely perfect in every detail. He would hide among the shadows of the Pantheon Church in his dashing rogue costume—perfectly tailored for him by his adoring mother—and move silently among the pillars as the object of his affections stood by the central altar. Then he would spring upon her, startling her there alone, and sweep her into his arms as he proclaimed his adoration of her beauty.

Unfortunately, the priest, who had no appreciation for romantic adventurism, had mistakenly told the girl to wait for him under the great tree in Chestnut Court.

Unfazed by this news, Percival determined at once to improvise. As the sun set, he donned his rogue's outfit, examined his looks thoroughly in the polished metal mirror in his mother's fitting room, and then bounded into the twilight with his cape held across the lower half of his face's chiseled features. He stealthily made his way down the now completely deserted Butterfield Road, turned toward Blackshore at the crossroads all of two hundred feet distant from his back door, and crossed the East Bridge onto Boar's Island. It was a long, circuitous route, permitting him to leave the island by South Bridge, cross the Wanderwine again, and reenter the town from the south. Dark was falling quickly as he approached Chestnut Court and the enormous chestnut tree at its center.

The cloaked Percival stopped at the edge of the courtyard and frowned.

The lamps bordering Chestnut Court were all dark. No pixies illuminated the courtyard with their bright glow, although he could see lamps illuminated on Cobblestone Street north and south of the courtyard.

Percival smiled. Fortune, he believed, had smiled on him. He had intended to surprise the object of his desire in the church. Knowing that there was no way to sneak up on anyone under the tree in the middle of the courtyard, he had thought that part of his plan would have to be abandoned. Now, however, a new plan—a brilliantly improvised plan—sprang into his head.

Percival looked about him and, confirming the courtyard still deserted, dashed to the massive chestnut's trunk. Grasping its lowest reaching branch, he scampered up into the tree.

Jarod sat behind the altar of the church, musing in the darkness.

He was uncomfortable, and not just from the etched stone that dug into his back where he sat. Everything he felt for Caprice Morgan was too big for the words he had been considering for months now. The Dragon's Bard had done his best to coach him—much to the amusement of Farmer Bennis—and he had rehearsed any number of speeches, all of which sounded stiff in his ears and nothing close to what he truly felt.

Jarod turned the Treasure Box over and over in his hands, questioning once again if he were doing this right, if she would like the gift, or if he could even find the courage to give it to her. The hat it contained was ridiculous. Would Caprice think so too? Would she laugh at him? Could he even speak?

*That was the point, wasn't it?* he reminded himself. *I'm sitting here in the dark so that I can say to her in the darkness what I can't say to her in the light.* He had even gone to the trouble of getting Xander Lamplighter to keep all the lamps around Chestnut Court free of pixies so that he could speak to Caprice without seeing her face. Now, he knew, the courtyard was dark for nothing as he waited here—and for what? To be rejected? Or worse?

Jarod made his mind up to go home and was about to stand up when he heard light footsteps coming into the church.

Something stirred within him. He had wondered if the heroes in the stories and legends who fought the dragons and the terrible ogres and giants of the midlands in the Epic War also felt this fear and, in that moment, gathered their courage and stood up to do the great deeds for which their songs were sung. Jarod suddenly knew that it was time—that this was his moment to face his fear and Caprice.

A thousand words rushed through his thoughts as he stood up, but they all fled him. All he said as he turned was, "I brought you a present. Will you come to the dance with . . ."

He froze, the box held between his hands.

He was looking into the gloriously pretty face of Vestia Walters.

Caprice Morgan stopped at the edge of Chestnut Court and frowned. The instructions from Father Patrion had been specific, but there was something about the courtyard that she did not like.

It was dark, to be sure, especially after the bright pixie light from the lamps lining Cobblestone Street, but this alone was little cause for alarm. It was something within the magic of herself—the inner sense of a wish-woman—that told her that the courtyard held her destiny but in the strange way of her broken well.

Caprice had worn her best dress, a plum-colored fabric with elegant brocade panels and a high collar. It had been her mother's, and although the fabric had faded slightly over time it fit her perfectly. She wore a short jacket against the evening chill, but she hated hats and never wore one if she could avoid it.

Still, the priest had been quite specific about the time and the place. She had participated in the Ladies' Dance in the Cooper's Hall—Jep Walters's place of business on the south side of Charter Square—and come directly here. Shrugging, she stepped into the square and crossed directly to the base of the chestnut tree.

It was difficult to see, as her eyes had been accustomed to the lights of Cobblestone Street. She found the trunk of the tree, turned, and, crossing her arms, waited.

She could hear the distant sound of the troubadours' music drifting down the river from the Cooper's Hall to the north. There was a rustling and creaking sound from the branches overhead. A twig snapped.

Suddenly, a shadowed form dropped directly down in front of Caprice, its dark face a mystery. It fell to the ground, struggling with its cape for a moment before it rose up and turned toward her.

Caprice screamed, instantly drew back her right arm, and drove her small, clenched fist with all the might of her shock with such force into the nose of her assailant that it lifted both his feet free of the ground and sent him sprawling across the frozen ground.

Still screaming, Caprice ran back up Cobblestone Street, leaving the groaning figure of a rogue moaning on the ground.

"For me?" Vestia squealed as she reached forward and snatched the box from Jarod's hands.

"No . . . I mean . . ."

"Oh, you mean what's *in* the box is for me, don't you!" Vestia teased.

Vestia Walters was the daughter of the town's leading matron and patroness Livinia Walters. Jep Walters was her father. She was as lithe as a lily and as deep as a sheet of parchment—a blank parchment at that. She was the undisputed beauty of the town, a perfect statue to look at and admire, and about as good at conversation as shaped marble can be. This is not to say that Vestia was foolish: she possessed considerable cunning and uncanny sense when it came to society. She knew what she wanted out of life, believed she had the physical assets that would allow her to acquire it, and possessed a romantically sensible disposition that allowed her to always better her position.

Tonight she was dressed for the hunt at the dance in a fabulously cut hunter green silk dress with white, fox-fur trim. It showed her figure to its best advantage. Even in the darkness of the church, Jarod could see that her golden hair had been carefully prepared to frame perfectly the curve of her jaw and her small, upturned nose.

Jarod pulled at the collar of his doublet, panic rising perceptibly from somewhere near his stomach.

"How do you open this . . . oh, here's the latch!" Vestia bubbled at the thought of her gift. She threw open the top of the box and gasped.

"It's not . . . I mean, it wasn't meant . . ."

"Oh, but it's *perfect!*" Vestia cooed. She reached into the box and removed the sleeping dragon hat.

She tossed the Treasure Box casually aside, its wood banging against the floor as it fell on its side.

Jarod, horrified, reached down at once, retrieving the box from where it had been discarded. He quickly pressed the catches and was relieved to find that the box still functioned, folding itself down until he could hold it in his palm and out of sight.

"Why, it's absolutely adorable!" Vestia continued, her entire world revolving around her present for the moment. "You know, everyone in town who is anyone got one of these hats today, and I was absolutely sure that I wasn't going to get one because Mother was in such a snit about Merinda Oakman this morning, but here you've gone and given me the best one of all! Why, Jarod Klum, I had no idea that you even thought of me that way!"

"Well, Vestia, you're a nice girl and all, but I—"

"Now, you didn't invite me out here to this church with some other purpose in mind, did you, Jarod Klum?" Vestia teased.

Jarod felt the heat rush to his face. "No! I wouldn't . . . I didn't . . ."

"You're right," Vestia continued the conversation on her own since Jarod obviously was not going to participate as quickly as she liked. "There's probably not enough time now, so we'll just have to think about that later. We've got to get back to that Couples' Dance that's coming up! I want to show this hat off to all the girls in town and you with it!"

"But Vestia . . ."

"Say, where's that box my hat was in?" Vestia glanced around her.

"I've taken care of it," Jarod said.

"Good!" Vestia smiled brightly as she took Jarod's arm and led him out of the church. "We wouldn't want anyone knowing we were here by leaving junk around."

Jarod, with the splendid Vestia on his arm, stepped off the bridge at Bolly Falls into Charter Square and stopped.

Warmth and light poured out from the large open doors of the Cooper's Hall on the south side of the square. The sounds of the crowd within rolled in muffled tones into the night. The square itself was brightly lit by the pixies in their lamp prisons, illuminating the heavy flakes of a late snow beginning to fall.

Caprice Morgan stood beneath one of the streetlamps, brushing a tear from her eye. She did not see him standing there watching her as she gathered her jacket about her and stepped into the Cooper's Hall alone.

Jarod could only stare.

"What is it?" Vestia asked with a bright innocence, even though this was one area where she was uncannily aware and knew a threat to her when she saw one.

"Oh, nothing," Jarod said, though in his heart he knew it was absolutely everything.

"Come on, then," Vestia tugged at his arm. "Let's show this town how a Couples' Dance is done!"

Jarod looked down into her radiant, beautiful face and felt nothing except his own sense of obligation and a kind desire not to embarrass or hurt this lovely creature who had been thrown in his path through no fault of his own.

Jarod managed a smile. "Very well, Vestia. You need to show off your hat."

Jarod vaguely wondered as he stepped into the Cooper's Hall why the troubadours were not playing. Indeed, the crowd in the hall was milling about excitedly and muttering in harsh undertones.

"What's going on, Jarod?" Vestia asked.

Jarod was craning his neck, trying to see over the heads of the throng around him. "I don't know. Something's wrong."

"You don't think it will delay the dance, do you?" she asked with genuine concern.

"I don't know . . . Father!"

Ward Klum, looking, if anything, more grim than usual, turned toward his son's voice and motioned Jarod toward him.

"You wait here, Vestia," Jarod said, then abandoned her as he pushed his way carefully through the party costumes and dresses of the evening. "Father, what's happened?"

"Beulandreus Dudgeon. Xander's placed him under arrest."

"Arrest?" Jarod was incredulous. "For what?"

"It's Livinia Walters who's made the charge but her evidence is so unusual I just don't know . . ."

"What is he charged with, Father?' Jarod repeated.

"Theft," his father answered. "Theft and fraud."

## · CHAPTER 9 ·

# The Curious Dwarven Smith

arlier that same evening, in the deepening blue twilight of the early spring night, a dwarf had stood atop a crate in the shadows behind the Cooper's Hall. There, in the settling chill of night, he had gripped a windowsill with his large hands and peered quietly inside.

On the other side of the slightly distorted glass, the women of Eventide gathered together in the open center space of the Cooper's Hall for the Ladies' Dance. Under the bright glow of a half dozen pixie lamps provided by Xander Lamplighter, and with a roaring fire in the enormous hearth casting warmth and a cheerful glow over the crowd, a tradition as old as anyone's memory joyfully began once more. All of the eligible young women of the town pranced lithely into the cleared center of the floor, fluttering like butterflies from the streams of colorful ribbons each had tied to their wrists. Vestia Walters, Evangeline Melthalion, Megeri Kolyan, the Bolly twins, and all three of the Morgan sisters—with Sobrina doing so under only the slightest of protests—all these and a dozen more from beyond the town boundaries fluttered together. Many of the younger girls joined in out of sheer exuberance, and occasionally one or two of the older ladies—usually including the Widow Merryweather—had been known to take a turn or two during the dance. Ariela Soliandrus, the Gossip Fairy, hovered among the Spring Revel hats of the married women, watching intently but never once joining in, as she had made a point of abstaining at every Ladies' Dance since she came to the town. The young men were also watching intensely, though their motives were easier to guess than those of the Gossip Fairy.

Aren Bennis, the centaur who generally kept to himself, watched with several visiting centaurs from where they stood together near the door. Bennis had managed to comb his hair and shave for the occasion. There were several fillies among the visiting centaurs, but they would hold their own dance later out at the Bennis farm. Ten years before there had been an attempt to integrate the centaur fillies—most of whom came from Butterfield—into the Ladies' Dance, but the results had been nearly disastrous for everyone involved. Since that time the centaurs were always invited to attend the Ladies' Dance, where they would politely decline to participate—an expected ritual much to everyone's mutual relief.

Jep Walters, his plump cheeks flush with a rosy glow—it being entirely a matter of speculation as to whether the color came from the heat in the hall, the mead he had downed, or just excitement at commanding the event—banged his long staff down on the floorboards of the stage he had built for the occasion.

"Oyes! Oyes!" he bellowed. "Let the dance begin!"

The Flag Four Troubadours struck up a lively reel. The young women reached out their hands and began the dance—a weaving reel with three circles that intertwined as they passed one another from hand to hand, whirling in time with their ribbons fluttering about them.

Outside in the deepening cold of the night, Beulandreus Dudgeon took in every step, every turn, and every pose of the grace and beauty beyond the glass, his hobnail boots—as quietly as possible—mimicking the steps atop the crate that supported him.

The dwarf longed to dance.

Beulandreus Dudgeon was a dwarf from the Eastern Mountains. That fact meant that he was an expert blacksmith. What else could he be? Everyone knows that dwarves are good only for ironwork, and it would have been foolish to expect them to entertain any other profession when they were so obviously good at smithing. No one ever questioned why he had come to Eventide, what would cause him to leave the deep mountain home of the eastern dwarves, or anything about his past. They already knew everything they needed to know about him: he was a dwarf, therefore gruff, rough, and unsociable—an outsider with skills the town needed, whose strange, foreign ways could be politely tolerated.

It was this general expectation of the Eventide townsfolk that Beulandreus tried to live up to. He was gruff and abrupt. He had no talent for small talk, which, in his view, was the only kind of conversation in which most of the humans in the town were ever engaged. There were some in the town—Farmer Bennis chief among them—who tried to befriend the dwarf, but Beulandreus always became guarded when anyone threatened to get to know him.

The deep truth—deeper than the farthest mines of his ancestors' dwarven home—was that he found it too painful an expectation. He felt desperately alone but feared being hurt or, worse, hurting someone else. More vulnerable and fragile than anything was the tender, kind heart of Beulandreus Dudgeon, and he kept it locked safely behind his leathery skin and his iron will.

So Beulandreus came up into his shop each morning, stoked the fires, tested the bellows, and began to work the metal as he had done every day since coming to the village. Each night he banked the coals, secured the shop, and then walked down the short stairs into his home that was more underground than not. He would unlock the door with a large key and step inside, leaving the world untroubled by him until the next morning when he emerged again to open his shop.

Occasionally he would make the trip down King's Road and cross the bridge from Charter Square to the traders' market. His boots would resound against the cobblestones as he moved from stall to stall and picked out meats, fruits, and vegetables. He always spoke quietly and never bartered too much with the sellers, his eyes downcast and his voice almost too quiet to hear. Arms full, he would then turn and make his way back home.

Were someone to stand outside the dwarf smith's door for months on end, they would agree with the consensus of the town that there was nothing more to this dwarf than his ironwork, eating, and breathing.

And never once would anyone have seen him smile.

Yet somehow, Jarod Klum had made the dwarf dare—if only just a little—to open the locked secrets of his heart and allow a sliver of his life behind his locked front door to come out. The boy's desperate yearning to win the heart of his young love had found an unguarded seam in the dwarf's armor. Beulandreus had been filled with a sudden desire to help the boy and had run down the stairs to his front door, pulled out his large iron key, and entered his secret world. When he emerged, Beulandreus had the Treasure Box in his hand. The genuine appreciation and admiration offered by the earnest Jarod as well as Aren Bennis and that Edvard fellow touched the dwarf more deeply than he had expected. It became a wedge of longing that opened in the dwarf the thinnest line of hope.

Beulandreus had surreptitiously watched every dance that had been held in Eventide since his coming—sometimes from the shadows of an alley near the square or sometimes from a rooftop where he knew he would not been seen. Spring, summer, fall, or winter, at every dance he would be in attendance, and no one in the town was the wiser. He had watched every Ladies' Dance at Spring Revels, and although the crates he used had changed each year, he always watched from some unnoticed window or hiding place, his heavily booted feet shuffling to the music.

He would imagine himself in the hall, his hands reaching up above him and holding hands with the lithe human girls whose form he found artfully beautiful. He envisioned himself dancing with them, their smiles falling like impossible grace upon him, their ribbons flying as he moved with them, a glorious gap-toothed smile beaming from his rapturous face.

And then, each time the dance concluded, he would weep hot tears at the glass that separated them and, unnoticed and unseen, retire behind the locked door of his cellar home.

But not this year, he said to himself. This year he had hope.

Beulandreus took in a deep breath, stepped down off the crate, and stomped around the building to enter the Cooper's Hall.

Livinia Walters stepped onto the stage platform that Jeb had built for her to the sporadic applause of the crowd in the Cooper's Hall.

"Thank you! Thank you all!" Livinia said in her pinched, nasal voice that pierced the air to every corner of the room. The crowd quieted down and turned their attention to her. She noticed at once that there were a number of young people who had managed to escape before she had begun. That charming Dragon's Bard fellow was no longer to be seen, but she noticed that his apprentice, at least, was still in the hall trying to get the attention of Melodi Morgan—so there was at least the possibility of her practiced words being recorded for posterity. "May I take this opportunity to offer my personal thanks to each and every one of you for gracing our Hall this evening. You honor us and our Hall."

It was a well-known fact in the town that Livinia had campaigned hard to have the evening festivities of Spring Revels in the Cooper's Hall. Previous years had seen the dance and contests held in the larger Guild Hall across the river on Trader's Square. The choice ultimately had more to do with giving in to Livinia than it had with honoring her or her Hall.

"Master Abel, are you getting all this?" Livinia called down from her perch on stage.

The apprentice scribe waved at her but did not look away from Melodi.

Livinia continued, "For generations we have celebrated our Spring Revels with dances and contests of prowess, craft, and artistry. While some of our contests have sadly been curtailed in recent years . . ." Livinia nodded with condescending sympathy toward Melodi. The popular afternoon Wishing Contest had had to be abandoned after the wishing well was broken, and its absence was an annual reminder of the Morgans' change in fortunes. " . . . still, one of our finest traditions—the Local Crafts Contest—endures."

"As we endure it, Livi!" a man called out from the back of the hall, drawing a laugh from a number of the other men present.

Livinia magnanimously ignored the remark. "We've had a number of magnificent entries this year, but I must report that the final judging was unanimous."

A murmur went through the crowd at this news. The judges for the contest included not only Livinia Walters but Daphne Melthalion, the wife of Squire Melthalion, and the Widow Marchant Merryweather—three women who had never agreed completely on anything between the three of them in their lives. For them to reach a unanimous consensus on anything was itself worthy of an award.

Livinia turned to the Flag Four behind her. "Are you ready, gentlemen?"

The troubadour troupe readied their instruments.

"Awarded the yellow ribbon and third place in this year's Crafts Contest . . . number fifteen!"

A delighted squeal came from the side of the Cooper's Hall. Deniva Kolyan pushed forward through the crowd toward the stage. She was an enormous, stocky woman who some said could have worked the docks at Blackshore but preferred her bakery instead. She usually preferred to wear men's trousers while working at her shop—the subject of constant speculation by the ladies of Cobblestone Street—but tonight was in her best dress. Her flat face was beaming as she held aloft her numbered square of parchment signed on the back by Xander Lamplighter, the Constable Pro Tempore. The Crafts Contest had become so heated between the ladies of Eventide, and suspicion in the judging so rampantly fueled by the Gossip Fairy, that each entry was received by the constable and matched with a number so that the judges would have no idea which person had submitted which entry.

Xander brought out Deniva Kolyan's submission from the workroom behind the makeshift stage—a cake platter carved from a single piece of wood and polished to a shine that gleamed in the light of the pixie lamps. Xander showed the platter to the crowd and handed the baker her large yellow ribbon award. The appreciative applause of the crowd was genuine if somewhat restrained.

"Congratulations, Deniva," Livinia smiled. Then, turning back to her audience, she announced, "Earning second place and the red ribbon this year is . . . number seven! Number seven, please!"

"Here!" called out the cheerful voice of Winifred Taylor from just below the stage. She too was waving her square of parchment. She was helped up on stage at once by her proud husband, Joaquim. There she bowed profusely as Xander came back again from the workroom, looking terribly uncomfortable as he carried a magnificent dress fitted with faceted sequins in patterns along the bodice, high collar, and sleeves. An appreciative murmur came from the crowd pressing forward in the Cooper's Hall, and their applause was heartfelt.

"Thank you, Winifred," Livinia said through a tight smile. All the townspeople present knew that Livinia was wondering why Winifred Taylor's son, Percival, had not asked her daughter to the Couples' Dance later in the evening. Awarding her second prize was testing her limited diplomacy. Xander gratefully delivered the dress back to Winifred, handed her the elaborate red ribbon award, and hurried back into the storeroom.

"Now, for our first prize and the unanimous decision of our judges, I am thrilled to announce that the blue ribbon and the grand prize winner of this year's Crafts Contest goes to . . . number thirteen!"

Xander came at once out of the workroom holding a tapestry.

The crowd gasped. The tapestry was set on an easel that supported it for its full twelve-foot height so that it could be seen throughout the hall, but everyone present, including the centaurs watching from the back of the hall, was drawn toward it at once. The pixies pushed against the glass of their lamp prisons in wonderment.

It was the most exquisite tapestry anyone there had ever seen. The tiny stitches were impossibly close together, their silk shining in the pixie lights. It was a mountain scene with a waterfall of silvery threads that seemed to cascade as the light shifted against it. The clouds, too, seemed to move beyond the mountain peaks. There were a lake and pine trees with a spindly white tower emerging above the tree line. In the foreground were two figures facing each other—undeniably Queen Nance and King Reinard—in their coronation dress and mantles, each rendered in exquisite detail.

Someone started clapping amid the appreciative murmurs, joined quickly by others until the entire Hall was filled with applause and shouts of congratulations.

"Number thirteen!" Livinia called out to the crowd, standing on the tips of her pointed shoes trying to see who might acknowledge creation of this amazing work. "Please! Number thirteen step forward!"

From the back of the crowd she could see people begin to part, though for some reason she could not see who was approaching. In a few moments the people moved aside and she gazed down in shock.

Standing before her at the front of the stage stood Beulandreus Dudgeon. His hands were scrubbed nearly raw in his attempt to get the smithy stains of years of work out of them. His face behind his neatly combed beard was equally pink, as was his shiny, bald head. He wore a leather coat over his threadbare shirt, and his nicked and cut hobnail boots had a dull polish to them.

In his right hand he held a square of parchment—signed by Xander Lamplighter—with the number thirteen.

Livinia gaped at him for a while. The applause died down in anticipation but was only filled with Livinia's silence. At last she spoke with the only explanation that made sense to her.

"Master Dwarf," Livinia said as though speaking to a naughty child, "you're from a different land and I'm sure you just didn't understand the rules of our contest. You were to submit only work that you did yourself—not something made by someone else."

"Made it myself," the dwarf nodded, thrusting the square parchment slip up toward the woman. "Number thirteen . . . that be mine."

"The dwarf made *that?*" someone called out from the crowd.

"Yeah," called someone else, "with his hammer, he did!"

A tittering sound rolled through the crowd. They had come to have fun and now their celebrations were taking a strange turn. They wanted to get back to having a good time.

"It must have been a very *small* hammer!" someone called back.

An explosion of laugher broke in the Hall.

Livinia's face went flush. "You're a smith! A dwarf! You *can't* have made this—"

"It are mine and I made it," Beulandreus said, his cheeks flushing to a brick red as the laughter grew behind him in the Hall.

Livinia's shrill voice cut through the Hall. "Thief! Liar! Xander! Arrest this dwarf!"

"Theft and fraud?" Jarod repeated. "Father, that can't be true."

"I know," Ward Klum answered, shaking his head. "But where did that tapestry come from? He insists he made it, but I've been to court in Mordale, Son, and there's nothing remotely that beautiful even in the halls of the king's palace there. If he were capable of creating art that's more beautiful than the craftsmen to the king can produce, why would he be in Eventide? That tapestry alone is worth more than our entire town. And if he didn't make it, where could a dwarven smith get the wherewithal to buy such a treasure?"

"It doesn't make sense, Father," Jarod said, shaking his head. "I know the smith—better than most, I think—and he just couldn't do that. Where is he now?"

"Xander and Aren took him over to the lockup," Ward replied, taking off his hat and pushing an uncharacteristically out-of-place lock of hair back where it belonged. "I think Aren mostly went to show Beulandreus support and to stay with him. Livinia's convinced most of the town—thanks to the unfortunately rapid assistance of the Gossip Fairy—that Beulandreus must be dealing in stolen goods. But if that were the case, then why expose himself by trying to pass off a tapestry as his own in front of the entire community?"

"How's Beulandreus?" Jarod asked. "What does he say?"

His father drew in a considered breath. "He never says much anyway, Son. The more we talk to him, the quieter he seems to get. He did ask me to find you and have you get a few things for him from his house."

Jarod looked down. His father held the dwarf's great iron key.

"You're coming with me," Jarod said, taking the key. "Right now."

Jarod turned the key in the lock and pushed the door slowly open.

It was extraordinarily dark inside. No lamps were lit, and there were no windows in the subterranean apartments of Beulandreus Dudgeon. Jarod's father stood behind him with the lantern, but Jarod was blocking the light into the room. He took a step inside as his father pushed the lantern to the side.

The rooms were more spacious than Jarod had imagined—and filled with artistic treasures that took his breath away. Among the chairs, tables, and couches that furnished the room were paintings, sculptures, and tapestries ornamenting every wall, each exquisite in its own way. Some lay casually propped against the wall. There was jewelry as well, and gems and wooden cases filled with expensive silks and threads.

Ward shook his head. "This won't help his case, Son. This is a king's treasure he has hidden in his home. It looks as though he *is* a thief or at best is assisting a thief."

Jarod walked over to a workbench at one side of the room. He stopped and gazed down at the pieces of wood partially assembled on the table. They looked familiar to him, reminding him of . . .

Jarod reached into his pocket and drew out the Treasure Box.

The pieces were the same. Beulandreus had not just given him a Treasure Box—the dwarf had *made* the Treasure Box.

Jarod cast his eyes quickly about the room, his eye settling on a shadowy form around a corner at the back of the main room.

"Come on, Father," Jarod said, moving quickly around the corner. "I know what the dwarf needs."

The dwarf shivered, huddled on a stool in the dungeon cell behind the iron-barred door that he had installed just three weeks before. The cots had not yet been replaced, and a stool from the countinghouse above was the only readily available seating that Xander could find for his prisoner.

Outside the cell, Ward Klum stood with Jarod and the Constable Pro Tempore.

"You think Aren will be much longer?" Xander asked.

"I think your answer has arrived," Ward replied.

"We're all very busy women," came the unmistakable voice of Livinia Walters echoing down the dungeon corridor. "Everyone is waiting for the Couples' Dance!"

"They'll wait," said Aren Bennis without the slightest tincture of sympathy in his voice.

"Really, Farmer Bennis!" said Daphne Melthalion. "I thought we had all this settled already!"

"There'll be a complaint to the town fathers about this!" added the Widow Merryweather.

The three women appeared at the base of the stairs, urged onward by the uncomfortably bent form of an aging centaur filling the stairway behind them.

"I'm just following orders, ma'am," Aren Bennis said, giving them a polite shove down the dungeon corridor.

Livinia saw Ward, Jarod, and the constable at once and stepped quickly toward them. "What is the meaning of this, Ward Klum? You've apprehended the criminal and . . . oh, what kind of sad joke is this?"

Livinia had turned toward the dungeon cell and discovered

what for her was the incomprehensible sight of a dwarf sitting on a wooden stool in front of a tapestry loom frame. A box of silk threads sat next to the dwarf, but Beulandreus himself sat with his back toward the cell door, slumped over and making no move toward either the loom or the spools of thread.

"You've really gone lunatic this time, Ward Klum!"

"It wasn't my idea," Ward replied calmly. "It was my son's."

"You're going to blame your son for this?" Livinia shrieked. "Sitting that fool dwarf in front of a tapestry loom like some kind of bizarre River Fairy tableau? You might as well try to convince me that my dog can play cards!"

"Livinia, you don't have to get so—"

"I do *too* have to get so, Daphne Melthalion!" Livinia snapped. "That dwarf tried to make a fool of all of us by passing off his stolen property as his own, thumbing his nose at the lot of us while he uses our town—our town!—for his criminal deeds!"

Xander shook his head. "Now, there's no real evidence—"

"No evidence? Are you blind?" Livinia's face was nearly purple with rage. "He's a *dwarf!* He's a smith from under a *mountain!* They're all the same: dirty, smelly creatures whose only worth is in beating things into shape with a hammer. They have no grace . . . no appreciation for the finer things in life . . . no understanding of art. I mean, honestly, all you have to do is look at him and . . . what does he think he is doing?"

The dwarf offered no reply. He put his hands to the loom and began to weave.

What emerged with incredible speed was a tapestry of the finest detail using impossibly narrow silken threads. The dwarf's thick fingers moved with unmatched skill. Silence fell in the dungeon even over Livinia, who stood with her mouth stuck open in midlecture.

For some time they all watched as a perfectly beautiful face emerged in the tapestry.

It was the face of Livinia Walters.

Not the line-creased, careworn face of the screaming, scolding woman, but her face as she might have been in joy and peace. The lines at the corners of her eyes and mouth were still there, but there was the hint of bliss in their turn. Her eyes shone from the silken threads with an inner contentment. Her head was tilted slightly as though inviting conversation. It was a more beautiful Livinia—it was the woman she longed to be.

The dwarf dropped the shuttle and turned to look at the woman whose image he had just completed.

Livinia Walters fell to her knees on the dungeon floor, covered her eyes, and wept.

The crowd in the Cooper's Hall was tiring of the Flag Four Troubadours. They had long since exhausted their repertoire several times over, but no one was willing to leave until the Couples' Dance was accomplished.

Livinia Walters returned to the Hall to the accompaniment of relieved applause and cheering. A few noticed that her eyes were bloodshot and her face flushed, but mostly they were astonished that she was followed by the dwarf who had been arrested in front of them—and whose guilt so many had been convinced of—only an hour before.

Ariela Soliandrus, the Gossip Fairy, fluttered her wings madly to carry her fourteen-inch height over to Aren Bennis, who had motioned her toward him. It was the first time the centaur had ever deigned to speak to the fairy and, as he whispered in her tiny ear, her eyes widened perceptibly.

Livinia did not take her place on the stage but stood next to the dwarf. She could not find her voice even though the apprentice scribe was prepared to record her words precisely. Instead, overcome as she was, she allowed the Gossip Fairy to spread the word of events quietly throughout the Hall, which grew more silent by the moment.

Livinia took the blue ribbon from where she had left it on the stage and, with tears in her eyes, quietly knelt and handed it to the dwarf.

At the back of the hall, Jarod Klum stood next to Vestia Walters, who was looking on in open-mouthed astonishment at her mother. Jarod looked around the silent hall and caught sight of Caprice Morgan, standing alone next to the large double doors that opened out into Charter Square. He slipped away from Vestia and, filled with an idea that overcame his fear, he stepped up to Caprice and quietly spoke to her.

"You don't have a partner for the Couples' Dance?"

Caprice looked away with a wry smile. "I did . . . or thought I did."

"May I make a suggestion?"

Jarod whispered to her, and her smile widened. "Yes, I'd like that."

Caprice Morgan walked down the length of the Cooper's Hall past the brightly colored costumes and hats of the silent crowd and stepped up to the dwarf, whose head was bowed down as he held the blue ribbon in both his large hands.

"Master Dudgeon," she said across the silence of the Hall. "It's good luck to dance with a dwarf. May I?"

Beulandreus turned his face up, gazing at Caprice in wonder.

She reached down and took his hand, leading him to the center of the floor.

"What shall we dance?" she asked him.

"I . . . I watched the Ladies' Dance," he mumbled quietly.

Caprice smiled. "Do you mind? It *is* the Ladies' Dance . . ."

"No! I don't mind!" the dwarf blinked.

Caprice looked around at the stunned occupants of the Hall. She spied a familiar face and called to her. "Evangeline! It's a reel. We need someone else for the dance!"

Evangeline shook her head emphatically. Daphne Melthalion, watching next to her daughter Evangeline, turned to her and whispered insistently, then gave her daughter a shove. Evangeline stumbled onto the floor and took the dwarf's other hand. "It's . . . it's good luck to dance with a dwarf?" she said uncertainly.

At the back of the hall, Jarod Klum walked Vestia Walters onto the floor and left her there with the dwarf. "It's good luck," he said to her.

Vestia shot a questioning glance at her mother, but Livinia only smiled back and then turned to the troubadours. "The Ladies' Dance reel . . . now, if you please."

As the first notes rang through the hall, every young woman of the town—urged quietly by their atoning mothers—rushed in to join the dance.

The heavy footfalls of the dwarf resounded through the hall, his hands reaching up above him and holding hands with the lithe human girls whose form he found artfully beautiful. Their smiles fell like impossible grace upon him, their ribbons flying as he moved with them, a glorious gap-toothed smile beaming from his rapturous face.

From that time onward, if you were so fortunate as to visit Eventide on the night of Spring Revels, you would be astonished to see all the prettiest maidens of the town lining up with delight to take their turns dancing with a dwarf. They all see him with different eyes than a stranger might, for behind his shining eye and the clumsy steps that pound the cobblestones beneath his feet, they see the beauty of song, poetry, and art—and to dance with such handsomeness, any maiden knows, will bring her good fortune in her life.

And the dwarf would be smiling all the while.

The Couples' Dance was finished. Jarod had dutifully done his turn about the floor with Vestia Walters—who continued to go on and on about her marvelous hat and how much she must have meant to him in order for him to give her such a wonderful gift. He was gracious as his parents had taught him to be and left her at her door as soon as decorum would allow. It was, after all, a very short trip, since Vestia lived above the Cooper's Hall with her parents.

Jarod turned and stepped into the deserted Charter Square. The early spring moon cast its blue light over the scattered vestiges of the celebration. Spring Revels were over, and with them had flown the great plans of his quest on behalf of his beloved . . .

"Jarod?"

"Caprice?"

She leaned against the low courtyard wall on the west side of Charter Square overlooking Bolly Falls. The pixies in the lamp next to her had since been released so that only the moonlight illuminated her. "I was just waiting for my sisters. They've been talking with Merinda over at her shop about a hat for Melodi."

"Oh, a hat," Jarod said casually, wondering why it was easier to talk to her now than ever before. He strolled nonchalantly toward her. "You should have gone with them. I hear Merinda is the woman to see about hats."

Caprice laughed. "No, thank you. I hate hats!"

Jarod smiled as he answered, "Me too. You have no idea how much."

"I wanted to thank you for getting me a date," Caprice said.

"The dwarf?" Jarod laughed. "You're welcome—but I think I could have managed someone better."

Caprice stood up and faced Jarod. "Yes, I believe you could have."

"Caprice!"

Jarod winced. He turned to see Melodi and Sobrina crossing the deserted cobblestone square. Sobrina held a lantern in her hand.

"We must be getting home," Sobrina said with a glance at Jarod. "It's late and there *are* highwaymen about."

"May I . . . may I walk you ladies home?" Jarod offered.

Caprice smiled. "Why, Jarod Klum, that is most kind of you—"

"No, that won't be necessary," Sobrina interrupted. "It's too many to protect."

"I'm sure I can handle—"

"No, Jarod," Caprice said gently. "She means that *you* would be too many for *her* to protect."

"Caprice, I wish—"

"*Don't* wish," Caprice said, touching her hand lightly on his chest. He dared not move, afraid to break the fragile, glorious moment. She stepped quickly away to follow her sisters north past Fall's Court to the Mordale road. "I'm a wisher of the well . . . I don't need wishes!"

Jarod watched her vanish into the moonlight with her sisters. He worried for her traveling at night up the Mordale road. Dirk Gallowglass was abroad near Eventide—the notorious highwayman who, upon seeing Caprice, would no doubt swoop down upon her from astride his midnight black horse, sweep her up in his powerful arms, and carry her swooning into the night.

At least, that was what he would do if *he* were Dirk Gallowglass.

# THE NOTORIOUS
# STRATAGEM

❦

*Wherein Jarod tries to be
an infamous rogue and discovers
it's not nearly as appealing as
the Bard's stories make it out to be.*

## · CHAPTER 10 ·

# The Gossip Fairy

If you walked down Cobblestone Street south from Chestnut Court you would see rows of small, cozy homes lining both sides of the street. Each one would be charmingly individual in some detail but on the whole of approximately the same height and construction as the next—all, that is, except one. The uniform row of thatched rooflines would be broken in the middle by one very small house, built specifically to accommodate the short form of Ariela Soliandrus, who tried her best to fit in with her neighbors—despite the fact that she was a fairy.

Her home was a miniature of those around it and completely unsuitable for human occupation. It had been built for her by the Black Guild Brotherhood—the secret guild to which most of the men in the town belonged—largely at the insistence of the women of Cobblestone Street, who had come to accept her with remarkable ease once her value to their ladies' community had become quite obvious. The house stood on a four-foot foundation of stones and mortar so that the small front porch would be at the same level as those of the homes on either side. This necessitated the construction of a narrow stairway with miniature treads, although Ariela flew everywhere and had never used them. The look of her home was identical to that of the townhomes on either side, with half-beam frame construction and wattle and daub filling the walls between the timbers, forming square and triangular shapes in the walls, each fitted with leaded glass panes and the ubiquitous painted front door. The primary difference lay entirely in its scale, for everything was adjusted in size to Ariela's fourteen inches of height. Her extravagant green door was a full two feet tall, and the three stories of her home reached a lofty ten feet above the surface of the street if one counted the foundation. Nor were its sideways dimensions out of proportion; hence, it could have no common walls with the neighboring townhomes. It stood apart in the center of her parcel of ground, which was fine by Ariela, as that left more room for her extravagant garden.

Each day, Ariela went out calling. Dressed most impeccably in a silk dress with an ornate brocade bodice, a straw bonnet tied firmly to her head with a scarf, she flitted from home to home among her neighbors, visited with the women of her acquaintance in their gardens, and gave them her advice on the plants . . . as well as the latest news from around the town. Ariela was known somewhat unkindly among the men of Eventide as the Gossip Fairy, and there was no bit of news on which she could not amplify, exaggerate, or speculate wildly. If gossip ever ran through the town like wildfire, you could be sure that Ariela was at the front of it, actively fanning the flames with every beat of her wings.

While the Gossip Fairy had a most vocal opinion regarding the background and secrets of nearly everyone in the town, she was silent about her own past. That Ariela was a River Fairy who had abandoned that wilder existence for a life among the inhabitants of Eventide was obvious, but why a River Fairy would do so had long been a matter of speculation among the women of the town.

Some of the women claimed that she was really the queen of the fairies in disguise, hiding among the villagers of Eventide, and that if her true nature were discovered they would all be murdered in their beds. Others—mostly the younger women—were convinced that Ariela was fleeing from a tragic past where she had fallen passionately into a doomed love affair with a merman . . . or a selkie . . . or a fairy prince. Most of the men were convinced that she had simply been thrown out of her own tribe for causing too much trouble.

Ariela had heard all of their stories about her—and even repeated them to others—without ever confirming her true reasons for being there . . . except, possibly, to the scribe Abel, who noted that Ariela loved her garden above all else and that the roving River Fairies were never in one place long enough to establish one.

She sowed seeds of all kinds around the village, both in the gardens and in the ears of her eager listeners. Unfortunately, the fruits of such seeds were often both unpredictable and dangerous.

For example, when Jarod had his rather fated chance encounter with Vestia Walters . . . well, there were just not enough known facts to make a proper telling, so the Gossip Fairy felt perfectly justified in filling in the unknowns with what she considered the most plausible fabrications. This ability was precisely the aspect that qualified her to be considered an expert on any subject concerning the town or world beyond.

So it was that as spring warmed into a verdant summer, so, too, blossomed the speculation around Vestia Walters and Jarod Klum, and with every telling by the Gossip Fairy another nail was driven into the coffin of Jarod and his hopes for winning Caprice Morgan.

"So I don't know what to do," Jarod concluded, lifting up the sluice gate to Farmer Bennis's south field as he saw the water approaching down the ditch from the north. "Vestia Walters thinks I'm interested in her and somehow staked out a claim on me when I wasn't looking."

"I thought that Percival fellow from the town was chasing her?" Edvard said casually. He was sitting on the rail fence, leaning into the post next to him as he nibbled at the end of a long stalk of green wheat.

"He was," Jarod sighed. "He got his nose broken back on the night of Spring Revels. It shifted his nose to one side, which ruined both his looks and Vestia's opinion of him. No one ever found out how he broke it . . . he always changes the subject whenever it's brought up."

The Dragon's Bard frowned. "The nose looked straight the last time I saw him."

"That's the strangest part," Jarod said, looking up into the bright sky. "It had just started to heal when it broke again—only this time he was right in the middle of Trader's Square with Jon Zwegan and Merlin Thatcher. They were just walking across the square when Percival cried out and fell to the ground, his nose broken again. This second time it healed straight and looks as though he had never broken it at all—but he had to go through the pain twice, the swelling in his face and the bruises under his eyes. He looks fine now, but Vestia still won't have anything to do with him."

"Bad wishcraft that," Farmer Bennis said as he removed his hat and wiped his brow. "Put the nose right but in a bent way. That's a broken wish for you."

"Well, whoever wished it didn't do me any favor," Jarod groused. "Vestia couldn't stand to be around him, so now the town thinks she and I are a couple and Caprice doesn't seem to even know I exist."

"I'm sure she does," Bennis advised. The massive centaur was trotting along next to the approaching water, his shirt sleeves rolled up and his enormous brimmed hat shading his eyes. He held the handle of a long shovel in one hand, resting it back over his left shoulder. "The Morgans are having troubles of their own, Jarod. It's been hard enough on them these years since their wishing well was broken—and losing their mother in the bargain—but it's been especially difficult these last two months."

"That foolishness about a wishing well in Butterfield?" piped in the Dragon's Bard from the fence. "It was nothing but a ruse by an itinerant charlatan preying on the innocence of the unsuspecting and easily persuaded!"

"An expert opinion, indeed," Bennis nodded.

"But they caught the man in the act," Jarod said. "Ran him out of Butterfield."

"Yes, but not until two months had gone by for the Morgans without any wishers at all," Bennis concluded. "Their position was not good to begin with, but now they're in serious trouble—Abel! Please turn the water in there!"

The scribe, standing next to the ditch with his own shovel in hand, nodded and quickly pushed the spade down into the path of the water, turning it into the channeled furrows of the field.

"This were far easier when the wishcraft was working," Farmer

Bennis said as he carefully walked along the northern edge of the field, checking the water as it slowly moved down the channels between the rising stalks of grain.

Jarod shook his head as he knelt next to the sluice gate, holding the wooden dam in his hand. "I know it's been hard for her family, but I just wish she would see that I'm here. But I'm no different than anyone else—just another face in the village."

The Dragon's Bard sat up suddenly on the fence, his face brightening. "Of course! That's it!"

Jarod glanced up warily.

"You need to stand out, be distinctive . . . dashing, daring . . . mysterious . . ."

Jarod started shaking his head. "Wait a moment! I don't want—"

"I've got it!" the Bard shouted. "A brilliant idea!"

"No!" Jarod yelped.

"You just need to be noticed!" Edvard pushed himself off of the fence, his hands flourishing in the air as he spoke. "To stand out from the crowd—"

"No, not again!" Jarod jumped up so quickly that his boots slipped on the wet bank of the ditch. He slid into the water, then regained his footing as he stepped out toward the Dragon's Bard. "The last time you tried to make me into someone I wasn't—"

"But that's not what I'm talking about, my boy!" The Bard laughed heartily, clasping his hand on the boy's shoulder. "I'm not talking about changing who you are—just who everyone thinks you are! Perception is everything, the very key to being noticed! The repentant sinner is ever more quickly noticed than the saint! The scoundrel with the heart of gold ever so much more attractive to romantic young women than the honest farmer with a stable income—get it? Stable income, eh?"

"A scoundrel?" Jarod snorted. "So now I'm supposed to be some knave blackguard? That's not me!"

"You don't have to actually be scandalous, just have the slightest taint of it," Edvard said. "Of all the stories I tell, the ones that the women love most are those filled with rogues, rascals, and scalawags! Take the stories of this local ne'er-do-well . . . this highwayman chap . . ."

"Dirk Gallowglass?"

"Yes! Dirk Gallowglass!" The Dragon's Bard rolled the name off his tongue again in the most dramatic fashion. "Dirk Gallowglass! There's a name that makes men tremble and women swoon! He is a scoundrel who glides along the roads beyond the town by night, his black domino flying in the wind behind him as he plunges down the moonlit lanes! He robs trade merchants from distant lands, but his strange code of honor never permits him to raid the town of Eventide. No doubt he has a secret lover in the town who holds his heart bound never to harm or disturb the good citizens of Eventide as he hides among the rooftops, prancing along the ridgepoles in the silence of the—"

Edvard stopped abruptly.

Jarod, the centaur, and the scribe were all staring at him in dumbfounded silence.

"Now, there is a man whose name is known to everyone in the town," Edvard continued, undaunted by his audience. "You cannot purchase that kind of notoriety!"

Farmer Bennis raised a single eyebrow. "You do know that there is a difference between notoriety and being notorious, don't you?"

Abel tried unsuccessfully to stifle a sudden laugh.

The Dragon's Bard stared at his scribe as he spoke. "Of course, but the slightest hint of the notorious can buy you a lot of notoriety."

Bennis shook his head, swinging his shovel down from his shoulder. "And some of us want neither, as you all too well know. A reputation, especially in a town like Eventide, is a fragile thing." Bennis gripped the Bard's shoulder hard enough to make him wince. "None of us want anything so fragile to be broken."

"I assure you again," Edvard said, "at least one reputation here will remain intact . . . even after I am allowed to leave."

Edvard gingerly held the small teacup handle between his thumb and index finger, his pinky extended as he spoke. "Have I told you what a remarkably lovely garden you have, Miss Ariela?"

Ariela Soliandrus sat across the garden table from the Dragon's Bard, perched atop her smaller chair, made especially so that she could sit at the table built for her human neighbors. "You have, Mr. Dragonguard."

"That's Dragon's Bard," Edvard corrected with a slight tip of his tiny cup.

"Yes, yes, yes," the fairy said with a bored air, waving her tiny hand. Her voice was higher pitched than most humans', yet remarkably melodious. "But it is most vexing that you have taken this long to call on me, though hardly surprising inasmuch as you are a man and, as such, have little comprehension of the refinements of polite society."

Ariela had polished condescension to a fine art.

"I would agree with you in the general case," Edvard cooed, "although in my situation, I have had cause to immerse myself in society and, as such, am on good acquaintance with the finer nuances of grace and decorum."

"Indeed, Mr. Bard?" Ariela raised both her tiny eyebrows.

"Please, call me Edvard," the Dragon's Bard said, flashing a smile filled with endearing teeth. "I dare hope that we two shall be on such good acquaintance."

"Hmmm." Ariela turned to face her servant's quarters—a small but well-kept one-room shack at the back of the garden. She called out, "Lucinda!"

There was a sudden scrape of a chair leg and the bump of a table before a young servant girl popped out of the door with a tea-kettle in one hand and a plate of scones in the other. She was human and no more than fourteen years old by the look of her. Her round face was a ruddy color and her hair somewhat disheveled from its intended form. She quickly approached and navigated the garden paths, balancing her cargo precariously as she moved. Coming at last to the table, she made a quick, if awkward, curtsy, set the plate of scones on the table with a clattering sound, and then proceeded with nervous care to pour the tea, first into Ariela's miniature cup and then into that of the Bard.

"That will be all, Lucinda," Ariela said with a dismissive, humorless smile.

The girl curtsied once more and then bounded back down the garden paths and into the painted box that passed for her home.

"She is a good girl, though, sadly, her parentage will condemn her to a life in service for the remainder of her days," Ariela said with a tragic shake of her small head, the curls in her carefully coifed hair quivering ever so slightly. "The young Duke Hareld, third cousin once removed to the king, often passed through Meade—and not entirely for the ale manufactured there, it is said. Lucinda's mother was a foolish woman who had dreams of bettering her life without much concern for the means by which she achieved position—or, it seems, for the position by which she might acquire her means. Ample proof was delivered some months later, but the duke never acknowledged the responsibility. It is true that the woman had fallen before the duke had her, and more than once—so they say—but as there had never been an issue before she met the duke, the child's parentage seemed certain—the poor dear! Imagine the struggle it must be for her to have to live with such tragedy, especially when it is so often retold, never to be forgotten?"

"Most tragic, indeed," Edvard replied with great sincerity, "and I shall tell it in those same tragic terms at each opportunity."

"As I would hope you would," Ariela nodded.

"Still," the Bard said, carefully setting down his cup in its saucer, "I have come with troubling questions, my dear Ariela."

"Troubling?" Ariela asked.

"Yes, and concerning someone in the town."

"Indeed?" The fairy leaned forward in her chair.

"It's this question of Jarod Klum," Edvard said, furrowing his brow with his best concern.

"Jarod?" Ariela leaned back at once. "He's fine enough for a young human male . . . and your friend, I believe."

"So I thought," Edvard intoned with resonant concern. "But the more I get to know him, the more troubled I become."

Ariela leaned forward once again. "Why ever so?"

"Perhaps I shouldn't say anything." Edvard shook his head as he frowned. "I'm sure it's nothing."

"Let me judge its worth," Ariela said through her smile. If there were anyone in Eventide who could make something out of nothing, it was the fairy.

"Well, have you ever seen him and this Dirk Gallowglass at

the same time?" Edvard leaned forward himself, lowering his voice dramatically.

"In truth, sir, I have never seen Dirk Gallowglass at all!" Ariela answered, her own voice lowering in return.

"But especially not with Jarod Klum," Edvard said. "I've never seen him at night when the highwayman is about. No one has! And he has a magical treasure box . . ."

"No!"

"Yes. It's hidden near his desk in the countinghouse," Edvard said, his eyes shifting left and right before he continued. "He's always visiting it. Who knows what he keeps in there!"

"But he works in the countinghouse," Ariela said, shaking her head. "His father is in charge of the arrest record . . . the town dungeon is right beneath him . . . he sees the Constable Pro Tempore every day . . ."

"And what better position to have if one were the highwayman!" Edvard exclaimed. "Privy to every move made by the very constabulary tasked with his apprehension? And what of this Vestia Walters, eh? How is it that such a common-seeming young beard as Jarod would turn the head of the town beauty? It would take more coins than an apprentice accountant earns to hold her attention. I think there may be more to this Jarod Klum than meets the eye!"

"I never considered the possibility . . ."

"I fear I must leave you at once," the Dragon's Bard said, standing quickly from the table. "I have said too much, and if Farmer Bennis thinks that I have been gone too long from his company he will be vexed—and I will be all the more sore for his vexing."

The Bard flourished his hat and all but ran from the garden.

"Do call again!" Ariela yelled after him.

Edvard smiled to himself. He did not think it would be

necessary to call again. As he proudly recounted later to his horrified scribe, he had helped his friend the best way he knew how.

By afternoon, Jarod noticed that people in the town were looking at him differently. They would whisper to each other as they passed him; they would stare, only to look quickly away whenever he caught their eye. No one was so tactless as to mention it to him directly or to his parents—but the insinuation of his being a rogue was otherwise of general knowledge.

By nightfall, everyone in the town except his parents and Jarod himself had heard the rumor connecting Jarod with the highwayman. This included Percival Taylor, who took a sudden aversion to the apprentice accountant, and Vestia Walters, whose interest in using Jarod to torture Percival increased proportionately.

It also included Dirk Gallowglass—the highwayman.

# CHAPTER 11

# The Highwayman

Dirk Gallowglass! A name that struck terror into the hearts of travelers! Whenever he rode on his midnight black horse and brandished his blade, merchants and patrons caught on the road would cower in fear. Grant him whatever he asked of you, it was said, and he would leave you in peace. Cross him, and there was no end but a death as black as the masked hood that he wore.

At least, that was what Henri Smyth hoped everyone believed.

Henri was a son of a farmer in Farfield. His tall, strong body and ruggedly handsome features had somehow not served him well behind a plow. He was a proud and moody youth whose eyes were always looking past the horizons of his father's fields. Josias Smyth, Henri's father, tried his best to keep his son's interest, teaching him what he knew about swordsmanship and the greater world, but the elder Smyth had come to realize that his headstrong son could learn the realities of life only by having them pummeled into him by experience. It was only a matter of time before he left his home against his father's advice. So Josias gave his son what little money he had, his sword belt, and his rapier from his service in the Epic War—and prayed to whatever gods might be listening to take care of his wayward boy.

Experience wasted no time before starting the pummeling. Henri had started out in the belief that he could somehow make a living off of his charm alone, but for some reason, people did not toss coins at his feet simply because he smiled at them. He took a few working jobs along the way, telling himself they were just temporary until someone recognized the glory that was in him and saw that taking care of him was something he deserved. After several months, he came to the startling realization, while cleaning out a pigsty in Meade, that handsome, comely people can starve to death just as quickly as ugly ones. He finished the job and got on the road back to Farfield.

He was on that road, considering returning to his father's farm and resigning himself to get back behind that mundane plow, when he came upon the highwayman, peacefully swinging by his neck at the side of the road.

Henri considered this amazing sight for a number of minutes. The legend of Dirk Gallowglass had, in the end, apparently not served him well. Other than his name—which may have been made up entirely, for all anyone knew—and his profession as a highwayman, no one knew anything about him. Where did he come from? Did he have parents? Well, obviously he had parents, Henri thought to himself, but what did they think of their son's choice of vocation? Did he have a woman somewhere wondering where he was? Did he have several? Would any of them remember him? It occurred to Henri in that moment that being a highwayman was the most anonymous activity one could engage in, for no one knew who highwaymen were, and their actions were veiled behind a forgetful obscurity.

It sounded perfect!

Not one to pass up an opportunity—even a dead one—Henri noticed that the highwayman had a striking costume and was close to his own size. He cut the man down with his father's rapier and noted that the highwayman's boots were also about his size and of a much higher quality construction. He considered this for a moment amid the buzzing of the gathering flies. At length he concluded that a dead highwayman had no further need of such accoutrements and decided to try on the clothing. He donned the boots first and was relieved at their fit. The doublet was too wide in the chest, but serviceable. The cloak, however, was a good length. He clasped his father's sword belt back around his waist and dropped the black hood down over his head, taking a few moments to adjust the holes to fit his eyes. He then drew out his father's rusting rapier and began striking a series of dramatic poses.

He was still admiring his dashing looks in the still surface of water pooling on the road when, as fortune had it, a tradesman on horseback happened by. Henri turned—the grip of his father's rapier blade still in his hand and a stripped corpse at his feet.

The tradesman let out a cry, gibbered for a moment, tossed down a bag of coins, and then put the spurs to his horse, screaming all the way back down the road.

Now, *that,* Henri thought, was more like it!

Soon it was known throughout all of Windriftshire that the highwayman Dirk Gallowglass was not dead, as the sheriff of Meade insisted, but was now a ghostly highwayman riding the roads of the county and striking his victims without warning.

It was a slightly different perspective from the highwayman's point of view. Henri was happy enough to take on the name of Gallowglass—since the real Dirk Gallowglass would no longer be needing his name any more than his boots—but he was determined to go about this highwayman business in a more professional and thoughtful manner. He needed a place where he could barter goods, and he determined Eventide to be the most centrally located of the towns about which he hoped to ply his highwayman trade. Then he carefully chose only those targets who could be quickly and easily frightened into paying his ransom. When merchant traders began traveling with armed escorts, Henri improvised, shadowing the merchants as they traveled the roads through the woods. Eventually the long journey would require the trader to relieve himself. Henri felt some guilt at surprising these merchants in the middle of their urgent duty, but at least he found them far more readily compliant in such circumstances. On occasion he would also be following a wealthy patron along the road who would leave his entourage with a young damsel in tow. Startling these couples not only proved lucrative but, in Henri's thinking, also rescued the damsel from distress—although on occasion the damsel in question seemed more upset than grateful about having the moment interrupted.

These merchants and patrons were naturally embarrassed about being thus taken off their guard, and so, in their recounting of the incidents once back in town, the legend of the power, stealth, and deceit of Dirk Gallowglass grew with each telling. The fear of the black hood and rapier blade of Dirk Gallowglass made Henri's job all the easier. He became a legendary figure about Eventide—a town that, rumor had it, was under his protection.

And that was true, although not for any of the reasons anyone in or out of the town imagined.

Henri pulled down the hood and became Dirk Gallowglass. It was late in the evening, a twilight ribbon fading at the horizon. Down the road came a single rider, his livery fine and his person fat. Dirk was in the shadows of the wood at the edge of the road between Welston and Eventide. No one else had passed by his hidden location in over a half hour. It looked like another easy mark. The highwayman adjusted his costume, drew his rapier, and leaped out in front of the horse.

"Haha!" he shouted in his most practiced and effective Dirk-voice. "Stand and deliver, lest you feel the wrath—"

He got no further with his speech.

The rider immediately dismounted without a word and drew his saber from its scabbard, closing directly with Henri, his blade rising at once. Henri barely countered a succession of swift cuts and thrusts that pressed him back before he could set a proper stance.

"Wait!" Henri cried out.

The elder man in the twilight only grinned.

The saber crashed against the thin rapier again and again, each blow shaking the grip in Henri's clenched hand, threatening to break the blade. Suddenly the saber swung in a spiral, steel singing against steel, pushing the rapier out of the way as the mysterious patrician lunged, plunging the blade just below Henri's left shoulder.

Henri cried out in pain, taking a great step backward. He swung the rapier in a wide circle in front of him to clear his opponent's blade . . . and then turned and bolted for the woods.

Henri was panicked. It wasn't supposed to happen this way— not to him. He could hear his opponent crashing through the underbrush behind him, chasing after him. The light was nearly gone and it was increasingly difficult to see in the deep woods. Yet, although the old man was obviously skilled with a blade, he was, nevertheless, still old. Henri outdistanced him quickly. It wasn't until he had lost him altogether that Henri realized he was feeling very strange, indeed. The wound to his shoulder was bleeding and he was starting to feel light-headed. He got his bearings with some difficulty and made his way back to his camp. Pulling himself up on his legendary black horse, he hurried to seek help in the nearest town . . . which happened to be Eventide.

"Shall I take Lord Gallivant up to his room?" Evangeline asked.

"Yes, Daughter," Squire Melthalion answered wearily as he cleaned the last of the spills off the long bar of the inn. He made his way around the room, snuffing out the lanterns as he went. "It's time to close—there'll be no more excitement for him tonight."

Evangeline was a lithe beauty. Many of the women on Cobblestone Street thought her too thin, but her slenderness only accentuated her large, brown eyes and black, curly hair. She had a wide, generous mouth that was quick to smile when she had the time. She crossed the common room of the Griffon's Tale Inn and took the old stubble-bearded man by the arm, helping him to his feet. Lord Gallivant tried to focus on her but gave up, taking her arm and moving across the room.

Evangeline had just reached the base of the stairs with Lord Gallivant when the door burst open. The Squire turned from the great fireplace of the inn where he was banking the fire.

Framed in the doorway and silhouetted from behind by the still-glowing pixie lanterns of Charter Square was the tall form of Dirk Gallowglass. His right arm still held the rapier, but he was leaning heavily against the door frame on that side. His left arm hung limp at his side, a glistening stain flowing from his shoulder.

Lord Gallivant turned as Evangeline gasped, raising one of his grey, bushy eyebrows. Squire Melthalion rushed toward the figure, trying to get between the man and his daughter.

It was a fortunate move, as the highwayman pitched forward into the room, barely caught by the Squire before crashing into the hardwood floor.

"Who is it, Father?" Evangeline breathed.

"Who is it!" the Squire answered in strained breath as he struggled to lower the man to the ground. "Evangeline Drusilla Melthalion, who do you *think* it would be, wearing a black hood and cape at this time of night? It's Dirk Gallowglass—and by the looks of him, he's bleeding to death."

"Dirk Gallowglass?" said Lord Gallivant. "Why, I haven't seen him in more than a month."

"A month?" the Squire chirped.

The old man chuckled to himself as he strode over to where the highwayman lay insensible across the Squire's legs. "He was such a young rascal in those days. Handy to have around if you needed to get through a locked door or avoid a deadly trap on the way to some ancient treasure room. I wonder if he's changed much since . . ."

Lord Gallivant reached down and snapped the hood off the highwayman's head.

He frowned.

"What's the matter now?" the Squire asked, trying to shift his legs out from under the weight of the highwayman's body.

"This isn't Dirk Gallowglass," Lord Gallivant said simply.

"Oh, of course it is!" The Squire was quite upset.

The highwayman moaned loudly.

"We must get him into the kitchen," Lord Gallivant said at once as he deftly took the rapier from the young man's limp hand. "Lady Moonlake, will you please assist the Squire in helping this wounded soldier?"

"Yes, Lord Gallivant," Evangeline replied at once. Lord Gallivant had so often called the Squire's daughter "Lady Moonlake" that she had long since simply answered to the name rather than correct him. She grabbed the young man's right arm and managed to shift his weight long enough to free the Squire. "We've got to help him, Father! He could die! And he's so . . ."

"So what, Evangeline?" The Squire moved to the other side of the limp man, and together he and his daughter managed to get him to his feet.

"Well," Evangeline said, struggling herself to hold up the limp body, "he's just so . . . well, he's too pretty just to let him die."

"Evangeline!" the Square exclaimed.

"Come, there's not a moment to lose," Lord Gallivant said.

"Are you certain?" the Squire huffed under the limp weight of the roguishly clad young man. "He surely looks like a highwayman . . ."

Since that night, six months before, the legend of the highwayman had only grown and, in a certain way, lent an air of distinction to the village of Eventide. The town was under the protection of the highwayman, it was said, because he was secretly in love with a woman there. Of course, no one knew the identity of this woman since that was, after all, a secret carried in the heart of the highwayman alone. But every young woman in the town fancied herself the secret desire of the dashing rogue Dirk Gallowglass and they all wondered in their dreams just when he would fly into the village on his midnight black steed, sweep them up, and carry them off in the best romantic fashion of the Dragon's Bard tales.

That was, until the rumor about Jarod Klum being the highwayman in disguise began to circulate.

Vestia Walters lay in her bed awake.

She had been thinking all evening about Jarod Klum being the highwayman and how perfectly this was all working in her favor. Percival Taylor was being driven insane by the mere possibility that his rival for Vestia's affections was actually a daring rogue. For that matter, Jarod Klum was even beginning to look like a serious contender for her affections, as the idea of him being a dashing, troubled, and conflicted highwayman had genuinely piqued her interest.

But which one should she choose? Percival was easily controlled, something she rather liked about him. He would give her no trouble at all, and his parents were well enough off that Percival and Vestia might live comfortably with her parents' assistance even in Mordale.

On the other hand, if Jarod actually were the highwayman, he could have a substantial treasure horde hidden, she did not doubt, somewhere in the woods. A highwayman's treasure could set them both up forever in style and possibly even buy them a position at court in Mordale. And it would make her a highwayman's wife, who might be so outlandish as to get away with wearing breeches and brandishing a sword or a knife or something when the mood suited her.

Maybe Jarod had even hidden his ill-gotten fortune in the bottom of that broken wishing well tended by the smirking Caprice and her two sisters. Vestia had gone to the well for a wish of her own not long ago and, although the results were eventually to her liking, it had looked disastrous at first. The more Vestia thought about it, the more certain she was that the well was the location where Jarod the highwayman had buried the immense wealth of his treasure.

Yet Vestia knew that Jarod would not be so easily manipulated as Percival . . . he might even go so far as to possibly act on his own without asking her permission at all!

So she tossed and turned in her bed, unable to make up her mind between her two suitors and her own destiny.

Vestia sighed for her own benefit and got up out of her bed. She crossed to the window of her room. Her parents' lodgings were above the cooperage and most of the windows were in dormers on the north side overlooking Charter Square. Vestia unlatched the casement window and swung it open so that she could find some solace or inspiration in the night.

Vestia gazed out through her window over the square and the Cursed Sundial at its center. The pixies had long since been released by Xander from their lanterns in Charter Square, and the windows of the town were all dark. However, the moon was nearly full that night, casting a bright blue pall over the town. It was a beautiful, calm night. The murmur of the Wanderwine River came up from its banks on the west side of the square, and the rustling of the waterwheel from Bolly's Mill put a deep rumbling under the otherwise still of the deep night.

Then came the sound of horse's hooves at an easy walk drifting into the square. It was curious, indeed, for Vestia had come to think of herself as the only person awake in the entire town. She craned her head out the window, trying to see whose steed might be abroad in the quietest part of the night.

From King's Road a single horse and rider came slowly into the square, the horseshoes clacking noisily against the cobblestones. A cloak was drawn about the figure closely, and a dark hood, blacker than the night, completely covered his head.

Vestia drew in a quick breath, then murmured quietly, "It's Jarod . . . the highwayman!"

The highwayman turned around the corner of the Griffon's Tale Inn, his shape silhouetted against the cobblestones shining in the moonlight. There he pulled on the reins, stopped his horse, and, turning, gazed upward . . .

. . . into the open window of Evangeline Melthalion.

Vestia's eyes widened, her nose wrinkling in a most unbecoming fashion.

The slight figure of Evangeline leaned out the window. Vestia did not have to hear the words being spoken to understand their intention. Evangeline disappeared from the window, and for a moment Vestia thought she might be mistaken—but only for a moment. Then the door to the inn opened with studied care and the unmistakable figure of Evangeline emerged. She quickly made her way to the highwayman, who swooped her up in his arms, setting her in front of him on his horse and riding northward up the Mordale road.

Vestia, jaw slack in anger and surprise, turned away from the window and sat down on the floor.

"No one walks away from me!" she seethed. "You'll pay for this, Jarod Klum!"

# CHAPTER 12

# Guilty Associations

arod Klum whistled as he tripped happily down Wishing Lane. The Mordale road was behind him now and the apple trees to either side were losing the last of their blossoms in a beautiful light shower of petals. It could not have been a more perfect setting, place, or time—not even Abel, the Bard's quiet scribe, who trod at his side, could dampen his spirits.

Caprice had sent word through the rather overly enthusiastic Edvard for Jarod to meet her at the footbridge over the Wanderwine near the well. Abel begged to accompany him on the short journey, as he had discovered his missing book to have ended up in the hands of Melodi Morgan and was anxious to meet the youngest of the Fate Sisters.

"Isn't it a great day?" Jarod beamed as he walked, taking great strides down the road and swinging his arms freely. The scribe was having a difficult time keeping up. "I mean, I think the sun is shining brighter—actually brighter—and the colors in the woods are outstanding, wouldn't you agree?"

Abel nodded enthusiastically.

"Now, you remember our bargain," Jarod said. "When we come to the footbridge, I'll introduce you, but you excuse yourself and go straight up to the house. I'm sure that Melodi will be there or somewhere nearby. I'll just stay at the bridge with Caprice. Look, there she is now!"

Caprice stood in the middle of the footbridge, leaning against the railing and gazing into the waters of the Wanderwine River rushing below her. The course of the river had cut a slight crevasse into the landscape here that the footbridge connected on either side.

"Caprice!" Jarod called, waving his hand vigorously.

The woman turned toward the two men as they quickly approached, her face troubled.

"This is Abel, who . . . what is wrong, Caprice?"

The green eyes that had so captured his heart turned toward him, filled with tears. "Oh, Jarod, I . . . I just don't understand it all . . . the things I've heard . . . the things they've been saying . . ."

Jarod was truly puzzled. He had not known what to think when Caprice had sent for him, but this was not among the dozen wonderful possibilities he had concocted for himself. It was obvious she was distressed, and he had no idea why. "Oh, Caprice! I'm so sorry! What have you heard? What is it?"

"Here," she said, pressing an amulet into his hands, "it's the best I can do to help you. It's broken, of course, but maybe some good will come out of it for you."

Jarod gazed down at the simple medallion. "It's a wish?"

"I got it from the well this afternoon, so it's still fresh," Caprice sniffed. "It will keep in the amulet, though, for a long time. Use it when you think it best—when it will help you the most."

"Well, of course," Jarod smiled. "That's a very thoughtful gift!

I . . . I've been working on a gift for you . . . a gift of my own, I mean, and as soon as I've got enough money, I'll . . ."

Caprice suddenly slapped his face.

"I don't want your tainted money, Jarod Klum!"

Jarod's face reddened to match the growing mark on his cheek. "And what's wrong with my money? I work hard for it!"

"You know very well what's wrong with it!"

"I do not . . . but I'm beginning to wonder what's wrong with you!" Jarod felt his own tears rising in his eyes. "You asked me to come, remember? What do you want?"

Caprice's green eyes softened suddenly. "I want you to give yourself up, Jarod."

"You want me to . . . what?"

"I want you to give yourself up," she repeated, throwing her arms around his waist and holding him tightly. "You must turn yourself over to the authorities immediately. Xander Lamplighter's a good man—so are the town patrons. Perhaps if you confess, they will be merciful to you and save you from the hangman's rope . . ."

Jarod was in a whirlwind of confusion and conflict. On the one hand, his beloved Caprice Morgan was holding him tightly to her and the sensation filled him with elation—and yet the few words he caught between the beats of his pounding heart and the sudden rush of blood to his ears were ominous and more than a little bizarre. He gazed toward the scribe for help, but Abel seemed to be looking anywhere but where Jarod might catch his eye.

Caprice had begun sobbing into his shirt.

"There, now," Jarod said in soothing tones as he awkwardly put his own arms around her shoulders to comfort her. "It's going to be all right . . . what is it you want me to confess to? I can go see Father Pantheon right away if—"

Caprice pulled back from him. "Oh, Jarod, this is no time for making jokes!"

"Caprice, I don't understand what you're talking about," Jarod said, once more thrown into confusion, especially after having managed momentarily to hold her in his arms only to have that thrilling moment yanked away from him. "If I've done something wrong . . ."

"Something wrong!" Caprice gasped. "Of course it's wrong . . . you know it's wrong!"

Jarod stood for a moment, words having failed him utterly.

Caprice looked down at her feet and then took both his hands in hers. "Perhaps you're not the man I hoped you were, Jarod. We all have our wishes . . . maybe it's time that I realized that mine are broken, too . . . just like everyone else's."

"No, Caprice," Jarod said. "I . . ."

A loud voice called out from behind him up Wishing Lane.

"JAROD KLUM?"

Jarod rolled his eyes, turning slightly so as not to pull his hands away from Caprice. "Yes? Who is—Father?"

He dropped Caprice's hands at once.

Not just his father, he noted, but Xander Lamplighter and a number of the men from the town were with him. His intimate tryst had somehow turned into a community meeting. "What are you doing here?"

Ward Klum's hat seemed particularly square on his head today, his face grimmer than usual. He bowed slightly to Caprice. "Mistress Morgan."

"Master Klum," Caprice curtsied in response.

Ward Klum turned to Jarod. "I need you to tell me what's going on, Son."

Jarod flushed. "Well, Caprice . . . Mistress Morgan . . . asked me to meet her here so that she could tell me something."

"And what did she tell you?"

Jarod grinned with embarrassment. "Well, I didn't understand it, really. She told me I should turn myself over to . . ."

Ward Klum shook his head. "I'm afraid it's too late for that."

Jarod gaped. "Too late for . . . Father, what's going on?"

Ward looked away. "I think you had better come with us, Son."

Abel followed Jarod as the men led him back up Wishing Lane. He did not get to see Melodi Morgan that day to ask her about his book, and Caprice was left standing alone on the footbridge, quietly crying.

"But I'm not the highwayman!" Jarod, red-faced and frustrated, insisted yet again.

"That's just what I'd expect the highwayman to say!" growled the Constable Pro Tempore as he pushed the young man into a dungeon cell.

"Xander! Please!" Ward Klum spoke as sharply as Jarod had ever remembered. "You're not helping the situation at all. Of course, he isn't the highwayman!"

"Then why are we arresting him?" Xander fumed.

"Because there's been a complaint lodged officially with my office," Ward replied evenly, regaining his composure. "Once the complaint is registered, there is a procedure that has to be followed . . . and I'm afraid in this particular case it gets rather complicated."

"Complicated?" Xander looked at the elder Klum slightly askew. "I don't much like the sound of that!"

"Well, in this particular case, it is—"

"Where is he?" came an anxious voice from the top of the dungeon stairs.

Ward and Xander both turned toward the sound.

Squire Melthalion came down in a rush, his feet sliding down the last two treads before he came to a jarring halt at the base of the stairs. He barely stopped to catch his breath. "Where is he? Do you have him?"

"Who?" Ward asked in astonishment.

"The highwayman!" The Squire gulped once before rushing forward. "I heard that you had the highwayman in custody and were . . ."

The Squire stopped suddenly as his eyes fixed on Jarod's cell.

"Why . . . that's not . . . that's your son, Ward!"

"Yes," the elder Klum replied flatly.

"But he isn't . . . I mean . . . he, uh, he couldn't be the . . . the highwayman."

"But he is," Xander said with a great sniff. "Near everyone in the whole town says so!"

"But that's just Gossip Fairy nonsense!" The Squire seemed almost amused at Jarod's predicament. "Why, he doesn't even look like . . . er . . ."

"Look like what, Tomas?" Ward asked, his eyes narrowing as he gazed on the innkeeper.

"Why, he doesn't even look like . . . like . . . like a highwayman!" the Squire stammered. "I mean, where's the . . . the black . . . you know . . . cape-thing and the . . . the . . . the . . . hood?"

"Well, you wouldn't exactly expect him to pass among us during the day in such a getup, would you?" Xander countered, his big fists planted firmly on his hips.

"No, of course not!" Tomas answered, the blood rushing up into his wide face. "But, I mean, look at him! It's only Jarod! There's nothing dashing about him!"

"What do you mean by that?" Jarod complained.

"Eh? Oh, sorry, Jarod . . . no offense meant at all! You're a fine man . . . just fine! But, in all seriousness, you?—the rogue raider of the night? I mean, it's laughable!"

"Could you please stop trying to help me?" Jarod groused.

"What you think, or Xander thinks, or what I think, for that matter, is of no consequence," Ward said, his voice rising slightly to that commanding tone that Jarod knew and feared all too well. "The complaint has been registered, and it must be prosecuted according to the King's Law."

"Here now!" Xander said indignantly. "There's no need to persecute the boy!"

"I said prosecute—not persecute!" Ward snapped. Then he shrugged his shoulders and lowered his voice. "There is a process that must be followed, and there are circumstances regarding all questions of Dirk Gallowglass that require special care."

"Well," Squire Tomas said, blinking as he thought, "what are the charges against Jarod? Maybe there's a problem with the original complaint."

"The charges are clear and supported by evidence," Ward said. "Last night a large sum of money—three sacks of coins, to be exact—vanished from the cooperage. Jep Walters has made a thorough accounting, with my help, and it does appear that he was robbed in the night. The main doors to the cooperage were locked the night before and found unlocked this morning. The only things missing were the coin sacks and the only unsecured entry was those front doors. Vestia Walters—"

"Vestia?" Jarod exclaimed.

"Vestia Walters," Ward continued, "claims that she had the key to those same doors with her earlier the previous day when she met Jarod for an assignation on Boar's Island."

"Assassination!" Xander was deeply concerned. "Why, that's worse than I thought!"

"Not . . . that's *assignation!*" Ward fumed. "A tryst . . . like a meeting between two lovers. By the heavens! How I wish you people read books!"

"So Jarod met Vestia on Boar's Island," Squire Tomas shrugged. "Couples have been meeting there since before even you and I were young, Ward."

"Yes, but Vestia doesn't remember having the key after they met," Ward continued. "Then there's what she saw out her window last night."

The Squire raised his eyebrows.

"She says that she saw the highwayman riding away from the cooperage north past your inn, Squire Tomas," Ward continued.

"What?" Jarod whined. "I was out at Farmer Bennis's last night! I even told you where I was going."

"I know, Son," Ward said. "You said you were going to spend the night at Aren's—which, you must admit, is north of town. Xander and I did a little investigating on our own. There are a number of shod hoof marks that pass north across the stones next to the inn. There are also several places where the mud has covered over the stones during the winter and they have not yet been cleared. Interestingly, it seems that not only did a horse and rider pass that way but it looked to me as though they stopped for a time under one of the corner windows of your inn, Squire Tomas."

Tomas blanched.

"Squire?"

"I didn't hear anything!"

"No one said you did," Ward continued. "What's the matter?"

"Nothing at all," the Squire gulped. "Well, I'm sure you'll get all this cleared up in short order. Jarod's name will be cleared in no time at all!"

"I'm afraid that's the complicated part," Ward said with a look on his face that was, if possible, more grim than usual.

"Father?" Jarod asked. "What is it?"

"About five or six months ago, the highwayman made the mistake of surprising Lord Pompeanus on the road between here and Welston."

"Lord Pompeanus? Cousin of the king?" Squire Tomas gasped.

"Yes," Ward said, tugging uncharacteristically at his collar. "The king's favorite cousin and, as fate would have it, the field marshal of the Eastern Wall Armies."

"Bad luck that for you, Jarod," Xander nodded. "He's a cold killer with a blade in his hand. You'd have done better with a different mark."

"It wasn't me!" Jarod said, emphasizing each word.

"Oh, right you are," Xander replied with an exaggerated wink.

Jarod rolled his eyes.

Ward continued. "The warrant stated that Lord Pompeanus believed he had pinked the rogue but couldn't be certain. What *was* certain is that in pursuing the highwayman into the woods, Lord Pompeanus's foot found a gopher hole, which wrenched his ankle and broke his foot. For this offense, Pompeanus issued a warrant to every county and shire in the kingdom demanding jurisdiction if this rogue is discovered—and the extinction of all gophers, although that part of the warrant certainly does not apply here."

The Squire squinted. "So, what does that mean for Jarod here?"

"It means that Lord Pompeanus is being notified that Jarod has been arrested as the highwayman," Ward answered. "He will come here personally to take charge of the investigation."

"But they'll find Jarod to be innocent!" Tomas urged.

"Justice is rarely about the truth, Squire," Ward replied. "Even if Lord Pompeanus released Jarod, there would still be the matter of Vestia's report and the evidence in the courtyard. Pompeanus will not let the matter go. He will find his highwayman, and when he does, the matter will be out of my hands. His punishment, I've no doubt, will be swift and most final."

"Of course," the Squire said, licking his lips. "I . . . well, I'd best be off! Sorry to have bothered you!"

"That seems a rather sudden leave-taking there, Squire," Xander commented.

"No more so than the coming," Ward observed. "Tomas, you seemed to get here rather quickly after the arrest."

"Well, you know . . . incensed townsperson and all . . . concerned for the theft of a fellow merchant . . ."

Xander snorted. "Since when have you become concerned for the welfare of Jep Walters?"

"No, really, I must be going," the Squire continued, hastily backing toward the stairs. "Glad to see you've got this well in hand! Nicely done, Constable!"

"Constable Pro Tempore!" Xander yelled down the dungeon hall.

But the Squire had already bolted back up the stairs.

"Father," Jarod said with all the earnestness of his soul, "this is lunacy! I'm not all that certain I could ride a horse at a gallop, let alone be this highwayman."

Ward pressed his hands together, his two forefingers against his lips as he considered. "Xander, you say everyone in the town is sure that Jarod is the highwayman?"

"Aye! It's common knowledge."

"In my experience, 'common knowledge' is neither common nor at all knowledgeable," Ward replied. "More to the point, if what I hear about Lord Pompeanus is even half true, his dictation of justice is ruled more by his passions than by his head."

"What does it mean, Father?" Jarod asked as Xander closed the dungeon cell door.

"It means we have a week at most to prove your innocence to the satisfaction of a man who is not known for valuing proof," Ward said.

He reached out between the lattice of the cell's bars and, for the first time since Jarod was a child, took his hand.

"You're not the highwayman, Son," Ward said. "And what we have to do is find a way to convince everyone you're not."

## · CHAPTER 13 ·

# Dirk's Last Ride

It happened in the darkest and deepest part of the night.

The lamps in the streets of Eventide were all dark. The pixies had, many hours before, all been released from their confinements. Only the narrow crescent of the moon gave the barest light to the courts and alleys of the town, and that was occasionally shuttered by the passing of low clouds caught in the breeze in the night of an early summer.

Through the darkness—through the night—rode the highwayman.

The clatter of his black steed's hooves rattled down the streets. His shrill cry echoed between the walls like the wail of a banshee spirit. It startled the sleep of many as he passed up Cobblestone Street. Ariela shrieked in her own small house, adding considerably to the commotion as the dark form of the highwayman rode madly through the town at full gallop. His black hood obscured his face from any who leaped from their beds in panic and managed to open the shutters on their upper floor windows in time to catch a glimpse of the dark form, cape flying behind the rider's shoulders.

The highwayman pulled up his steed slightly as he entered Trader's Square, rounding the countinghouse. Deniva Kolyan, peering through the slits between her bakery's front windows, saw clouds part for a moment, the moon illuminating the square and the silhouette of Dirk Gallowglass on his steed, the horse's steel-shod hooves scraping against the stone, sparking in the night. She was surprised by this, as the legend of Gallowglass had it that he was an expert horseman. The figure astride the mount certainly looked shorter and somewhat heavier than she had thought would fit his description, no doubt the purpose of his disguise as he rode. The highwayman pulled the horse to his right, his arm flashing a blade in the night as he screamed, "Evangeline! Evangeline!" Mount and rider plunged through the night toward Bolly's Bridge—with Charter Square and the Griffon's Tale Inn just beyond.

In that moment, the clouds veiled the lunar light, plunging all the streets in the town again into darkness.

Dirk never made it across the bridge.

There was a horrible crashing sound and the distressed whinny of a horse. Angry shouting carried above the muted rumble of Bolly Falls and the Wanderwine River rushing beneath the bridge. Then the distinct ring of steel on steel pierced the night on both sides of the river.

A sudden, terrible squeal rent the air.

There was a loud splash from the river.

The night was silent once more . . . except for the clopping of the riderless horse of the highwayman walking aimlessly back into Trader's Square. When the clouds parted again, the moonlight re-vealed an empty saddle on the horse's back, glistening darkly.

Ward Klum, dressed unconventionally in his nightshirt, boots, and official tasseled cap, emerged moments later from the counting-house with a storm lantern held high. Garth Bolly was also rushing into Trader's Square from the mill, a stevedore's hook in his hand. They met, speaking with each other for a moment before Garth pointed and the two of them ran toward Bolly's Bridge.

At nearly that same moment, Jep Walters—at the most urgent insistence of his wife, Livinia—burst from the cooperage red-faced and gripping an antique casting wand in one thick hand and a sputtering torch in the other. The wand looked like a relic crafted from the time of the Epic War and had most probably not been re-enchanted or fired for more than twenty years. Jep looked encouraged when Joaquim Taylor and both Harv and Merinda Oakman came out of their shops—Joaquim brandishing shears and Merinda her largest rolling pin. Harv had his own torch as well. All three of them rushed toward the west side of Charter Square—from where they had heard the cacophony.

Both groups converged on the bridge at nearly the same time—and were brought to a sudden halt at the tableau that was revealed under the lantern and torch light.

The crimson shine of blood was everywhere. Squire Tomas Melthalion knelt on the bridge breathing heavily, his clothes stained in scarlet. He still gripped a long, elegant saber in his right hand. The blade, too, was streaked with blood. The Squire was shaking from head to foot and gasping for air.

"The . . . the highwayman," the Squire gasped.

On the bridge nearby lay a crumpled black hood and a trampled black cape.

Merinda Oakman, seeing the Squire's blood-soaked shirt,

dropped her rolling pin and rushed forward. "Tomas! We're here for you! Where are you wounded?"

"No, I'm not harmed, Merinda," the Squire croaked, trying to catch his breath. He pushed himself up to stand on his feet but his legs were not quite up to the task. Ward Klum and Jep Walters rushed forward to catch him before he collapsed again.

"You said it was the highwayman?" Ward asked, an urgent brilliance in his eyes as he held the Squire firmly on his feet.

"Yes," Tomas answered with a hoarse voice through a long, shuddering breath.

"Dirk Gallowglass?" Harv Oakman asked in astonishment.

Tomas cast his eyes to the ground. "Yes. Dirk Gallowglass."

"Tomas, you idiot!" Jep Walters said with some heat in his voice as he too held up the Squire. "What were you thinking, going up against a man like that? You could have gotten yourself killed!"

The Squire turned toward the cooper and smiled faintly. "Why, thank you, Jep. That's the kindest thing you've said to me in years."

"Over here, Jep," Ward urged the cooper, indicating with his head the north side of the bridge. The two of them helped Squire Melthalion to the low wall and leaned him against it. The Master of the Counting Guild then looked into his friend's face. "Where is he, Tomas . . . where's Dirk Gallowglass now?"

The Squire gazed back steadily as he croaked out the words. "Dead, Master Klum."

Ward reached down and forced the fingers open on the innkeeper's hand, freeing at last the bloodied sword from his grip.

"Dead," Tomas repeated in a raspy voice. "I killed him."

The double doors of the Guild Hall swung violently open, banging against the walls loudly as the imposing figure blew into the room like a violent summer storm. He wore an ornamental breastplate covered in golden filigree signifying his rank. The pauldron on his right shoulder was also of a distinctively decorative and unique style. He had a jutting jaw and deep-set eyes that shifted to each face as he entered the room. His golden hair was graying slightly but still flowed from a high forehead back into a tightly tied tail. His eyes were of a brown color so dark as to be nearly black. Twin long scars ran down his right cheek, one continuing down his neck and out of sight beneath his armor. He presented at once an image of authority and officious impracticality, as the village was hardly under siege, and, other than to impress the locals, there was absolutely no reason for him to be wearing the armor at all.

"Who thinks they are in charge here?" he boomed in a voice used to issuing commands from a distance.

Everyone turned as one to face the newcomer. The Guild Hall was packed with as many of the townsfolk as could manage to fit inside the doors.

Ward Klum, adorned not only in the hat of his Guild office but also in his official mantle as the town clerk, stood at the opposite end of the hall. "I am, my Lord Pompeanus. I speak for the village elders and all the people of Eventide when I bid you welcome and—"

"By the authority granted me by his most august personage, King Reinard, I, Lord Pompeanus, claim the right of jurisdiction over matters before this inquiry and to the prosecution of those parties found guilty in the eyes of justice and the King's Law!" Two enormous men followed Lord Pompeanus into the hall, both more sensibly dressed in linen shirts and matching doublets. Everyone in

the hall knew at once that they were knights in Lord Pompeanus's service, as the power of their form was exceeded only by the enormity of their contempt. They followed their master as he moved forward, limping with each step to heavily favor his right leg on his march toward Ward Klum. Dust from their lord's cape and leggings gathered on the long ride from Mordale now billowed onto the polished floor around him with every stride down the center of the room. "I will conduct this inquiry as I see fit, is that clear to everyone here?"

"We had news of your coming," Ward Klum offered the rapidly approaching warrior. "We trust we have anticipated your needs and—"

"Yes, yes, yes." Pompeanus pulled off one of his gloves as he stepped onto the raised platform at the end of the Guild Hall. He sat down at once in the guildmaster's chair. His companion knights took positions on either side of him, folding their arms across their massive chests. "You seem to know the particulars—who are you?"

"I am Guildmaster Ward Klum, my Lord," he replied with a slight bow. "I am also the King's Clerk in Eventide."

"Very well, Master Klum," the old warrior said, waving his gloves in his hand. "Present the proceedings."

Ward nodded and then turned to face the assemblage. "By decree of His Highness, King Reinard, and in his Most August Name, we proclaim open the inquest into the death of—"

"HOLD!" bellowed Lord Pompeanus.

"My lord?" Ward said evenly as he turned to face the king's cousin.

"The arrest of the highwayman Dirk Gallowglass is what interests me," Pompeanus said under his barely controlled breath. "It is

the only reason I have ridden all these hours to this pointless little collection of huts!"

"Aye, my lord," Ward nodded with a calm that astonished everyone in the room, including the escorting knights of the lord.

"Then what's this Blue Lady baggage about an inquest?" the lord bellowed.

"It is an inquest into the death of the highwayman Dirk Gallowglass," Klum answered.

"He's dead?" It was Pompeanus's turn to be astonished. "When?"

"Last night," Ward answered.

Lord Pompeanus leaned forward, a dangerous edge to his voice. "He died in your custody?"

"No, my lord." Ward cleared his throat. "The man originally arrested as Dirk Gallowglass later proved to have been falsely accused as a ruse by the highwayman to divert suspicion from himself. He was a most sinister and cunning rogue."

The lord's eye's narrowed.

"He died in a most gruesome manner," Ward added. "Would my lord care to hear the particulars?"

Lord Pompeanus sat back. "Proceed."

Ward turned to face the assemblage. Jarod sat on a bench in the front row next to his mother, who held his hand tightly in her own. Orlynda had been in a panic ever since her son's arrest—even though it largely involved him moving from his small room above the countinghouse into the dungeon two floors below. No amount of coaxing by Ward, however, would convince her that the distance was trivial. She visited him several times a day, bringing him so many tarts, breads, and apples that he had to start sharing them with Xander Lamplighter. Tomas Melthalion and his wife, Daphne, were in the front row on the opposite side of the aisle from Jarod although their daughter, Evangeline, was conspicuously absent. Even that fool Bard stood leaning against the back wall, his scribe near him in the corner faithfully and completely recording every nuance of the proceedings—for which Ward would later be most grateful.

"The inquest calls Merinda Oakman to answer truthfully in the name of the king!"

"Constable Pro Tempore, you examined the area where Dirk Gallowglass died?"

"Aye, sire, that I did, with utmost care of duty! Wouldn't want nobody thinking that the Constable Pro Tempore were not doing his job right proper!"

"Please, just answer my questions," Ward sighed. The constable was the fifth of his witnesses after Merinda and Harv Oakman, Garth Bolly, and Jep Walters. By far the constable had been the most troublesome of the witnesses, most likely owing to the fact that he was an official and, as such, knew less about what was going on than anyone else. In truth, it had taken a troubling amount of time to even find the Constable Pro Tempore, who had not been discovered until after sunrise this morning.

"That are what I be doing, yer sireship!"

"What did you see on Bolly's Bridge?"

"It were a most horrible sight indeed, Master Klum! There were blood everywhere . . . beggin' your pardon, ladies! It were even on the highwayman's horse when I examined it later."

"Thank you, Constable," Ward said as if to dismiss Xander. "You may sit down now."

"That's Constable Pro Tempore, Master Klum. Oh, and it were

all down the horse's flanks, that blood was, and on them saddlebags, too, and—"

Ward called out loudly as he ignored Xander, "The inquest calls Tomas Melthalion to answer truthfully in the name of the king!"

"Yes, he was very much a rogue," Tomas said, standing with his hat in his hands before the platform. "And a man whose acquaintance I was sorry to make."

"Then you had met this highwayman before?" Ward asked.

"Yes, Ward . . . er, sire. He came to the inn in the middle of the night just nigh over six months past, banging on the door and threatening us all. He forced his way into the Griffon's Tale and threatened not only myself but my daughter, Evangeline, and Lord Gallivant as well."

Lord Pompeanus leaned forward. "Lord Gallivant, you say?"

"Yes, your lordship."

"Can't be the same," the lord muttered, shaking his head and leaning back. "Go on."

"Well, he threatened us with our lives!" Tomas continued. "He was wounded bleeding in the shoulder—and demanded that we treat him or he would kill everyone in the house and burn it to the ground!"

A murmur ran through the crowd in the hall.

"Just a moment," Pompeanus interrupted again. "You say this was about six months ago?"

"Yes, my lord."

"And he was wounded in the shoulder?"

"Aye . . . most seriously, sire."

"HA!" Lord Pompeanus smiled, banging his fist on the arm of the chair. "Sir Konrad! You lose! Settle up!"

One of the escorting knights sighed, drew out a coin purse, and slapped it into the beckoning hand of the lord.

"Proceed!" said the grinning Pompeanus.

"So you treated his wounds and he left?" Ward prompted.

"Would that were all there was to it," Tomas said, shaking his head. "His wounds were deep and required some time to heal. We had no choice but to keep him hidden in the inn on the very threat of our lives! Sadly, it was my dear daughter, Evangeline, who was forced to care for him the most . . . and in that dark time the villainous highwayman began making unseemly advances on my innocent daughter!"

Several of the Cobblestone ladies gasped and the Widow Merryweather threatened to swoon. Even the Gossip Fairy managed to appear shocked.

"He became obsessed with her," Tomas continued. "I turned him out as quickly as I dared, but on those nights when the moon shone brighter he would come to the inn and try to coerce my daughter away from her home and her friends!"

"And did she go with him?" Ward asked.

"No, sire, she did not!" Squire Tomas asserted. "My daughter was not so easily persuaded!"

Lord Pompeanus leaned forward. "You are an innkeeper?"

"Aye, my lord."

"And she was an innkeeper's daughter?"

"Aye, my lord."

"And you say she was not easily persuaded?"

"As I have said, my lord."

Lord Pompeanus shrugged. "How odd."

"She was engaged to be married, my lord . . . to a farmer."

"Did anyone else know of this engagement?"

"No, sire. It was not announced, as we feared it might incense the highwayman's wrath. Evangeline tried otherwise to dissuade him."

"And still the highwayman pursued her?" Ward asked.

"He was a scoundrel, sire! Two days ago he discovered that Evangeline was to be married—in Welston. He went mad with jealousy—like some highwaymen do, I believe—and in the middle of the night rode into town at a full gallop yelling the name of 'Evangeline' at the top of his lungs with such force that he nearly lost his voice from the effort. I heard him coming. I grabbed that saber and ran out to stop him before he could reach my Evangeline and do her harm."

"A unique weapon," Pompeanus mused as he examined the sword. "A fine edge, although it's been abused . . . nicked in several places on the leading edge. So you ran toward the highwayman?"

"Yes, my lord . . ."

"You managed to wake up, dress, grab this saber, and run all the way to the bridge after hearing the highwayman riding and shouting from the south end of the village?"

"Yes, my lord. I was already awake and dressed, sire. I had a pair of hogs to be butchered in preparation for the wedding."

"The secret wedding?" Pompeanus asked quietly.

"Yes, my lord."

"Bloody business, butchering hogs," Pompeanus said. "You dealt with a lot of blood last night, didn't you, Squire?"

Tomas gulped once. "Yes, my lord. I reached the center of the bridge just as Gallowglass started across it. I challenged him, blocking his path and startling his horse. The horse braced to a stop so suddenly that the highwayman was tossed from the saddle onto the bridge. He rolled toward me, then sprang to his feet!"

The townsfolk of Eventide leaned forward—the silence in the room was profound. Squire Tomas had always believed himself to be a storyteller, and, for the most part, the citizens of Eventide had ignored his tales. But this was the most important story of his life, and from somewhere deep inside he found the courage to tell it with style, conviction, and power.

"His sword slid almost without a sound from its scabbard. 'Evangeline will be mine or no one's,' he says to me.

"'She will never be yours, accursed rascal!' says I. Then he lunged at me with his blade. I countered at once and our weapons crashed together in ringing blows—steel sliding against steel! The cut and parry drove our blades against the railing of the bridge, stone shattering to shards from the fierce blows.

"'I am the highwayman!' cries he. 'I take what I want!'

"'And I keep what is mine!' says I to him, turning his blade aside and thrusting my own into your lordship's previous wound!"

The townsfolk drew in a collective breath.

"As he staggered back, I shouted, 'You will haunt us no more!' And with a stroke of my saber blade, I severed his head from his body, knocking it completely off the bridge and into the swirling waters of the river below!"

No one moved. Not even Widow Merryweather dared to swoon for fear of missing what might come next.

Lord Pompeanus leaned forward. "Excuse me?"

Ward Klum turned to look back at the lord. Tomas looked up expectantly.

"You say you took his head clean from his shoulders?" Pompeanus asked.

"Yes, my lord."

"Knocked it right into the river?"

"As I said, my lord."

"And you did this with a saber blade that had already lost its edge from these repeated furious blows of your sword against the stone of the bridge walls?"

Tomas paused. "Yes, that's how it happened, my lord."

"That accounts for the head . . . but where's the body?"

"Sire?"

Lord Pompeanus opened his hands in front of him. "Well, you took off this knave's head and knocked it into the river—but the body remained."

"Oh, no, sire! It fell into the river too."

"Ah!" Lord Pompeanus smiled. "I see. So you knocked both the head and the body into the river?"

"Well, I'm not sure . . ."

"So who bled on the bridge, Squire?" Pompeanus continued. "If the head and the body are in the river, where did all the blood come from?"

"From the body, sire," Tomas said. "I had taken off his head with the saber."

"So, if I am to understand you properly," Pompeanus said with a venomous grin, "the headless body stood around at the side of the bridge for a while, bleeding on the stones and, apparently, on the horse, until, tired of the business, it pitched itself over the rail?"

"No, sire!" Tomas answered, sweat breaking on his brow. "The horse was not there then!"

"But the horse had blood covering it." Lord Pompeanus's grin deepened.

"No doubt, sire . . . no doubt the reopening of his previous wounds."

"But the blood was on the horse's flanks," Pompeanus said quietly. "It is your testimony that the highwayman was riding at a full gallop backward through the—"

The doors at the back of the hall opened.

Lord Pompeanus looked up, his grin suddenly falling.

Aren Bennis stood, hat in hand, at the back of the hall. "Sorry to interrupt," the centaur rumbled in his deep voice. "I have a message for Lord Pompeanus that must be delivered at once."

Lord Pompeanus stood up suddenly, staring at Farmer Bennis.

"If your lordship will join me outside for a moment, I will deliver my message," Bennis said, his deep-set eyes never leaving Pompeanus. "And if all you good people will just wait here, it shouldn't take but a moment, and things will be properly settled."

In the end, Lord Pompeanus never returned to the Guild Hall. Ward Klum was called out of the room a few minutes later, followed quickly by the lord's two escort knights. It was left to Ward Klum to return to the confused assemblage and pronounce the results of the inquest.

The highwayman was dead, his head and body lost forever to the Wanderwine River. Squire Tomas had killed him in defense of his honor, his home, and the community. The sad tale of the highwayman was closed.

All that was left was to celebrate the secret wedding of the couple who now were already settled in the reasonably distant town of Welston. Though the couple were not at the party that evening, Tomas assured everyone of the best wishes to them all from Evangeline Melthalion and her husband—a farmer by the name of Henri Smyth.

In the years to come, Evangeline occasionally returned home, but no one ever saw Henri Smyth in Eventide. However, Harvest Oakman reported many years later having visited a tall, strapping farmer with uncommonly good looks working a lovely little farm outside of Welston. He occasionally during conversation would reach up and rub his left shoulder. When asked about it, he replied it was an old injury from a previous job and the main reason why he had taken up farming. His name was Henri Smyth, and with his happy wife, Evangeline, he had five children—four daughters and a son by the name of Dirk.

Jarod slipped through the celebration crowd in Charter Square outside the Griffon's Tale Inn with a large piece of hog's meat in his hand. He was a free man—which meant that he could move the two floors back up to his room above the countinghouse instead of below it—and although his name was cleared of all charges, the slight aroma of his having been associated with such a scandalous tale had made him more noticeable after all.

Perhaps, he reflected, too noticeable. He was as much trying to avoid Vestia Walters as to look for Caprice Morgan. Jep Walters's missing money had not, it now seemed, been stolen at all but had somehow reappeared in the cooperage in the bottom of one of Vestia's trunks, where it had mysteriously fallen. Now Vestia was more interested in Jarod than ever.

Jarod took a bite from the hog's meat and turned again in the crowd—running directly into someone he had not seen behind him.

"Oh, pardon me, sir, I . . ."

It was Meryl Morgan—Caprice's father.

"It's all right, Jarod," Meryl said with a distracted chuckle.

"Oh! Master Morgan!" Jarod blurted. "I see you're out for a . . . I mean, it's terribly good to see you, sir!"

"You mean it's good to see me out in the town," Meryl nodded. "Caprice and Melodi insisted. It's a wedding celebration, after all."

Meryl looked away for a moment, apparently to a distant, happier time. Jarod, shocked at finding himself unexpectedly in the encounter that he had occasionally daydreamed about, suddenly realized his mouth was saying things before his mind could stop him.

"Father Morgan," Jarod heard himself saying, "I have the utmost respect and esteem for your family and, in particular, your daughter . . ."

Meryl came back from his painful, joyful memories at the sound of his name. "What, Son? Oh, of course you do."

"May I have your permission to call?" Inside, Jarod began to panic at the words, having been so long rehearsed in his head, coming out of his mouth of their own volition.

"Of course, Jarod! You are welcome to call upon me and my daughters at any time. I've been thinking lately that I need to see to that part of my daughters' lives. I've been meaning to get around to that, but . . . well, there's been so much to do. If only Brenna were still here, she would know how to take care of it."

"Thank you, sir!"

"I really must see to the girls," Meryl said. "Especially Sobrina. She has to be married first, you know."

"I didn't . . . what do you mean 'she has to be married first'?" Jarod asked quickly.

"It's bound up in being wish-women," Meryl said. "I wish Brenna were here to explain it. She knew all about it and was so smart and wise. The firstborn must be married before the others may be courted or the well may fail altogether. So, feel free to come calling on Sobrina anytime you like, Master Jarod!"

Meryl spied his daughters through the crowd and moved quickly toward them, leaving Jarod standing with what seemed like hog's meat in one hand and his heart in the other. The assistant accountant saw Sobrina towering above her sisters, her stern look a permanent fixture on her face.

"Oh, joy," Jarod thought without any joy at all. "Not only do I have to win Caprice for myself but I have to find someone else who will wed the frost queen of the well!"

# COURTING FATES

*Wherein Jarod tries a conspiracy of
wishes with another suitor of the
Fate Sisters . . . and discovers that good
wishes can have dire consequences.*

· CHAPTER 14 ·

# Broken Wishes and Mended Hearts

Y ou're sure he's the one?" Jarod said, his eyes stinging, filling with tears.

"You can believe in me, Jarod, when I tell you there isn't another man in all of Eventide who desires Sobrina Morgan more than this man!" the Dragon's Bard choked out. "I've had it on . . . just a moment . . ."

Edvard took a step to the side, turned his head, and gagged.

Abel, standing behind the two, was forced to hold his stylus in one hand and his writing tablet in the other and therefore was unable to shield his nose in any way except by the conscious effort not to breathe more often than absolutely necessary.

"I've had it on good authority," Edvard continued, his right hand pressing a scented handkerchief to his nose. It was like trying to hold back the tide with a teaspoon. "Both Beulandreus Dudgeon and Alicia Charon confirmed it to me in the most ardent terms. This is the man we want!"

The three unhappy callers stood at the southern end of Boar's

Island just above the confluence of the West and East Wanderwine Rivers and the marshes beyond. The enclosure took up nearly half an acre of property, with the rooftops of low buildings just visible over the high walls. A massive double gate stood closed before them with a weathered and nearly illegible sign next to it proclaiming: "Visitors Welcome—Please Pull."

Jarod tried to take in a deep breath, coughed, and then reached forward and yanked hard on the chain that ran over the wall next to the sign.

A loud bell clanged in the space beyond the gate. Nothing happened for a full minute, and Jarod was just reaching for the chain again when he heard the lifting of a heavy crossbar and saw the gate swing partly open inward. A swarthy face between two large ears and an explosion of jet-black hair pushing outward from around a gleaming bald dome of a head popped out of the opening.

Jarod, Edvard, and Abel all took an involuntary step back with the sudden onslaught of aromas pouring through the open gate.

"By the heavens! Jarod, how are you?" Lucius Tanner exclaimed as his face broke into a wide grin. He extended his hand, then abruptly pulled it back, wiping it on his apron before extending it again with undiminished enthusiasm. "I can't tell you what a delight it is to see you here—you and your friends. Come in! Come in!"

Jarod could only nod. None of the rest of them dared attempt to open their mouths to speak.

"You know, we just don't get many callers here," Lucius chattered on as they stepped into the tannery. "But you're always most welcome. Our work is a little slow today, but we've got a shipment of new hides coming in tomorrow. Still, I'd be delighted to show you around!"

Lucius Tanner was slightly shorter than Jarod, with broad shoulders and a wide, sturdy build. He wore a long-sleeved shirt, canvas trousers tucked into the tops of tall boots, and a large, heavily stained leather apron. Thick gloves were tucked into the apron where they might be readily grasped and put to use at a moment's need.

The interior courtyard was littered with low-rimmed vats filled with noxious-looking liquids. Sheds and a handful of buildings ringed the interior space, and everywhere one looked there were gnomes—each one no more than two and a half feet tall, and each wearing a strange, orange, conical felt hat with a feather in its peak—dashing from place to place in a frantic rush.

"May as well give you the full tour," Lucius grinned. "Now, over here in this covered shed is where we keep the dried skins. They come in just the way you see them: dried, stiff, dirty, and largely with their gore still attached. Those we take over here and soak in water vats to get them all cleaned up and softened. Then we take them over to these sheds where you can see Jurt here beating the hides and scraping off all the old flesh and fat. Of course, we still have to get the hair fibers out, too, so we bring them right over to these vats over here."

Jarod was decidedly losing color in his face at this point.

"Here we soak the cleaned skins in these vats of urine," Lucius said proudly. "It's the best thing in the world for removing hide hair. Of course, it takes quite a while, and the process only loosens the hairs. The hairs have to be scraped off the hides with a knife. That's what Klisten's doing over there right now . . . how is it going, Klisten?"

The small gnome woman was nearly hidden by the enormous, reeking hide that she was scraping. She waved back at the group with her knife as she flashed them a bright yellow grin.

"Once Klisten's finished, the hide gets a dip in that salt solution over there and then we take it to the most important part of the process—the bating of the leather. That's right over here."

Jarod was having difficulty keeping his stinging eyes open.

"Here's Klauf and his wife, Enuci, giving their personal touch to the most important part of the art," Lucius said with pride, pointing toward the far corner of the tannery. "In these rather impressive vats is our special mixture of dung and some, well, additional unsavory ingredients. Dog feces and pigeon droppings are generally the best, although, as you see under that shed over there, we maintain a supply of all kinds of dung for every hide-tanning occasion. You see how Klauf and Enuci are stomping down through the mixture with their bare feet? That kneads the dung into the hides . . ."

"Master Tanner!" Jarod belched the words out.

"You had a question, Jarod?" Lucius asked with eager anticipation. "Was I going too fast?"

"We . . . we need . . ." The stench was overwhelming.

"We have a most important matter to discuss with you," the Dragon's Bard managed to force out in a single breath.

"Oh, of course." Lucius's smile fell slightly. "But I haven't shown you the drying and stretching yards yet—"

"Urgent!" Jarod had discovered he could manage single words but nothing more in the odiferous confines of the tannery.

"Oh, in that case, you have my full attention . . ."

"Outside!" Jarod blurted out. "Private!"

"Ah!" Lucius nodded with understanding although he did not understand at all. "As you wish . . . but I hope you'll all stay for lunch?"

Lucius and Jarod had one thing in common: since they were both young they had each been in love with a Morgan girl.

Lucius found the prickly, distant Sobrina to be an object of abject fascination for him. His father was the tanner in the town, as had been his father before him, so he grew up knowing the wishing well and the wisher-women who tended it. His mother, a free-spirited perfumer woman with the mysterious name of Khaisai Zarkina, had come from Mordale originally and insisted that Lucius be schooled under the tutelage of a young scribe who had recently started at the countinghouse by the name of Ward Klum. He had been dutiful and had proven himself to be an apt student until a tragic dung-cart accident took the life of his father when the boy was seventeen—just as the romance between Lucius and Sobrina was starting to blossom. Lucius took up the family business at the tannery, and the promise of their union evaporated with it.

This was because of the great Tanner blessing—and curse: Lucius, his father, his father's father, and his father's father's father before him all had one unique gift that ruled their choice of trade, their fortunes, and their fates.

Not a single one of them had *any* olfactory sense at all.

None of them could smell a thing.

In the tanning business, this was a tremendous comfort and blessing. The process of tanning hides into leather is the most onerously odiferous profession in all the known realms. The lack of any sense of smell allowed the Tanner family down through the generations to perform their seemingly destined trade far more efficiently than others of their profession in other towns.

But it may also have been a major contributing factor in the dung-cart accident that took Clifholm Tanner's life.

Worse for Lucius, it was the major reason his romance with Sobrina had gone sour. Working now in the tannery, rather than in the musty but reasonably odor-free countinghouse, Lucius rapidly acquired a distinctive scent that announced his approach to the townspeople of Eventide—depending upon the current wind direction—well in advance of his even being seen. Even Mordechai Charon, to whom Lucius sold all his leather and by whose artistry both of them profited tremendously, had to stand at some distance from the man in order to conclude their negotiations. Tryena, a mysterious trader in pelts who occasionally came to Charon's Goods, would never deal with Lucius directly—she would only sell her pelts to Charon, who in turn would deal with the tanner.

Lucius was at once keenly aware of the problem and incapable of doing anything about it. He knew that he smelled to other people although the concepts of "smell" and "odor" and "stink to the ninth heaven" were outside of his experience. He also knew that if he bathed and cleaned himself up, people found him more acceptable and he could get closer to them before they fled. But without any ability to gauge his own odor, he could never know if he were acceptable in company. He would occasionally scrub himself raw in the East Wanderwine River and risk a visit to the wishing well, but whenever he saw Sobrina—no matter how hard he tried—down the years she would stand farther and farther off and always upwind.

His mother moved back to Mordale, and for several years her son supported her there, but she passed away during an epidemic in the city. That left Lucius alone.

Then Klauf Snarburt, a gnome, had showed up at the tannery gates one day two years ago, seeking employment. When Lucius's wages proved to be more than fair, Klauf invited several family members to join him, and, as the Snarburt clan's abilities in tanning leather were unsurpassed, soon the success of the tannery was beyond Lucius's dreams. The output of tanned leather tripled, and a future filled with gold coins accruing in his account at the countinghouse seemed assured. He had nearly cleared all his father's debts on the land and the buildings and was starting to turn a nice profit.

He knew he would become wealthy in just a few more years, but Lucius found no solace in it. All he could think about was Sobrina Morgan still standing well upwind.

"I can sympathize with your problem," Aren said as he glanced over the top of his book. "But there may be some hope for you yet. Perhaps a wish is in order after all."

The centaur sat with his legs folded under him on a large floor cushion beside a fireplace that nearly filled the end of the room. A cheerful blaze crackled and hissed above the grate, illuminating Farmer Bennis's main room in this home. The evening had turned unusually chill for the early summer season, and the aging centaur felt the need for a little warmth. Jarod was glad, for the fire brought out the details of the room: the dented shields that were mounted decoratively on the walls and the pair of short swords crossed above the mantel. The fascinating was mixed in with the mundane: a helmet with a lobster-tail plating down the neck sat on a shelf next to a number of crockery jars. A jeweled dagger lay across a round of cheese. Most intriguing of all was the segmented suit of torso armor standing in the corner on a frame, nearly hidden by the farmer's leather coat draped over it. Jarod took it all in from his polished chair without questioning any of it while Abel sat opposite him enjoying a slice of rye bread and cheese offered to him by the centaur.

"But the well is broken," Jarod shrugged. "How can that help?"

"Just because the well is broken doesn't mean you can't make a wish," Aren chuckled as he rubbed his weary eyes. "I see you're wearing a wishing amulet. You could try that."

"No." Jarod shook his head. "I'm not ready to try this one yet. Caprice gave it to me, and she said it was broken."

"She should know," Aren mumbled as he turned a page. "She has enough broken wishes of her own."

"So what would be the point of—"

"Jarod, listen to me," Aren said, setting his book aside in frustration and looking straight at the young man. "There are things you need to know about the broken wishes of the well. The reason they were broken in the first place is because so many pilgrims were using the well to wish things for themselves. That's what the great wizard did when he finally broke the well, but it had been weakened long before that. A selfish wish is a hard wish because it does no greater good. It does not contribute to the spirit of the world from which it came. It is also a weak wish because it is self-serving. The best wishes—the kindest and strongest—are those that we wish for others. If you sincerely wish to help Lucius win the somewhat imperious Sobrina for himself, then perhaps your wish has a better chance than you think."

"I've got to go," Jarod said, suddenly jumping up from his chair.

"You've got to . . . but you just got here," Aren protested.

"I, uh, I forgot something I have to do," Jarod said. "Thank you, Master Bennis. I'm much indebted to you!"

Jarod had closed the front door behind him before the centaur could respond.

"You are welcome, young master Klum," Aren chuckled as he reached again for his book. "Would you care for another slice of cheese, Abel? Please help yourself."

The stars wheeled across the heavens on that chill night in early summer. The moon was full and stood directly above the broken wishing well. Bright stars stood in line with it, and the meager wishes in the well swelled and surged as they had not done in a very long time.

Unknown to each other, three separate people had determined to approach the well, all on the same night. Each came in his or her turn and left before the next arrived. None of them could have known it but, in the alignment of the heavens, each came for nearly the same purpose.

The first to the well was Jarod Klum. He brought with him the few coins he had managed to save over the last three months. It was not a great amount, measured against the fortunes of the prominent families of Eventide, but it was dearly purchased through his own careful efforts. Because of that, the power of the spirit that it carried was far greater than a hundred times its weight in gold. He put the coins in the metal box, heard their sound as they fell, and then stepped to the well.

"I wish Lucius didn't smell so badly," he said into its depths.

Then with a sigh he left down Wishing Lane so that he might not be too late for supper.

Next to come was Caprice, who did not check the box for coins but instead dropped a ribbon of her mother's into the well. She had kept it for many years, and its wishing was powerful indeed.

"I wish someone would marry my sister Sobrina," she said in carefully practiced words, for she was a wisher-woman and knew that the wording of a wish was critical, especially when the wishes were broken.

As she left, the third person was watching her from the woods to the south. He waited until she departed over the hill toward the Morgan home before he stepped up the grassy slope to the rotting well, careful of the direction of the wind blowing from the west so that he would not be discovered by the Morgan household.

He placed as many coins as he could fit into the box and then leaned over the well.

"I wish Sobrina could be happy," Lucius said, a single tear falling from his cheek down into the well.

After a moment's reflection, Lucius hurried quickly south into the woods to make his lonely way back to the tannery.

Wishing wells are, in the best of times, difficult in their dealings. Their understanding of speech is often uncertain and their willingness to properly interpret the wisher's intention is dubious at best. Yet with the stars and moon aligned, even a broken well could not help but do its best to grant the wishes of three aligned individuals wishing so hard for each other's welfare.

Lucius woke up in the morning to a strange and incredibly unpleasant sensation. At first he was not sure what to make of it. It seemed like tasting food. He smacked his lips and ran his tongue over his teeth, but he had not eaten anything. He was not sure what to make of it.

· Then he sniffed.

An overpoweringly horrible sensation filled his head.

Lucius sat up at once in his bed. He looked around frantically, searching for what might be causing this fearsome experience. He felt sick to his stomach, like the time he had eaten meat that had gone bad—only he had not eaten anything.

His stomach heaved.

He jumped out of bed and ran down the stairs into the tanning yard.

New sensations assaulted his nose here. Lucius cried out amid the urine vats where he stood in his nightshirt. All of the gnomes looked up at him in alarm.

Still yelling in terror, Lucius bolted for the tannery gates, yanked them open, and fled up the road toward the center of Boar's Island. The terrible sensations were abating, replaced with more pleasant ones, but still the persistent, sickly sourness followed him.

Lucius stopped suddenly in the middle of the road.

He sniffed again.

His eyes began to water. It was *him!* This horrible thing was coming from *him!*

Lucius turned toward the southern bridge and pulled off his nightshirt. He plunged naked into the chill waters of the Wanderwine River, furiously scrubbing at his arms and legs, his feet and his hands, his face, hair, and neck. Then he would sniff . . . and scrub some more.

At long last, shivering and with his skin rubbed raw, he managed to pull his nightshirt into the water with him and, after considerable effort, got it clean enough so that he could stand to wear it. He staggered out of the river, dripping and a little confused about his surroundings with every new sniff of his nose.

It was in this condition that he showed up on the doorstep of a very surprised Mordechai and Alicia Charon in his still-dripping nightshirt. Of two things he was certain.

Never again would Sobrina have to stand upwind of him.

And his business was ruined forever.

## · CHAPTER 15 ·

# There Are No Gnomes!

I didn't mean it that way!" Jarod thought darkly to himself with his arms folded tightly across his chest. "I wished that he would stop stinking, not start smelling well! This is all my fault . . ."

But he kept his faults to himself as he leaned against a post in middle of the small group gathering in the Charon's Goods store. Damper Muffe, Madeline's dumpling and doughy sixteen-year-old son, had come into the store, as he often did first thing in the morning, to look through the seven different maps that Mordechai Charon had for trade. He never bought any of them but liked to dream that he had a use for their distant places and the roads that might have taken him there. What he discovered was the shocking sight of Lucius Tanner sitting on a stool with a blanket pulled around him, complaining about how damp wool smelled. Damper fled the store to sound the alarm that the tanner was in town, but as Damper was known to tell a tall tale now and then—and since a single check of the air gave no hint of the tanner's presence—nearly everyone discounted the news entirely as a fabrication. Jarod, however, had come at once to Charon's Goods on the run—the sight of which drew the attention of Jesse Hall, a tinker setting up his goods early in Trader's Square, who commented on the fact to the passing Widow Merryweather, who was on her way with Ariela Soliandrus to call on Madeline Muffe to extend their sympathy on having such a foolish son as Damper. After that, it was only a matter of a very short time before the entire town knew of Lucius Tanner's plight. The news, however, did not translate into the kind of event where the townsfolk gathered, by and large. There were fields to be tended, grains to be ground, baked goods to brush with churned butter, and iron to be forged. None of those things could be left at the moment to see a man whose novelty was that he no longer stank.

This unfortunately meant that those who had nothing better to do were the ones, by and large, who appeared.

"It's those pixies, Lucius, just as sure as I'm sitting here," said the Widow Merryweather, her tone defying anyone to contradict her pronouncements. "They've been meddling with the town for quite some time and now they've gone too far! Someone needs to do something about it right now or, mark my words, there'll be more of this terrible mischief and worse upon worse until we're all murdered in our beds!"

Being murdered in her bed was Widow Merryweather's preferred expression of a romantically tragic ending. Ariela Soliandrus, the Gossip Fairy, had picked up on it early in their relationship and used the phrase constantly no matter how remotely it fit the situation. Unfortunately, through overuse its impact in the town had diminished to the point where no one actually was afraid of being murdered in their beds. Some had muttered under their breath that they hoped someone *would* be murdered in their beds so that at least the ladies of Cobblestone Street could talk about something knowledgeably.

"It's not the pixies," Lucius sighed, shaking his head. He sat in the middle of the floor on a chair, still in his nightshirt but now wrapped in a blanket. Alicia had offered him some of Mordechai's clothing, but Lucius had politely refused. He was confused and assaulted by new smells and sensations. It was difficult for him to think clearly.

"How do you know?" the Widow Merryweather exclaimed. "They could have come in the night . . ."

"Perhaps while he was *in his bed?*" Harv Oakman was leaning against the counter. His wife's millinery shop was next door to Charon's, and his woodworking yard ran behind both shops. Merinda could not leave her shop and so had insisted that Harv drop what he was doing and come over to offer their help in her stead. Harv had dutifully set aside his work and come to his neighbor's store.

"Precisely!" Ariela chimed in with her high, fluting voice. She fluttered about three feet above the ground in front of where the miserable Lucius sat.

"Good thing he wasn't murdered while they were at it," added the Squire with a quick wink in Harv's direction. Tomas Melthalion was between the early and noon meals and so had managed to cross Charter Square to offer what help he could.

"Who is to say or understand the whims of pixies or the gods?" Edvard exclaimed.

Everyone turned to look at him in blank incomprehension, except for Abel, who was used to such random and pointless pronouncements.

"What I mean to say is, perhaps your craft is not lost after all!"

the Dragon's Bard amended. "Perhaps you might, in time, get used to the smell of the—"

"I can hardly stay in this room, Master Bard. Mordechai is my biggest buyer, and the few leather goods he has in this store are making me feel ill. No, I think I'm dead to my trade," Lucius said, shaking his head. Then he sniffed. "Say, does wet wool smell funny to anyone else?"

The Widow Merryweather puffed herself up and drew in a deep breath. "Well, if you ask *me* . . ."

The door to the shop banged open so hard that Alicia was momentarily afraid it might come off entirely.

Jarod slowly unfolded his arms, standing as he gazed at the person in the open doorway.

Sobrina Morgan leaned into the room with both hands on the door frame. She was flushed, and her breath was coming in quick gulps. When she caught sight of the people in the shop she let go of the frame and stood her slender, tall figure once more erect. Her hair was pulled back into its customary bun but somewhat off center and with strands of long hair sticking out of it. She stood still, affecting the cool detachment that everyone in town associated with her.

But her lower lip quivered.

Lucius looked up, drawing the blanket self-consciously around him.

"Is it true, Lucius?" she said.

"Yes, Miss Morgan," he replied quietly. "I may be presentable in polite company now, but I'll never be able to go back to my work."

Sobrina took two steps across the floorboards and abruptly stopped in front of where Lucius sat. "How did this happen?"

Lucius had not been this close to her since he was seventeen. He smiled shyly and looked down at her dust-covered shoes.

"A wish can be a powerful thing, Miss Morgan," he said.

She stood there before him as immovable as marble for a long moment. Then, hesitantly, she extended her hand toward him.

"I'm so sorry, Lucius," she said, her voice trembling for the first time in anyone's memory.

He looked at her hand in wonder and then slowly, carefully, as though afraid it would vanish into smoke, took it in his own. He looked up with wide, watery eyes. "I'm not, Bree . . . not sorry one bit."

Widow Merryweather and the Gossip Fairy rushed from the shop at once, which was a shame because neither of them was there when a loud, guttural cough shook the riveted attention in Charon's Goods away from Sobrina and Lucius.

There, standing in the store, was a gnome.

The reaction of the people present was decidedly mixed. Lucius smiled. Sobrina stared. The Squire looked away. Mordechai frowned, while Alicia simply turned and walked through the door into the back room of her shop. Edvard was curious. Abel picked up his writing tablet in anticipation.

Jarod was astonished. He remembered this gnome from their visit to the tannery just the day before. He was a bit too preoccupied to have caught the name at the time, but he seemed to recall that this was the father or husband of the gnome clan at the tannery— the leader of them in some capacity. He was no taller than two and a half feet and was wearing the pointy orange hat that seemed ubiquitous among his kin. He had on a pale green shirt with pants and doublet of leather. His shoes were pointed and curled upward at their tip. His skin was chestnut brown and his expressive eyes were dark green. A long, grey beard extended from his chin down to where it nearly touched his waist.

Most astonishing of all to Jarod, the little creature did not carry a whiff of a scent about him.

"Klauf!" Lucius said. "Good morning."

"Master Tanner," Klauf replied in a low, gravelly voice. He reached up quickly and snatched the orange hat from his head, revealing a gleaming bald spot at its crown.

"Oh, where are my manners?" Lucius said. "Mordechai, have I introduced you to my foreman, Klauf Snarburt?"

"No," Mordechai answered in a tone that left little doubt that he had no desire to meet the gnome.

"And you, Squire, have you . . . Squire?"

Tomas was looking in any possible direction but where Lucius might get his attention.

Jarod frowned deeply in thought.

Klauf sighed, then continued. "Begging your pardon, sir, but we were wondering when you might be coming back to the tannery?"

Lucius looked up at Sobrina and then back at the gnome. "I'm afraid I won't be coming back, Klauf. I'm . . . well, I'm quitting the tanning craft."

Klauf pursed his lower lip, causing his long beard to jut forward. "Then you'll be selling the tannery, I suppose."

"I suppose so," Lucius said. "I hadn't really thought about that. I'd have to find someone interested in—"

"We'll buy it," Klauf said at once.

Sobrina caught her breath.

Lucius looked at the gnome in amazement. "You? But how can you possibly have the money to—"

"We got some little saved by," Klauf said, "and you've seen us work. We could pay it out to you regular-like from a measure of our increase until—"

"No, it won't work," Jarod said, his forefinger pressed against his chin as he stood in thought.

"What do you mean, 'It won't work'?" Lucius was incredulous. "It's wonderful! I'd have enough to start over again . . . get married . . ."

"You can't sell the tannery to Klauf," Jarod sighed.

"Why ever not?" Sobrina demanded.

"Because there *are no gnomes!*" Jarod said in frustration.

There were in those days, by royal decree, no gnomes. Their existence as a race went entirely unrecognized by the crown, who, having never met one and finding tales of them to be entirely fantastical in nature, had mandated that there were no such beings.

This news came as something of a blow to Klauf Snarburt and his clan. Klauf's family—his wife, Enuci, brother Laut, and son Jurt, as well as his cousin Grig Philput and sister-in-law Klisten Brinswart—all worked at the tannery at the far southern end of Swamp Lane. They had all come to Eventide after Klauf, a tanner by trade, had come into the village and had immediately found employment from a very grateful and relieved Lucius. Klauf sent word at once to the Foglaiden Mounds in the South Country for his family and relations to join him here, and all found welcome employment from Lucius. The increased production output at the tannery proved a boon both to Lucius and to Mordechai Charon, whose sale of leather-tooled goods was also able to increase manyfold and provide the foundation of his family's meteoric rise in both the financial and social circles of the village.

The problem was, of course, that Klauf Snarburt and his kin were all gnomes.

And now, by decree, they didn't exist.

This proved to be an awkward challenge for the townsfolk who were used to trading with Klauf's people. Some now felt duty bound *not* to acknowledge their existence out of a sense of loyalty to the king. Others tried politely to suggest that perhaps the Snarburt clan should move away so as not to embarrass the town by making everyone look unpatriotic. Some secretly voiced the nasty opinion that Klauf was intentionally insisting on being a gnome just to foment a rebellion against the crown.

Gnomes were ignored, suspected, dismissed, talked about, and occasionally sympathized with, but there was one thing that was clear to Jarod from all the years he had been working in the countinghouse: No gnome could legally own land or enter into a binding contract . . . because gnomes did not exist.

Ward Klum was flipping at a furious pace through an enormous book on his desk. Around him seethed a sea of individuals arguing back and forth within the walls of the countinghouse.

"It's sedition! Sedition, I tell you," Jep Walters shouted, pounding his fist on Ward's desk, causing the accountant to grab both it and the book to steady it. "The just rulers of our land have decreed there are no gnomes, and it's up to every servant of the kingdom to uphold the letter of their law!"

"Man the barricades!" shouted the Dragon's Bard while his

scribe stood in the corner furiously scribbling in a vain attempt to keep up. "The gnomes are threatening!"

"There are no gnomes!" Jep insisted.

"But he's standing *right there,* Walters!" Lucius shouted into the cooper's face. "He's no figment of imagination!"

"But the law says he doesn't exist," the Squire insisted.

"I would that *you* didn't exist!" Sobrina fumed. Even in her agitated state, she knew better than to use the word *wish.*

"Listen, everybody, we've just got to calm down," Harv Oakman pleaded. "Why can't we just arrange among ourselves for the bargain? Why can't the . . . the . . . you know, why can't Klauf here just pay Lucius the money and we all just recognize who owns what around here. Nobody in Mordale needs to know . . ."

"And what happens when the tax collector comes," Ward said, his eyes still scanning the book, "and he finds all these nonexistent creatures operating the single largest revenue-producing effort in the county?"

"Really?" Lucius asked with a grin. "Are we really doing that well?"

Ward looked up. "Actually, your earnings prior to two years ago were flat, but your increase in the last two seasons alone was—"

"None of that is to the point!" Jep shouted. "The law is clear! Tanner here is a member of the Guild, and that's guild law! These . . . *things* do not exist by law and therefore they cannot join the Guild . . ."

"Or pay guild dues," Mordechai interjected.

"Or pay guild . . . that's not the point at all!" Jep was quivering in his rage. "You're a fine one to speak, Mordechai Charon! Your business is on the line if these illegal creatures are turned out. You've been making money off of them!"

"Because they do fine work!" Mordechai shouted back. "If your barrels were half the quality of their workmanship, you'd be doing far better in your own craft."

"Please," the Squire said, pushing his way between Jep and Mordechai. "Can't we all just agree to be loyal subjects of the crown?"

"Are you questioning my loyalty?" Lucius exclaimed. "Just because I have gnomes working for me?"

"But the law is clear: *there are no gnomes!*" the Squire bellowed.

Jarod rolled his eyes. "Well, the nonexistent gnome is almost standing on your foot, Squire, and I hope he kicks you in the shins with his nonexistent pointed shoes!"

This set off another round of general shouting until, at last, Ward Klum, towering over them at his high desk and tall chair, slammed shut the great book.

Everyone stopped and looked toward the Master of the Counting.

"Listen to me, all of you," Ward said. "I am the king's appointed representative here, and I am a keeper of the law. The decrees are clear—regardless of the evidence before us. Gnomes do not exist by express decree of the crown; they have no rights or standing before the law and cannot purchase property. Were such nonexistent persons to be found in the possession of such property, it would be confiscated by the crown—which would do neither Klauf nor Lucius any good. I would be expected to enforce such a law, and even if I chose not to do so, the tax collector would discover it on his first visit after the fall and the result would be the same. There are no gnomes—the king has proclaimed it thus—and therefore they cannot possess property or enter into any contract."

A silence fell over the assembly, each counting the costs of their victories or their losses and none feeling the better for it.

Then, Alicia Charon, who had been standing at the back, timidly raised her hand.

Ward sighed. "Yes, Alicia, what is it?"

"Well," she said in halting, shy tones. "Do they *have* to be gnomes?"

Ward squinted slightly and turned his good ear toward the woman. "What do you mean?"

"Well, I mean, what if they *weren't* gnomes?"

"But, Alicia," Jep Walters said slowly, "they *are* gnomes."

Alicia turned to the cooper. "But I thought you said there weren't any gnomes?"

Jep opened his mouth to answer but no words came out.

"We have dwarves in town," Alicia said.

"We have one dwarf," Ward nodded. "What's your point?"

"I was just thinking," Alicia said as she stepped forward toward where Klauf had stood wringing his hat in his hands during the entire ordeal. "What if these little people weren't actually *gnomes?* What if they were a new kind of—short dwarf?"

"Alicia," Mordechai whispered, "dwarf *means* short."

"So we'll call them dwarf-dwarves," Alicia said, kneeling down in front of Klauf. She held out her hand. "Would you mind terribly, Mister . . . uh . . ."

"Snarburt," the small man said with a wide, yellow-toothed grin as he grabbed her hand as best he could. "I'm Mister Snarburt . . . a dwarf-dwarf from the Southern Hills."

Jarod watched Sobrina and Lucius walk northward across Fall's Court toward the Mordale road, hand in hand. She would be taking him home to see her father, he thought. He smiled, thinking of the day when he would be making that same walk with the same purpose and Caprice on his arm.

"I think they are adorable, don't you?"

The bubble of Jarod's dreams burst in a moment.

Vestia Walters coiled her arm around his. "I only hope that he has enough put away for the bride price."

"What?"

"You're funny!" Vestia cooed, pushing up against him. "The man who wishes to wed must pay a bride price to the girl's father. The higher the price, the greater the honor for the bride. I suspect with all that money in that countinghouse of yours you'll be honoring your bride-to-be most handsomely. I myself expect to fetch a bride price higher than anyone in this town has ever seen before."

She stepped back and patted him on the cheek.

"So you had best start gathering your treasure together, Jarod!"

Vestia giggled and skipped off toward her home across Charter Square.

All Jarod could think of was his empty Treasure Box still sitting in his cupboard . . . and how he vowed to fill it for his Caprice. He needed a treasure worthy of her, and he knew only one man who might know how to come by such wealth in a hurry.

He'd have to ask the Dragon's Bard.

# FAIR HERO

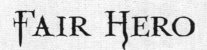

*Wherein the Fall Festival provides
Jarod the opportunity to gather sizable
wealth . . . with disastrous results.*

· CHAPTER 16 ·

# River Fairies

A great trumpet sounded in the evening air!

Merinda Oakman heard it from inside her shop, glancing up as a smile bloomed on her face. With giddy delight she ushered her clients out the door, locked it, and hastily hung up a sign saying only that she was closed.

The two notes came again, deep and resounding in the twilight.

Jep Walters arrested his hammer in midswing in the cooperage and left the hoop sitting on the anvil to cool while he wiped off his hands and tossed aside his apron.

The heralding sound called again through the streets of Eventide, seeming to dance the autumn leaves across the cold cobblestones under the fading light of day and whirl them down the darkening alleys.

Both Deniva Kolyan and Madeline Muffe anxiously watched the goods in their ovens, willing them to cook faster, and they waited not a moment longer than they had to before pulling out their goods and hastily banking their fires.

Townsfolk were pouring out of their homes and shops under the deepening hue of an autumn sky, drawn toward the sound of the horns. They grabbed their shawls and their jackets, their coats and their hats against the chill of encroaching night and danced among the bright dry leaves that spiced the streets.

Beulandreus Dudgeon smiled his wide, gap-toothed grin and quickly set about closing up his own shop, much to the confusion of the Dragon's Bard and his scribe.

"Whatever are you doing?" Edvard exclaimed to the dwarf. The Dragon's Bard had been canvassing the town since spring, cataloguing everyone's stories with his tireless assistant in tow. He had insisted that Abel meticulously record a seemingly endless cascade of tales whose content was of dubious universal interest and had been in the process of asking the dwarf a series of the most mundane and pointless questions Abel had ever heard. At such times, the scribe found better use in sketching illuminations, as he felt sure his editorial judgment at leaving out the entire history of steel tempering would somehow not adversely affect their next volume.

"Did you not hear the horns?" the dwarf exclaimed with delight as he banked his forge fire. The street outside the smithy had been nearly deserted in the deepening evening but was suddenly filling with humans, a few centaurs, and a number of dwarf-dwarves who seemed to appear out of nowhere.

"Well, I most certainly did, and a fine-sounding set of notes they were," the Dragon's Bard said. "But what do they mean? Where is everyone going?"

"It is the River Fairies," the smith exclaimed as he grabbed his leather coat and broad-brimmed hat. "'Tis the harvest, and they've come—and that signals the Festival! Now, out with you two!"

The dwarf grabbed Edvard and Abel by their arms and ushered

them with considerable strength out into Hammer Court. He pulled the last of the shutters closed on his open-sided shop and secured them with a great lock and key. Then, with astonishing speed, Beulandreus rushed down King's Road, one hand holding his hat firmly on his head against the autumn wind. Even the pixies had joined in the excitement, forgetting their usual antics and flashing back and forth above the crowd as if they were actually excited to light the way.

The Dragon's Bard and his assistant quickly joined in the growing stream of laughing children and giddy adults. Several dwarf-dwarves passed them doing backflips in their overflowing exuberance. It seemed that the entire town was turning out at a moment's notice as the quiet streets were suddenly alive with laughter and filled with boundless energy. Edvard gazed about him with slack-jawed wonder while Abel, faithful to his calling, quit his doodling with his stylus and, unbidden by the awestruck Bard, began taking notes of his own accord.

The crowd moved north across Fall's Court and spread out along the place where the Mordale road slopes down gently to the banks of the Wanderwine River north of town. The treeline of the Norest Forest stood on the other side just to the west. Everyone stood on tiptoe straining to look north up the course of the river, the pixies hovering above the crowd and bathing everyone in a softer glow than usual. Farmer Bennis stood athwart the road, his presence recognized by everyone there as the boundary of the town's gathering. Even the grizzle-chinned centaur looked happy, with a twinkle in his eye.

The horn once again sounded its two notes, one low and one high, from somewhere up around the bend in the river.

The town cheered.

Seven boats emerged from the forest canopy beneath a darkening indigo sky, gliding gently down the Wanderwine. Their hulls were elegantly shaped, each with a long keel curving to an elegant, high prow in the front and a raised afterdeck at the end. There was a sleekness to their hulls, with long, flat slats running bow to stern, widening to nearly flat in the middle, giving the boats a shallow draft. None of them had a mast or sail or any oars to be seen, yet each glided swift and sure across the waters heedless of any currents.

Within the boats, singing as they spun and wheeled above the decks, were the River Fairies. Their bright and garish costumes flashed in the air. Their tambourines banged and rattled in tempo with their swaying and their song. Along both sides of the lead boat's bow were fixed two enormous horns, which were sounded again, each in turn, by fairies at their narrow mouthpieces amidships. None of the boats were more than thirty feet long, but to the scale of the fairies who manned them, they were enormous craft. Each was also laden with the fairies' provisions and a few tents brought along for the benefit of any larger guest creatures that they might wish to accommodate in their encampment along the way.

Yet it was above the hulls and fairies that the greatest wonder was seen. There, woven in light and haze, was the dream-smoke of the fairy folk, drifting upward from the brazier near the center of each of their boats and weaving images shaped from the thoughts and dreams of the people at the river's edge. A tumbling cascade of visions formed, dissolved, and then re-formed above the ships—passionate, beautiful, vengeful, innocent, suggestive, sad, joyful—the softly glowing images in the dream-smoke delighted, embarrassed, and thrilled the townsfolk as the boats turned as one and rode up onto the far bank of the river.

Edvard's smile broadened. "I know of these fine fellows,

Abel! These are the River Fairies of Clan Obsintia! They are famous—or infamous, depending upon who you ask—throughout Windriftshire. I knew that they made a circuit of the rivers every year, but I had no idea that Eventide was graced by their presence. Wherever they stop, there is cause for celebration indeed, for their camp is renowned for its performances, dances, music, and entertainments . . . not to mention less scrupulous dealings that, now that I think of it, might be turned to one's advantage."

Abel gave the Dragon's Bard a dubious look.

"Excuse me!" Edvard called across the crowd. "Lady Merryweather! Yoohoo!"

Abel cringed as the stately woman pushed her way through the crowd. "Yes, Edvard, how delightful, is it not? The Fall Festival has begun at last!"

"Delightful indeed, Lady Merryweather . . ."

"Ah, alas, you must call me the Widow Merryweather," she said with a practiced sigh in her voice. "My dear late husband left for sea some fifteen years back and has never returned to me."

"Then he is late, indeed, madam . . ."

Abel kicked his master in the shin.

" . . . and I do share your loss. Would that I had met the, uh, captain . . ."

"My good Neddie was a Sailing Master, sir," the Widow Merryweather said, raising her chin imperiously. "So he would tell you, were he with us here today."

"As we all wish he was," Edvard smiled, "but please tell me about the River Fairies."

"Oh, you don't know them?" the widow chirped. "Well, let me tell you! They are vagabonds of the water, sir, carefree wanderers of the world. The gods alone know how they get *up* the river, but they come *down* the Wanderwine each fall and arrive when it is harvest time. They stop here above Bolly Falls for a week while the citizens of the town help them transfer their boats down past the falls. They set their camp in the Fae Grotto just to the west of here and provide all kinds of entertainments. The Dance of the Leaves is the traditional opening of the celebrations—although it is a far too refined entertainment for the young. When the fairies leave at last on the seventh evening, then the town holds its own celebration fair, often featuring some of the clever things we have bartered from the fairies while they were here. And, of course, there is the baking contest sponsored by Deniva Kolyan and Madeline Muffe that evening for the Festival Prize. Between you and me, Edmund—"

"That's *Edvard*," the Dragon's Bard corrected.

"Well, between you and me, the competition in this town for that prize is more pitched than the Battle of the Five Kings. Livinia Walters has taken that prize for the last three years running. No one knows how she's doing it since none of the women in the town have ever seen her lift a finger in her kitchen. Daphne Melthalion—the Squire's wife—has been fit to be tied each time; she would do anything to beat Livinia at any given contest. Of course, both Winifred Taylor and Orlynda Klum try each year as well, and I myself have come close a time or two."

"I see!" Edvard nodded. "Well, thank you ever so much, Widow Merryweather. You've been most helpful . . . by the way, have you seen Ariela Soliandrus? I've something urgent to speak with her about."

"Mistress Soliandrus?" The Widow Merryweather laughed lightly. "Oh, she never comes to this."

"Never?" the Dragon's Bard asked in surprise.

"Not as long as she's lived here."

Ariela Soliandrus sat on the back steps of her little home with her chin propped up by both her tiny hands as she looked out over her garden without seeing it.

Ariela had heard the sound of the trumpets coming from far up the river and the merry sounds of her fellow townsfolk making their way to the landing above the falls. The horns called to her, too, but in a different way. So she locked the doors of her home and hid inside until everyone had passed and gone their way. Then, as she had done every year, she sat on her back porch and waited.

"There, now, my love . . . did you think that I would not come?"

Her tiny heart jumped at the sound, as it had done for uncounted years before. She took a breath and counted as far as four before she felt she could reply.

"Coming was never your problem," Ariela responded, folding her hands as she sat up. "As I recall, staying was more the question."

The small, lithe figure emerged from the dark line of trees beyond the garden. He was tall for a fairy—nearly as tall as a gnome—but he had a strong body and a beautiful set of wings. His hair was the color of a summer sunset. His shirt was a deep shade of turquoise, while his vest was a profusion of colors patterned after a peacock's feathers. His hat was pushed back casually from his forehead, and his eyes were a brilliant green. He had no beard—few fairies could grow them well—so his face was smooth. Yet Ariela noticed the lines at the corners of his eyes and knew that time could catch up with even the Fae.

"And yet here I am now in your very garden once again, Ari," the fairy said with a slight bow as he drifted toward her in the cool of the autumn evening. "Same old garden, same old flowers, and all stuck in the same old ground, are they not, Ari?"

"Right as always, Lord Obsintia," Ariela said without enthusiasm.

"And here I find you planted right along with them, my dear," the fairy king replied. "Stuck with your feet in the same unmoving ground. But the water, Ari, the water! How could you set aside the motion and the challenge and the change of a world full of rivers to explore? How could you leave it, Ari?

"It left me," Ariela replied, her voice quiet. "I wanted a garden— a nice piece of ground filled with all the flowers that I loved. Storms come to the garden, but they pass, and the garden remains. There's peace in my garden."

"Well, I've ridden the waves of the Staymark River, sailed the glass surface of the Underground Sea, and shaken my fist at the Furies in the Lake of Souls! Now I've returned down my old friend the Wanderwine just so that I could see you, Ari! Just so I might float above your garden and hear your voice!"

"Quindonalas Obsintia, if that were true," Ariela replied, "then why are you doing all the talking?"

"Ah, and you have me there," he answered with a brilliant smile. "And you used to call me Quin. Couldn't you go back to calling me Quin?"

"Calling you Quin was what got me in trouble in the first place," Ariela sighed.

"Nonsense! You were a great queen to our clan!"

Ariela looked away. "But they were not that great to me."

"There you go again!" Quin said with affected hurt. "I've come for your help, and all you want to do is bring up old hurts."

"Help?" Ariela laughed. "When did you ever need anyone's help?"

"Well, I do tonight, my love, and you're my last hope."

"Me?" Ariela ran her fingers through her hair. "Please, Quin, it's hard enough having you here."

"I mean it," Quin said, fluttering nearer.

"I won't go," Ariela shouted at him. "I came here to get *away* from all that . . . away from you. I've built a life here with these people."

"A life with these people?" Quin scoffed. "What kind of a life can you have with these dull-witted giants? You dress like them, you talk like them, you've even got your pretty little garden, but what do they know about riding the wind? Do they understand you at all? Do you even understand them? You can try to fit in all you like but you're not one of them, Ari, no matter how hard you study them or try to mimic their lives. You cannot be one of them, Ari!"

"I *am* one of them, Quin!" she cried. "I love these people and I do my best to serve them the only way I know how. Maybe it's *you* who doesn't understand."

The two fairies sat on the back porch stairs for a moment in silence.

"Say, where's that largish servant girl of yours?" Quin said at last.

Ariela sniffed. "At the landing, probably, with everyone else."

"Look, Ari, I'm sorry about all this—what I've said and all," Quin said, putting his arm around her. "I miss you, is all . . . and I do need your help, just for tonight. And then in a few more days I'll be gone."

"What kind of help, Quin?" Ariela asked as she dried her tears.

"I need you to do the Dance of the Leaves for—"

"NO!" Ariela said at once. "I'm a respectable woman of this community! I will most certainly not—"

"It's a masked dance, Ari, you know that," Quin said, holding her shoulders so that she could not move away. "No one will know it's you, and there's never been anyone better at the dance than you were . . . than you *are!* Listen to me, please!"

Ariela looked sideways at Quin.

"Libithania tore a wing at our last camp, and Murialana is expecting again," Quin pleaded. "No one else knows the dance and none of them can perform it as well as you can."

"Quin, no, it's just not who I am anymore."

"I know," Quin said with a one-sided grin. "But just for one night, Ari . . . it could be you again. Think of it, Ari! Dropping those stays and corsets for one night and thrilling everyone in the town—in *your* town—with a dance that they'll be talking about for the whole year! It will be you behind that mask, behind their applause, and they never have to know, Ari, that it was you—their own garden-loving prim little neighborhood fairy—who made it happen!"

Ariela gazed thoughtfully over her garden.

"This town has looked forward to this night the entire year," Quin whispered. "Would you disappoint your entire village?"

Ariela fluttered unseen among the bushes just beyond the edge of the Fae Grotto, smoothing out a costume she had kept carefully hidden away for many years.

The gown was elegant even by fairy standards. The base of the skirt was woven specifically for her form and her skin tones so that the lines of the dance would be uninterrupted to the audience's eye. Over this was a diaphanous patterned cloth in fall shades nearly as light as the air around her, with carefully weighted hems that shifted the cloth around the base of the gown so that it could wind and unwind around her as she moved. The effect was suggestive but never revealing in performance—the conveyance of a dream far better than reality. She had known the Dance of the Leaves since she was a child and had still occasionally pirouetted some of the more complex movements in her home when the shutters were well secured.

Ariela looked out into the Fae Grotto. The pixies—unusually cooperative tonight—had formed a ring about the clearing, their light shining down on the faces from the town. Nearly all the adults were there, seated in a semicircle at the edge of the fairy encampment. The tents, Ariela knew, were for the benefit of the humans present—the Fae had no real use for such things, preferring to find their beds under open skies.

Ariela picked up her mask and gazed at it. She, too, missed sleeping under the stars, and there was a part of her that longed for the feel of the river. She had been a queen and revered among her kind, but something within her had grown weary of the constant course of rivers with no purpose and no end. She longed to *mean* something to someone somewhere beyond the blind adoration and the fawning of the fairy court. She wanted to make a difference in the world and not simply fade away to be forgotten and to have left no mark on the river that claimed them.

So she had left the river and taken up a new life. It was hard for her to fit in among the predominant humans of the town. There were nuances to human society that she still found baffling. Yet she had discovered that the women of the town loved to hear about each other and about themselves in turn. Ariela knew that she had a talent for telling a story and that unembellished truth did not make for interested listeners. So she gave the truth a little more structure and color and interest whenever she passed on the news of the town. Soon she found herself accepted into most of the homes in Eventide and invited to all the social events. She felt hurt and often a little confused that some of the people in the town looked down on her or considered her a menace or a nuisance or, worse, laughable. She kept all those stings to herself because she genuinely loved Eventide and the people in it. She had her home, she had her garden, and she was serving her friends in Eventide in the best way that she knew how.

Now she fluttered at the edge of the clearing with the mask of her old life in her hands. She could not disappoint them. They had to have their Festival, and she could bring it to them.

She pulled the mask down over her face and, reaching down, picked up the two silk leaves with wicker stays that were made to match the cloth of her gown.

"They will never know," she whispered to herself, then fluttered into the grotto. Through the mask she looked out on the faces of her friends and foes alike all looking back at her in wonder as though they had never seen her before.

And they all cheered.

The Dance of the Leaves performed in the Fae Grotto that night was talked about for many years to come. Those in the town who missed it counted themselves cursed. The youth, who were not allowed to go, speculated wildly on what was seen that night, making up their own visions because none of the adults would tell them. The men in the town who were present spoke of its passion, its power, and its aching beauty. The married women in the town spoke of its grace, its poetry, and its perfect expression of longing.

The women of Cobblestone Street, when they gathered like hens about Widow Merryweather in her parlor, had their own view of the event.

"Wanton exhibitionism, if you ask me," the Widow Merryweather sniffed. "Wanton exhibitionism!"

"I would not be the least surprised," stated Winifred Taylor with arched eyebrows, "if this results in an unfortunate jump in the population of Eventide."

A murmur of agreement ran about the circle of women in the room.

"Shocking, indeed, that such a display should take place so near our town," voiced Livinia Walters. "And that it should happen every year and next year as well!"

The women in the circle all sighed. "A whole year . . ."

Through it all, Ariela nodded her agreement with the Widow Merryweather and her companions as she sipped her tea and smiled politely.

And when the day was done, as she would for many years to come, Ariela went into her proper little house, climbed her miniature stairs, and opened her small closet to gaze with a smile on the jeweled mask, the gossamer gown, and two silk leaves that she kept in the back.

*"Jarod!"* the urgent voice whispered from below.

Another pebble bounced off his window.

Jarod Klum pushed open his window and stared into the dark plaza below. "Who is it?"

"'Tis I," came the dramatic voice. "The Dragon's Bard!"

"What now?" Jarod whined. "I'm sleeping!"

"There is work to be done and fortunes to be won!" Edvard said sotto voce.

"I don't gamble," Jarod said in a hoarse whisper back down the wall from his room above the countinghouse.

"No, you asked me to find you a business proposition that would reward you well," the Bard replied.

"Business in the middle of the night?"

"It's business best done in the middle of the night!" the Bard replied. "Get dressed—you're going to be rich!"

## · CHAPTER 17 ·

# Battle of the Five Pies

On the mantle above Livinia Walters's kitchen hearth sat an oversized, ornate chalice.

It was too big to be of any use as a cup and too small to be of any use to hold flowers. It was heavy in its construction and not of particularly lovely lines. It was too strange to sell and too useless to give as a gift. As to practical uses, it might best be put to use as a doorstop.

Yet, for five women in Eventide, it had become the focus of their desires, attention, efforts, and time.

The Fall Festival was being celebrated with dances being held in the Guild Hall, feasts being sponsored by the Griffon's Tale Inn, songs being sung once again by the Flag Four Troubadours, and a number of contests of skill and strength taking place. Evenings were filled with all manner of magical entertainments in the Fae Grotto, where the dream-smoke tableaus, fortune-telling tents, and the fairy dances and music continued for six nights. All this was organized around the chore of hoisting the seven fairy ships out of the Upper

Landing and moving them across Charter Square and Bolly's Bridge, then down Cobblestone Street so that they could be launched again into the Wanderwine River just below the confluence.

Yet, for these five women, the sounding of the fairy horns signaled not so much the start of the Festival as the first blow in an annual battle. The useless and unattractive chalice was the embodiment of the most fiercely contested prize in all of Eventide.

The Fall Festival Pie Competition.

Now, eschewing the parties and the joy abounding outside her kitchen door, Livinia stood in her kitchen, her arms folded tightly across her chest as she concentrated on the chalice and how she might retain it for yet another year.

Both Livinia Walters and Daphne Melthalion had, since their youth, been locked in a seemingly endless battle over ownership of the prized pie chalice. For long years, other challengers were counted of little consequence, until some seven years ago when the combat was joined in force by Marchant Merryweather (the local widow who joined the contest after taking umbrage at a rumor that Daphne Melthalion had once fixed a lunch for her husband), Winifred Taylor (who submitted her own pie after Livinia had refused to attend her thrashing party), and Orlynda Klum (who, it appeared, simply submitted a pie because she thought it might be fun . . . and thereby found herself in the middle of a withering crossfire from which there was no hope of escape).

Livinia considered the chalice. Her chances of retaining it were difficult for her to gauge. She had held onto it for the last three years running, but last year had been a very near thing. Both she and Daphne had submitted variations of apple pies, and if it had not been for Livinia's last-minute addition of a crumb topping, she might well have lost the contest altogether. As it was, Orlynda's plum fig pie had been a very close third and a much better showing by her than in previous years.

Contrary to the popular belief among the ladies of Cobblestone Street, Livinia had done her own cooking since she was very young. That she had a serving girl now was largely pretense for the benefit of the town. Eunice did the scullery work, which Livinia hated, and the general cleaning, which Livinia hated more than the scullery work. But when it came to cooking the meals in the house, this was one labor that Livinia thoroughly enjoyed. It was a matter of pride and accomplishment to her.

There was a sharp knocking at her kitchen door.

"Who is it?" Livinia asked loudly, still considering the chalice.

"Ariela Soliandrus," came the muffled response. "I have most intriguing news!"

"Come in, Ariela, the door is open." As the door opened, the cooper's wife's eyes remained fixed on the mantel.

Livinia just *had* to win the chalice again—whatever the cost.

Jarod Klum stood uneasily behind the small cart in Trader's Square. He had borrowed it from Farmer Bennis and fixed it up as best he could the night before to make it appear festive and presentable. There were a number of different spices arrayed across the top of the cart, small shingles with prices scrawled across them sitting before each. The spices were rather common—most of them Jarod had acquired from other vendors in the square, and their diversity was small.

Townspeople passing by were quite surprised to see the counting apprentice having set up a spice cart in the middle of the Fall

Festival. They were in turn more surprised by the prices listed on the shingles for each of his products—and continued passing by.

"I don't think this is going to work," Jarod said to the Dragon's Bard, who was leaning against the wall of the Guild Hall behind him, relishing a crisp apple.

"And why should it not work?" Edvard exclaimed, nearly spitting out a piece of apple in the process.

"Because we haven't sold a single thing all day," Jarod said, his voice forlorn.

"Of course you haven't . . . certainly not at those prices!"

"Maybe we should lower them," Jarod wondered aloud. "Bring them more in line with the other vendors . . ."

"Nonsense! This rabble is not your market, boy," Edvard exclaimed. "You'll never get rich selling pinches of spice! Your *real* mark . . . I mean, your real customers have not yet come to you. You remember what I told you, do you not?"

"Yes, I do," Jarod sighed.

"And you visited Lord Obsintia?" the Bard coaxed.

"Yes, he had exactly what you said I needed," Jarod replied, clearing his throat nervously. "Still, I'm not that sure that this is a good idea. I mean, it seems like there's something wrong with it."

"Nonsense, my good Jarod!" Edvard exclaimed. "It's business!"

"Still, after talking with the fairy king, I—"

An imperious voice called his attention back across the makeshift sales cart. "Jarod Klum?"

"Oh! Why, good morning, Madam Walters!" Jarod said, his voice rising half an octave.

"Good morning to you, Jarod." Livinia was dressed in her fur-trimmed coat and matching hat. Jarod wondered idly if she had killed the animals herself.

"I've got a fine selection of spices and herbs . . . for baking, I mean," Jarod swallowed hard. "There's . . . uh . . . some cinnamon here from the south, and that's . . . let me think . . . that's anise . . ."

Livinia cleared her throat. "Do you have anything . . . special?"

Jarod stared for a moment. The Bard kicked him to get him started again.

"Why, yes, I have something special," Jarod answered slowly, "but it's very expensive. I don't think you would be interested in it."

Livinia nodded. "You're probably right."

Jarod's face fell.

"Still," Livinia said, leaning over the cart and speaking in low tones. "If you were to meet me with it this evening around the hour after sunset behind the ruins of the old pottery kilns on Butterfield Road . . . and were willing to part with your 'special' spice . . . I think I could meet your price."

Livinia stood back up and continued nonchalantly down past the other stalls in Trader's Square.

Jarod turned to the Bard, a wide grin splitting his face. "She's going to *buy* it, Edvard! I can't believe it!"

"That's the beauty of this business. All you have to do is sell this one potion for a king's ransom to someone rich enough and desperate enough to afford it," Edvard said. "Then you'll have enough for the bride price of your darling Caprice."

That night, after his meeting at the ruins, Jarod quietly returned home to the countinghouse and pulled out his Treasure Box from the office cupboard where he had kept it since the spring.

With warm satisfaction he opened the box, unfolding it to a

pleasant size in his hands—a size that he felt was just right for the important occasion. He set the box on his desk, reached into the folds of his coat, and pulled out a heavy coin purse.

"One hundred gold crowns!" Jarod exclaimed. "All from buying a single cooking potion from the fairy king and selling it to Livinia Walters!"

Jarod calculated it as his father had taught him, just to make sure he understood the magnitude of what he had achieved. He had spent three silver leaf coins to purchase the potion in the first place. The Bard had negotiated with the fairy king a deal that the Fae could sell any kind of potion they liked to the townsfolk *except* baking potions. Jarod had paid one gold crown to hold that exclusive privilege. Having spent two gold crowns for the spices he placed in his business cart, plus another three silver leaf coins on fixing up the cart so that he could present a legitimate business appearance, Jarod tallied up his expenses at three gold crowns and six silver leaf coins. That meant, by Jarod's reckoning, that he had made a profit of ninety-six gold crowns and four silver leaf coins!

The young man carefully counted the coins into his Treasure Box and was about to close it when he stopped.

If he did it once . . . why not do it again?

There must be other ladies in the town who might like a little extra assistance with their pie baking this year and who would be willing to pay an outrageous price.

Jarod quietly took three of the silver leaf coins back out of the Treasure Box and a couple of gold crowns just to be certain. Then he closed the box and folded it up small, placing it back in the cupboard.

Filled with pride in his own business sense, Jarod went back out the door and headed toward the Fae Grotto.

On the seventh day of the Fall Festival, the townspeople gathered in Charter Square around the Cursed Sundial in the brisk fall air. Long tables borrowed from the Guild Hall were supplemented with several from the Griffon's Tale Inn. Each was covered with long linen, and the square was lit once more with the glow of the pixies—imprisoned again for some heinous if thus far unspecified offense.

Everyone in the town brought something for the Harvest Feast, a community sharing of the bounty from the growing season and, it would seem, the last great holiday for them all to gather together before the onset of winter and the long wait until the spring. Breads and stews, meat pies and vegetables, fruits and tubers—all were passed along joyfully down the rows and shared with each other.

The town had said farewell to the fairies earlier that afternoon. The tents and provisions were all secured aboard their seven ships and they sailed away somewhat earlier than expected. The fairy king—Lord Obsintia—seemed to be in a particular hurry to leave. The fairies sailed down the Wanderwine River toward distant Blackshore, waving and singing as they left.

Jarod, dressed in his best leggings and doublet, found Caprice in the crowd and sat down on the bench next to her. "Good evening, Caprice!"

"Why, good evening, Jarod," Caprice said, raising her eyebrows as she looked at him. "And may I say you are looking particularly well this evening?"

"You may," Jarod said with a smile. "I have been looking forward to this evening for quite some time and wanted to look my best!"

"You are a great supporter of the Fall Festival then, I take it?" Caprice's wide green eyes were filled with mirth.

"In more ways than you may know," Jarod answered, then leaned slightly toward her. "Caprice, would you meet me beneath the tree in Chestnut Court after the contest? I have something particular to say to you."

"You *are* saying something to me," Caprice said in a mockingly serious voice, matching Jarod's own conspiratorial tone.

Jarod laughed. "So I am . . . but I have something *particular* to say to you and you'll not know what it is unless you meet me there. Please say you will!"

"Of course I will!" Caprice smiled, and the world seemed brighter to Jarod. "After they award the chalice . . . I'll meet you there."

"Perfect!" Jarod exclaimed. He leaped up from the chair and ran down the row to find his mother, his feet seeming barely to touch the ground.

He found Orlynda fussing over her cranberry-apple pie. "Oh, Jarod, I just don't think the crust is right—and I practically stood over that Muffe woman while she baked it!"

Jarod swallowed. He could have told his mother that she shouldn't get her hopes up because he had personally seen to it that no matter what his mother baked, she was going to lose the competition. But he cared too much for her, told himself that it was all for the best, and said, "It will be fine, Mother. You wait and see."

Jep Walters was standing up at the table that seemed to have been arranged for the more important folk of the town—at least more important in the estimation of those who had arranged the tables.

"Ladies and gentlemen, friends and neighbors of Eventide!" Jep pronounced, his hands firmly gripping the lapels of his long coat. "It has been a wondrous celebration this year—a bountiful harvest for which each of us gives thanks to those gods whose largess smiles upon us. It behooves us at times like these to reflect back on—"

"Never mind that, Jep," yelled Joaquim Taylor from the back. "Let's get on with the contest!"

Nervous laughter ran through the crowd, but Jep was beaming. It seemed he, too, would like to have this final duty concluded.

"As you wish! It's time to judge the winner of the Fall Festival Pie Competition . . . the winner receiving this fine . . . this fine . . ." Jep was having a little difficulty lifting it up onto the table before him, "*this* fine chalice to keep for one year—until the next Fall Festival—in recognition of their achievement. Our competition is being judged, as usual, by Deniva Kolyan and Madeline Muffe— the fine bakers in our town—as well as our guest judge, Captain Hamish Pew, who has come all the way from Blackshore for the evening. Captain Pew!"

Jarod shook his head. Deniva Kolyan and Madeline Muffe had been made the judges of the contest partly because they could not be allowed to compete for the prize and partly because neither of them could ever agree on anything. All of this was supposed to be balanced out by the selection of a third judge from outside of the village, but this year's selection of a sea captain whose palate was probably used to salted fish and hardtack was probably not the best choice.

"Ladies," Jep said with a nod, "bring forward your pies."

Orlynda Klum took in a deep breath and stepped forward. Livinia was already at the table setting down her pie—a cherry and pear cream confection that caused those watching to draw in a breath. Next, Daphne Melthalion presented her rum-apple and cheddar pie, which also drew delighted sounds from the crowd. The Widow Merryweather and Winifred Taylor both arrived at the same time, setting down their walnut peach-berry and pink lemonade pies, respectively. Orlynda set her cranberry-apple pie down at the far end, feeling a bit sheepish about her humble-looking entry this year.

All five of the pies were lined up right next to each other—and that was when the trouble started.

Magic, as anyone with any practical familiarity with the subject will tell you, is a jealous and dangerous thing. Intention counts for little in its application of effect, and the simplest of instructions can go awry when placed in proximity with other instructions of supposedly equal simplicity.

One might be tempted to blame the fairies for providing the magical potions in the first place, but that would be unkind and unfair, for the potions performed precisely as specified. Perhaps Jarod was to blame for deciding that if one could make so many gold coins with the sale of a single potion, it would be four times better to sell four such potions. But that, too, would be less than generous, as his motives were good and his reasoning sound in terms of business. Perhaps the ladies themselves were to blame in their zeal to obtain the prize.

As to the results, no one was in doubt. Four of the pies had been magically enhanced with cooking potions, each of which caused that pie to assert itself as the best pie of all. Each pie would do anything—*anything*—to assert its supremacy over every other pie around it.

Deniva Kolyan and Madeline Muffe stood on either side of the Captain and approached the pies.

The Captain leaned forward over Livinia's cherry and pear pie with a knife.

A spark flew up from the center of the crust and burst into the form of a tiny, sparkling dandelion.

The thick brows of the Captain rose in surprise.

"Toot!"

The judges turned to look down the row of pies.

The walnut peach-berry pie had sounded a note.

Crackle! Snap! Livinia's pie was producing a spectacular display in light and sound above its cream crust.

Not to be outdone, Daphne's rum-apple and cheddar pie suddenly burst into flames across its surface, causing the Captain to push back his two fellow judges in alarm.

Winifred Taylor screeched.

Her pink lemonade pie lifted off of the table and flew about the heads of the judges.

The fiery rum-apple was forming images of pirates fighting each other in the flames.

The walnut peach-berry pie was whistling a jig.

The sparkling bursts over the cherry-pear pie were getting larger above the heads of the judges, exploding around the flying pink lemonade pie, which took exception to the barrage and dove down on the cherry, flipping it skyward with the rim of its pie tin.

The cherry recovered in midair, sectioning itself into eight wedges, each of which gave chase to the lemonade pie.

The townspeople scattered in a panic, knocking over tables and chairs in their desperate attempt to escape.

The rum-apple pie tipped on its side and rolled along the tabletop, shooting flames behind it at the cherry. The cherry, thus diverted, separated three wedges from its pursuit of the lemonade pie and began spitting cherries at the rum from above, the thudding impact of its fruit slamming into the table and spattering red syrup on the innocent bystanders seeking shelter nearby.

The peach-berry pie unrolled its crust and began flinging walnuts. One of them connected with a wedge of cherry, which broke in two and careened in a spiral downward, slamming into the face of Percival Taylor—counted afterward as the first man wounded in the action.

The rum-apple pie had taken a number of hits from the cherry and was wobbling in its course. It veered to the right, leaped a gulf between the tables, and drove straight on its edge toward the peach-berry pie, which immediately began screaming for help while diverting its walnuts toward the onrushing rum-apple pie.

Overhead, the lemonade was still being pursued by several slices of cherry but saw an opportunity. It dove down over the peach-berry and flipped over, spurting whipped cream down onto the peach-berry. The pie choked on the cream and was temporarily silenced.

Suddenly, Jep Walters appeared with his ancient wand in hand. This caused everyone to renew their efforts to flee, as no one could predict what the untested weapon might do.

The peach-berry leaped into the air, trying to avoid the juggernaut of rum-apple driving relentlessly toward it in its quest for pie supremacy. The rum was not fooled, however, and flew into the air as well, just as the remaining cherry wedges and the lemonade converged.

The resulting terrible explosion of pie was so cataclysmic that it covered the farthest corners of Charter Square—and everyone within it.

When the Captain drew himself up from behind the overturned table, his ceremonial saber in hand, he looked about at the carnage, and one thing caught his eye.

Orlynda Klum was holding her cranberry-apple pie—still intact. He declared her the winner at once.

Jarod never met Caprice that night.

The initial and universal reaction was to arrest the Bard, but Jarod could not live with that. He confessed everything to his mother and his father. Both were upset with their son, but mostly Orlynda Klum, who now was in possession of the Fall Festival pie chalice and was certain that the rest of the women in the town would think she had put Jarod up to this escapade. She insisted that he give every one of the women their money back at once.

Treasure Box in hand, Jarod made the rounds of the four women and called at their back doors. Their reactions, however, surprised Jarod. Each one of them took the money back but begged him not to tell anyone what they had done. He promised that he would keep their secrets, and each one of them was relieved and grateful to him.

Perhaps too grateful, in one case.

"Jarod, you're a good man," Livinia Walters said to him at her back door—being careful that no one else could see them.

"Thank you . . . and I'm sorry about all this . . ."

"No, you've shown a head for business and are honorable besides," Livinia said. "You keep our little secret, and I promise I'll do everything I can to help you."

"Well, thank you, but that isn't necessary . . ."

"You just leave it to me, Son," Livinia said, closing her door.

Livinia nodded resolutely to herself. Jarod Klum was a better man than she had thought.

She determined to do everything she could to square things between Jarod and her daughter, Vestia.

# TALE OF FRIGHTFUL MANORS

❖

*Wherein Jarod is inducted into the Black
Guild Brotherhood—the secret men's
society known to everyone in Eventide—
but only if he can pass a haunting
initiation test.*

# CHAPTER 18

# The Black Guild Brotherhood

The chill, northwest wind moaned through the Norest Forest, shivering the bare branches of the trees and skittering the dried leaves across the frozen ground. It swept across the deserted Fae Grotto, brushing with it the low autumn clouds as they crossed the full moon overhead. It passed again into the sleeping trees, all cowering from its frigid blast, and came at last, as if bidden there, to shake the shingles and rattle the dark windows of Forgotten Manor.

No one now recalls its former name. In happier years a wealthy family had built the grandiose structure as a palatial summer retreat for members of the court in Mordale, but for reasons never explained—though wildly speculated upon—the imposing building was abandoned shortly after it had been furnished. Most of the stories told about it in Eventide involved secret murders, dark, mystical practices in hidden rooms beneath the foundations, and the haunting of its halls. Only the young and foolish ever dared approach the ruin, for it remained in shadow even in the full light of day, and those who did were so shaken by their experiences there that they vowed never to return again. Occasionally, nervous reports of seeing shadows moving across the windows and even occasional smoke from the long-cold chimneys would come to town. Everyone who had been born to Eventide knew to leave such dark forces well alone. Slowly, over the years, the grandeur that used to be succumbed to the forces of decay as nature slowly encroached upon it. Now, the brooding edifice stood as a dark stain among the leafless trees and beneath the cold light of the harvest moon.

Xander Lamplighter, the Constable Pro Tempore of Eventide, stood next to the long dried-up fountain before the wide steps leading up to the manor, lifting his lantern higher with his left hand. The light barely penetrated the gloom, showing the dirty stone columns flanking the main doors to the house. The finish on the enormous double doors was weathered and cracking. The shifting light from the lantern played tricks on Xander's eyesight, suggesting something moving among the columns, but Xander steadied his hand and the illusion vanished.

Satisfied, the Constable Pro Tempore turned and moved along the gravel path that was laid parallel to the face of the ruin, his booted feet kicking the fallen leaves just enough for them to be caught by the wind. The dark windows of the three-story manor looked menacingly down upon the feeble circle of light that encompassed Xander and barely kept the smothering darkness at bay.

Xander made his way around the northeast corner of the mansion. There he came to a portico with steps leading up to a smaller entrance. There were double doors here as well, although not nearly as large or as grand as the main entrance. One of the doors slammed closed every few seconds, only to fly open again in the whirling eddies of the howling wind. Xander walked quickly up the granite steps and grabbed the door handle. He raised his lantern again into the opening.

"Who goes there?" Xander cried out loudly over the wailing of the gale behind him. "Answer in the name of the king!"

A faint light shone at the end of the rotting hall, just beyond the limit of Xander's lantern.

Xander stepped inside, closing the door behind him and making sure the latch caught. Slowly he began walking down the dilapidated corridor, his footsteps forcing the floorboards to creak beneath him. Portraits hung down the length of the hall seemed to follow him with their eyes as he walked. The dim, red-hued light from the room at the end of the hall beckoned him on.

He stepped into the drawing room, its ceiling high overhead. Heavy curtains closed off the windows to his right.

Embers glowed warm in the fireplace.

He felt a rush of air behind him that made the hair on the back of his neck stand on end.

A low moaning sounded in his ear uncomfortably close.

Xander spun around, his lantern casting wild shadows across the room.

"Boo!" said the pixie now hovering inches from his face.

Xander grimaced. "Glix! You little demon . . . you like to frighten this old man to death!"

Peals of laughter came from behind the faded settee, chairs, and tables about the room.

"Oh, and look who's taking himself too seriously now!" Glix chided.

"Well, it weren't right, you leaving the door open like that," Xander said, setting down his lantern on a polished claw-foot table.

"I thought some fool might have stumbled in here and found you lot."

"And what if they had at that?" Glix sneered. "The place is haunted, don't you know? We'd have run them out so fast their head would have had to hurry to catch their own feet, wouldn't we, lads?"

The pixies, nearly two hundred in all, had emerged from their hiding places. Now they were scattered all about the room, seated on the mantel, the backs of couches, and the edges of tables and lounging about on cushions. A dozen or so were struggling to toss a log on the fire to liven it up for the evening.

Xander removed his hat and coat, tossing them in the general direction of the couch, where several of the pixies intercepted them. The hat they laid carefully with its crown down on the table, while the coat they folded and draped across the back of the couch.

"That ain't the point," Xander said to Glix as he sat down with accustomed ease in the large chair near the fireplace. "The last thing we need is having anyone snooping about out here. So long as they be afraid of this manor house, then we've got the good life and that's a fact. If ever they get the idea of what's going on out here, then they'll be out to pin the lot of you in a glass display case and me along with you."

"What's with the lamplighter?" Plix said with both his fists on his hips. "Who put a gnome in his hat?"

"Maybe you lot don't remember," Xander said, taking off his boots and rubbing his feet. The fire was starting to brighten again. "Where were we before we fell into this, eh? That's right. Wandering about the country from town to town doing that 'Pixie Circus' act and then moving on when it all got stale. Starving half the time, we was. Then we lands here and sweet as you please we're set up for life—if we play it right. We get food, regular pay, and you lot get to sit pretty as you like in them lanterns every night making fun of the people what's passing underneath. They get their streets all lit up from your jollies and no one's the wiser, see?"

"Sure, and that's the beauty of it, isn't it, though?" Glix beamed. "Say, the boys and I were thinking it time to expand a bit, as it were—explore another room or two here in the residence . . ."

"There'll be no more talk of that!" Xander said emphatically, pounding his fist down on the arm of the chair and causing a cloud of dust to rise from its ancient upholstery. "I told you lot to leave the rest of the house be. There be something not right about that part of the house, and I don't want any of you causing trouble. We've taken rooms enough."

"Afraid of the ghosts, are you, Xander?" Plix sneered.

"Ghosts, bah!" Xander said with a wave of his hand. "The spirits don't frighten me near as much as the idea that some fool might come out here and ruin it for all of us! Mind you, if someone does come in here, you'd best show them the most frightening haunt that ever sprang out of a nightmare or it will be pitchforks and torches for the lot of us!"

Jarod Klum was forced to his knees and the blindfold was removed from his eyes.

Blinking, he knew at once that he was in the Hidden Chamber of the Black Guild Brotherhood located in the basement of the Guild Hall. He had been politely blindfolded by Harv Oakman and Joaquim Taylor after he answered their request to meet them in the alley behind Bolly's Mill. No doubt he was subsequently led through the secret door in the back of the third closet on the right in the main hall and down the circular stairs to the Hidden Chamber.

The Black Guild Brotherhood was, as everybody knew, a secret organization. Only the most successful and skilled tradesmen and craftsmen of the village were allowed into its ranks, and then only after a strenuous test of the applicant's courage and determination to be admitted. The men met in secret lairs—or the basement of the old Guild Hall—and they practiced unspeakable rituals—or played cards over drinks—while they plotted among themselves the future of the village. Who was listed among the society's secret ranks was known to everyone in the town, and to be counted among them was to have one's future assured.

It was for this reason that Livinia Walters insisted that her husband, Jep—the Supreme Shahanshah of the Eventide Black Guild Brotherhood—admit Jarod Klum into their ranks or suffer the wrath of the wife of the Supreme Shahanshah. Vestia wanted him, and the young man had proved himself to possess both business savvy and the ability to keep a secret with regards to the unfortunate pie incident. So Livinia told her husband to make sure that Jarod was properly initiated into the Black Guild Brotherhood and the sooner the better.

Jep dutifully carried out all the necessary preliminaries for Jarod's initiation. His name was brought up for recommendation as an *Initiati* and dutifully considered by the other Black Guild Brothers during a break between hands of cards. With the required unanimous consent of the attending *Corpus Brothus* achieved, a secret invitation was issued on special brown parchment written with red ink and sealed in wax with the Shahanshah's own signet ring.

By the time the invitation arrived in Jarod's hands, there was hardly a person left in Eventide who didn't know the invitation had been issued.

Now, kneeling in the Hidden Chamber of the Black Guild Brotherhood, Jarod looked up over the heavy table. On the right side of the table, with its tip pointed at Jarod, was a long, narrow knife with an incredibly sharp edge sitting next to a solitary lit candle. On the left side of the table were an enormous round of cheese and a basket of fresh bread. Directly behind the table sat the hooded figure of the Shahanshah himself, Jep's face obscured in shadow as he gazed upon the *Initiati*. Behind the Shahanshah on the wall hung the Secret Flag of the Black Guild Brotherhood: a black field embroidered with the symbol of five blades—signifying the five edicts of the Guild and, some say, the five cards dealt to each player.

"Bring the *Initiati* forward!" the Shahanshah decreed.

Harv and Joaquim glanced at each other. Both were also wearing their ceremonial cloaks but had not bothered to pull their own hoods up. Joaquim shrugged.

"He *is* forward, Supreme Shahanshah," Harv said.

The hooded figure seated behind the table shifted slightly so that the front of his hood could be raised.

"So he is," Jep said in a booming voice. "Is he willing to take the oath?"

Harv nudged Jarod.

"I am," Jarod answered, his voice nearly breaking in his excitement.

"Has his metal been tested in the Black Guild forge?" Jep's voice more than filled the basement room with its drama. The eighteen other members of the guild wished to themselves that he would tone things down a little but knew it was a forlorn hope.

Joaquim answered. "His metal has not been . . . has not been . . ."

"*Tried by our forge!*" Harv prompted under his voice.

"Has not been tried by our forge!" Joaquim finished with a grateful glance toward Harv.

"Place him in . . . LIMBO!" Jep's voice shouted dramatically as he pointed emphatically at the basement door, "where he shall stay until the *Corpus Brothus* can determine a suitable test of his worth!"

The blindfold was placed back on Jarod at once and he was led through the door and into an extra storage room, sat down on a chair, and told to wait for the decision of the members as to his test.

"How long are you going to keep him in there, Jep?" asked Harvest Oakman.

"Until I get a winning hand," Jep said, gathering up his cards.

"That could be a long time," Mordechai said, pushing a pair of silver coins toward the center of the table.

Joaquim nearly choked on his cider as he snorted, "Hey, maybe that could be his test—waiting for Jep to actually win a hand?"

"Laugh all you want," Harv said, fanning out his cards and examining them with care, "but we've got to come up with something for him to do."

"What about running through the town in a dress?" Joaquim offered. "That's always been a good one."

"That's just because you want to make the dress," Mordechai said in droll tones.

"Well, if I did, he'd be the prettiest *Initiati* we've ever had," Joaquim replied, tapping his own cards on the table.

"We could have him ride the water wheel three times around on Bolly's Mill," Harv said, pushing his own silver coins forward. "The water's cold enough and it's always a lot of fun to watch."

"Didn't we do that last time?" Mordechai asked.

"Yeah," Joaquim said, "and I believe it was *me* that was doing the riding."

"You looked so good doing it, too," Mordechai smiled.

Jep had kept quiet for the most part and let the conversation flow around him. The truth was that he liked Jarod but resented Livinia's bullying him into inviting him into the Black Guild just so Vestia could have a respectable beau. This was his Black Guild Brotherhood, his one refuge from all the cares of his normal life, and now that special place was being invaded too.

So he had thought long and hard about what kind of trial to put Jarod through . . . not so much for his torture but so that he might really earn the right to be here apart from Livinia's insistence.

"Well, I think I've got it," Jep spoke up.

Everyone at the table looked up and, as word was passed among the other tables, the general murmur of conversation died. All eyes turned toward their Shahanshah as he took a long draught from his mug of ale.

"That old summer house—the Forgotten Manor," Jep said. "It's a strange old place and the whole town thinks it's haunted. What if he spent the night out there?"

A cold silence greeted the Shahanshah.

"What's wrong with that?" Jep demanded, putting his cards facedown on the table.

"But . . . it *is* haunted," said Jesse Hall in a quivering voice. Jesse was a teamster at Bolly's Mill.

"Oh, that's just fairy talk," Jep said with a dismissive wave of his hand. He picked up his cards again. "It's just an old empty house! Besides, we won't actually have him spend the night out there . . . we'll march out there with him, tell him he has to spend the night. Harv, you go with Joaquim over to his store and get some sheets of muslin—enough to cover you up. Then, while we're out there, the two of you go in the back, cross through the salon and into the front hall. Hoot him up as though you were spirits in the house, and when he runs out we'll tell him he passed. If he's got enough man in him to go in the front door, that's good enough."

"So," Harv asked, "you want us to go now?"

"No," Jep said, tossing a few more silver coins into the middle of the table. "Not until we've finished this hand."

Flaming torches fluttering in the night, the men of the Black Guild Brotherhood, still clad in their ceremonial cloaks and hoods, marched down the Meade road and turned north to follow the overgrown and abandoned road that wandered into the Norest Forest. Pushed before them was a decidedly upset Jarod Klum doing his best to counterfeit some semblance of bravery, his hastily acquired bedroll squeezed in the crook of his arm. Jep Walters's firm hand was on his shoulder, pressing him ever forward down the dark road to a darker end.

The Black Guild Brotherhood came at last to stand before the imposing edifice of the Forgotten Manor, its columns and blackened windows barely illuminated by the dim light from the guttering torches.

"What is it?" asked Plix.

"Sure, it's an invasion, it is!" Glix said, peering out the window from the darkened room in the north wing. "Torches and all!"

"Should we be waking the constable, then?" Dix asked anxiously.

"And get him all bothered again? Forget it!" Glix said. "Gather all the clan. We'll handle this lot ourselves!"

"But will you look at that one!" Plix said, pointing. "He's going to the front door!"

"Then we'll cut him off . . . go through the house ourselves."

Plix's eyes went wide. "But the constable said—"

"Who's in charge here, Plix?" Glix answered at once. "I'm head of the clan, not the Constable Pro Tempore. Gather the sheets, boys. We're on the haunt tonight!"

· CHAPTER 19 ·

# The Frightening

Jarod could not stop shaking. He was squeezing the woolen bedroll under his arm so tightly that he thought he might have pressed it flat. He desperately wanted to close his eyes and run away, the combination of which he somehow knew was wrong. It would probably result in his running into a tree, but it was, nevertheless, how he felt.

The forbidding edifice rose before him, a dark, malevolent shape against the moonlit clouds racing on the wind. Leaves skittered across the wide, stone steps. His own shadow, cast by the torches of the Black Guild Brotherhood behind him, rose enormous across the face of the building, leaving the entry door completely dark.

*How did I get into this?* his mind raced. *How do I get OUT?*

He knew in his heart the answer to the first question. When the invitation had been extended to join the Black Guild Brotherhood, it had nearly made Jarod believe in miracles from the Lady of the Sky. Sobrina and Lucius were going to be married the following month, the banns having been read before the town by Father

Pantheon shortly after the Fall Festival's conclusion. This would leave Jarod free to court Caprice properly—but it still left him with the problem of what offering of worth he might put in his Treasure Box to take to Caprice and her father as the bride price. Then came the invitation to join the Black Guild Brotherhood—which practically everyone acknowledged to be the most influential society in the town—and it looked like the key to prominence in the community. Social connection might not fit in his Treasure Box, but it certainly would open doors all over town for him and show Meryl Morgan that Jarod was himself a prize worthy of his daughter.

As to the second question, his mind was desperately searching for an answer. He had feared the Forgotten Manor and quaked at hearing stories of the place since he was old enough walk. Tales of the family who once lived there, all horribly murdered in their beds. Tales of warrior spirits who had taken up residence in the halls after they were unable to return to their own homes. Tales of wishes gone bad accumulating in the halls until they awoke and wanted only to ensnare the living with them in their despair. Tales more recently of the ghost of Dirk Gallowglass, whose headless body no doubt now roamed the halls. Any who entered would surely be most horribly tortured by the spirits that haunted the abandoned ruin, losing their sanity and having their souls slowly devoured by the darkness!

Jarod gulped.

*Do it for Caprice . . .*

The young man blinked. He was not certain if someone had whispered it to him or if he had simply thought it.

*Do it for love . . .*

Jarod drew in a breath. Somehow he found that his feet were moving him forward. They carried him up the broad, stone steps to the front door of the Forgotten Manor.

He reached for the handle and pulled the creaking door open.

An abyss of blackness was on the other side.

Jarod stepped into it.

"I'm not so sure this is a good idea," Joaquim said from under his muslin sheet.

Harvest Oakman and Joaquim Taylor were both standing on the west side verandah draped in white cloth taken from Joaquim's stores. Necessity had required that they cut holes in the cloth through which they might see, which left Joaquim complaining about how he was ever going to get the Black Guild to pay up for ruining the cloth. Those considerations, however, had been set aside by the terror of standing at the dark manor's back door.

"Well, you heard the Grand Pashashashasha," Harv replied in a voice only marginally more steady than his companion's. "We just go in these doors, run straight through the salon and into the hall on the other side. We give Jarod his little scare and then we follow him out the front, easy as you please."

"Easy enough to say," Joaquim stuttered through chattering teeth.

"Soon begun, sooner done," Harv said, both for his own benefit and for that of his friend. "Let's get this over with."

Harv pulled open the door, gave Joaquim a push, and followed him inside.

Glix had just banked the fire in the drawing room. Throughout the room floated the sheets that had once protected the furniture, now suspended in the air by the pixies.

"All set then, boys?" Glix called out with determination as he flew up in front of the assembled haunting.

"Right enough," Plix replied, "but old constable told us not to go into that part of the house . . . I mean, what if it *is* haunted, Glix?"

All motion of the false spirits in the room suddenly stopped.

Glix paused, considered, and then shook his head as he spoke. "There's no spirits in this house, boys. The constable knows us pixies right well, and he'd never bring us to a place that's haunted—him knowing what a dreadful great fear we have of the dead. So there'll be no more talk of spirits! Follow me, lads! Let's do some haunting of our own!"

Glix pulled open the door and flew into the pitch darkness of the narrow gallery leading to the main hall.

Jarod stood still in the center of the main hall. Dim light filtered in from the full moon through the dirty windows high on the wall behind him. The hall was two stories tall and once must have been beautiful. Twin staircases curved upward at the far end of the hall to a balcony on the second floor. Numerous doors led off to the left and right to destinations that Jarod did not care to guess. Cloth-draped furniture was scattered everywhere.

The muted wind was the only sound.

Jarod stepped into the hall farther, wondering just how far in he would be required to go. He stopped in the center of the hall at a cloth-shrouded round table and decided that the only real condition he had been told was "inside" the house, and that meant he could probably get away with standing all night next to the front door.

He was just turning back.

The north door from the gallery burst open. Out poured the faint glowing form of spirits, their outlines like flying sheets flapping and cracking as they flew into the hall.

Jarod yelped! All conscious thought left him in that moment and he forgot how to find the front door. He backed away from the onrushing apparitions, his back pressed against a door on the south wall.

Suddenly, at the top of the stairs, two more ghostly forms materialized. These were larger in form and had taken on a heartier, more corporeal form. Their keening was deeper, too, and both appeared to be wearing boots.

The first spirits wheeled in the air, confronting the second pair of spirits as they both came to a sudden stop halfway down the stairs.

The flying spirits all shrieked an ear-splitting keening!

The two booted spirits screamed back!

"They'll be coming out any minute," Jep Walters assured the remaining assembly of the Black Guild Brotherhood. "Then we can all get back to our secret meeting—I left a pretty good winning streak and I don't want it to go cold."

A single cry from the house pierced the air.

Jep smiled with satisfaction. "That's Jarod . . . we're about finished now."

A bone-chilling, cacophony of screams filled the air, all coming from the house. Mordechai Charon and many others would later swear they saw glowing spirits flying behind the windows all around the front door.

Jep Walters's eyes went wide as his jaw dropped.

The shrieking of the ghosts would not stop.

There was no sign of Jarod Klum.

The flying spirits scattered about the hall in a panic, their glow suddenly intense as they rushed here and there in a fury.

The booted ghosts on the stairs also fell into a frenzy, one jumping over the railing and rushing down a service hall while the other ran back up the stairs, turned, and, still keening, bounced off a door before opening it and loudly slamming it closed behind him. Several of the flying spirits had followed them both by chance, and the screaming from all the spirits continued unabated.

Jarod blindly reached behind him. His hand came to rest on a latch. He quickly depressed it and fell backward through the door, slamming it shut after him.

Five people turned and looked at him.

"Oh, I beg your pardon, I . . ."

Jarod froze.

There was an elderly gentleman sitting in a large, upholstered chair. Next to him was a handsome couple holding hands where they sat on the divan. A young woman lay on a fainting couch, leaving the book she had been reading. A small, curly-haired boy sat on the floor of the parlor with his hands over both his ears.

It was a common and tranquil enough scene, except that Jarod could see *through* each of the family members.

The old man said, "Are you all right, boy?"

Jarod gaped.

"Oh, don't talk to them, Father," the woman said from the divan. "They never understand."

"I'll talk to them if I want to," the old man said. "Maybe if we did they'd leave us alone for a change!"

Somehow Jarod found his voice. "But you're . . . you're . . ."

"Dead?" said the man sitting with the woman. "You *can* say it, you know. It's not a dirty word. Everyone gets to be dead sometime."

"Oh," Jarod responded in a daze. "I suppose you're right."

"Who better to know than us?" said the old man.

"Please, Father, can't you just make him go away . . ."

"Now, daughter, just because we're dead doesn't mean we should forget our manners."

"And he is rather charming," said the young woman on the fainting couch.

A renewed shrieking passed by the door at Jarod's back.

Jarod flinched.

So did the ghosts.

"Blast that racket!" said the old man ghost. "We never should have come here!"

"Come here?" Jarod asked more boldly, seeing that these particular apparitions were not immediately intent on murdering him. "I thought this was your home."

"*Our* home?" said the ghost woman on the couch. "Fancy that!"

"No, my boy," said the old man ghost, shaking his head, "we came here to get *away* from that sort of noise. We're on holiday from Mordale."

"Mordale?" Jarod said. "What happened to you in Mordale . . . I mean, if it isn't impolite to ask."

"Oh, and he's so polite, Mother!" the young woman cooed.

"Now, Esmeralda, you know better than to get your hopes up," her mother replied from the couch.

"Oh, it's all so ridiculous," said the father from the couch. "Bad construction of a wall. Dreadful thing fell on our carriage—snuffed out the lot of us. Unfortunately, we all had a good deal of unfinished business to be done before we moved on . . ."

"Moved on?" Jarod asked.

"Don't explain, Philip," said the mother ghost, patting her husband's hand. "They never really understand."

"The point is that we've been working things out in the city," said the elderly ghost, "but it's so noisy there that we all felt the need to get away. We knew about this place in the country—word gets around among the spirits, you know—so we thought we would come out and rest in peace. But this is worse than the city . . . people coming in and out and screaming like this!"

"We came here to get away from all that chain-rattling," huffed the mother ghost as a renewed set of lusty screams and pounding feet passed the door.

Jarod drew in a slow breath. "You mean . . . those things out there *aren't* ghosts?"

"Those?" piped in the apparition of the little boy. "Not hardly!"

"Blasted intruders," grumbled the old ghost. "Waking the dead!"

Jarod took a careful step forward. "Please, I apologize for disturbing you . . . and for my friends outside . . . but if you're willing to help me . . . I think I can solve your . . . uh . . . infestation problem and give you some quiet after all."

The father ghost stood up. "Why should you do that?"

"Well, because I'm on a quest," said Jarod. "There's this woman named Caprice . . ."

Jep Walters wrung his hands. The rest of the Black Guild Brotherhood stood shifting back and forth, their torches guttering in the autumn wind, anxious to do something and yet powerless to make themselves move forward toward the horrible sounds coming from within the manor.

The sounds of the commotion were roaring all through the house. Flashes of light would pass a window with screams and sobbing on the upper floor only to be matched in the next moment by a crashing sound and more cries for help from the main floor.

"We've got to do something!" Mordechai pleaded.

"What can we do?" said Jep in reply. "What can *any* of us do?"

"It wasn't haunted, you said," whined Brody Muffe. "There's no danger, you said."

"Someone has got to do something!" Mordechai moaned.

Suddenly, the front doors of the manor flew open, banging against the walls as a figure emerged.

It was Harvest Oakman, still wearing the remnants of his torn muslin cloth. He stumbled down the stairs as several of the Black Guild Brotherhood rushed forward to catch the still shaking Harv.

"It was Jarod!" Harv said, out of breath. "He found me in that madness . . . he led me out!"

A bone-chilling shriek followed from the doorway and the Black Guild Brotherhood fell back.

Then a second figure shot out, running as fast as any man present had ever seen. It took several of the Brotherhood just to stop him before he passed them by. It was Joaquim Taylor, his eyes wide and his breathing hard.

"Shades! Spirits! Haunts!" gulped Joaquim. "Thought they had me for sure! Say—where's Jarod? He showed me the way to the door. I thought he was right behind me?"

The house shook with a terrible keening sound.

There, framed in the doorway, stood Jarod Klum. He was supporting the rather massive weight of a blubbering Xander Lamplighter, who was having trouble keeping his feet squarely under him.

Jep stood looking at Jarod in amazement as he turned over the Constable Pro Tempore to the arms of the Brotherhood. "That was the bravest thing I've ever seen."

Jarod looked Jep Walters squarely in the eye and said, "I've got to go back in."

"You WHAT?" squeaked the Supreme Shahanshah of the Brotherhood.

"There may be others still inside!" Jarod said nobly. "Besides—I have not yet finished my task."

Then Jarod turned . . . and walked back into the Forgotten Manor.

The young man had no sooner entered the house than the most horrible, frightening commotion heard yet roared from its open door. It was as though the house itself had been outraged and had taken Jarod into its insatiable maw. The sound carried as far as Eventide, waking the women of Cobblestone Street into a sudden fear.

The main doors slammed closed as if of their own accord.

Then, an instant later—silence.

The dawn rose cold. Jep Walters was exhausted, but he and the rest of the Black Guild Brotherhood had remained through the night, watching quietly and hoping against hope for the deliverance of Jarod Klum.

As the sun's rays peeked over the summit of Mount Dervin, Aren Bennis with Beulandreus Dudgeon on his back galloped up the old manor lane. Mordechai had gone for them in the morning and both had swiftly answered the call.

"What's going on here, Jep?" Aren asked in brusque tones as he reached back and helped the dwarf down to the ground.

Jep shook his head sadly, his face drawn. "It's . . . Jarod Klum, good man that he was. We need someone to go in and bring back whatever is left of him. It's the least we can do for his poor mother."

Aren eyed the house critically and then reached behind his back, pulling from under his coat an enormous, gleaming sword. "Come, Beulandreus—let's go find the boy."

The dwarf nodded grimly. Both were surprised to see Abel, the scribe, resolutely stepping forward to join them.

Sword drawn, the centaur walked up the steps with his two companions. Aren pulled open the front doors of the manor with his free hand and, bending over, led them inside.

Illuminated by the rays of morning light, streaming through the dirty windows, the entry hall featured beautiful architecture even in its dilapidated state. The matched curving staircases were impressive despite the broken railing on the left side. Most things were still covered in a thick layer of dust, but tracks led in every direction across the floor, and there were several pieces of furniture newly broken.

Rap . . . rap . . . rap . . .

Aren jerked his head up at the sound, raising his sword.

Beulandreus took out a hammer and adjusted his grip.

Abel drew out his pencil.

The soft sound had come from the top of the stairs.

Aren carefully advanced up the stairs, the great blade drawn back, his arms poised and tensed to strike. Beulandreus flanked up the opposite stairs while Abel followed at a discreet distance behind the centaur.

Rap . . . rap . . . rap . . .

The sound was moving.

Aren followed it south through a doorway and into a narrow corridor. Beulandreus closed ranks with Farmer Bennis as Abel scribbled a descriptive note.

Rap . . . rap . . . rap . . .

It came from behind a door to their right.

Aren carefully reached for the door latch and slowly released the catch. He gave a push to the door. It swung wide into the room with a terrible squeal.

It was a bedroom, and an opulent one at that. The bed was the largest that Abel had ever seen, fitted with a sumptuous mattress. Four tall posts stood at its corners, with curtains hiding its occupant.

Rap . . . rap . . . rap . . .

This time, from behind the bed curtains.

Aren approached slowly, motioning the dwarf over toward the foot of the bed. Abel held his pencil threateningly. The centaur thrust back the curtains around the bed.

There, blinking with the sudden intrusion of light, lay Jarod Klum. He sat up with a groan, rubbed his eyes, and then yawned. "What time is it?"

Aren chuckled as he lowered his blade. "An hour past dawn, young Master Klum. Sorry to awaken you, but you've kept the entire Black Guild Brotherhood up for the whole night."

"Truly?" Jarod sounded surprised. "They said I had to sleep here all night. That's all I was doing."

"All you was doing!" Beulandreus roared with a hearty laugh.

"Oh, please keep quiet," Jarod asked in a low voice. "I promised them we wouldn't disturb them while they're here. How did you find me?"

"We heard some rapping sound," Beulandreus said. "Led us to you straight away."

Jarod stretched. "Probably the boy. He was the one who found this bed for me. A pretty helpful lad once you get to know him, even if he is dead."

"Who?" Aren said with a quizzical look. "What have you been up to out here, Jarod?"

So it was that Jarod, still sitting in his comfortable bed, rehearsed to them what truly had happened—though he swore them all never to tell.

And none of them did . . . for a very long time.

Aren, Beulandreus, and Abel all stood in the main hall of Forgotten Manor behind Jarod, who had finished rolling up his blanket.

Aren reached over and messed up the young man's hair.

"Hey, stop that!" Jarod said, pulling away.

"You have to look the part," Aren said quietly with a smile. "Come on, now. Let's see about making you into a hero."

By this time, much of the town had turned out to witness the spectacle at the Forgotten Manor from a *very* respectable distance. When the doors opened, there was a great gasp from the crowd as Jarod Klum—the bravest man in Eventide—bounded out the doors.

A tremendous cheer erupted from the townsfolk.

"I am astonished, boy! Simply astonished and overwhelmed!" shouted Jep Walters, a tear of relief streaking his wide, cherry-cheeked face. He kept slapping Jarod on the back.

Jarod looked around him. Aren, Beulandreus, and Abel had all joined the crowd. Curiously, the Dragon's Bard was not there.

But Jarod's gaze was drawn at once to the edge of the cheering throng, where Caprice Morgan was smiling and waving at him. He raised his arm to wave back, but in that moment Vestia Walters ran into him, throwing her arms around him with such force that he was nearly knocked to the ground.

"A champion!" she cried as he struggled to keep his balance. "My true champion!"

By the time he had extracted himself from Vestia's grip, Caprice Morgan was nowhere to be seen.

# THE DRAGON'S TALE

*Wherein the brave Jarod is appointed*
*Captain of the Dragonwatch and*
*why slaying dragons is considered a*
*hazardous profession.*

· CHAPTER 20 ·

# Muster of the Dragonwatch

Father Patrion raked the dead leaves out of the flower beds surrounding his church with a distracted air. It was such a beautiful place, he thought. He had come to love it dearly—even as he knew in his heart that he had failed his church, his people, and his faith.

He had made a terrible and simple mistake in the face of the infallible divine.

Father Patrion sighed as he gazed at the columns supporting the roof over the church. They were all so straight and so true, he thought. Once again he felt ashamed for his shortcomings, for his inability to convert a single soul to the worship of his goddess and his utter failure in communicating his situation with his superiors in Mordale.

Now the wedding of Sobrina Morgan to Lucius Tanner had been announced. The banns had been read before the town and the date was rapidly approaching. He, being the person officially entrusted with the things of deity, had been called upon to seal the marriage before the gods—although which of the gods they intended had yet to be made clear.

How could he pronounce the blessings of the gods when he knew in his private, dark moments that he was a fraud . . . that the divine voice he thought he heard was only the echoing sound of his own imaginations?

A shadow moving among the pillars caught his eye.

Someone was in the church.

Father Patrion frowned for a moment and then set down his rake. His hands were dirty from tending the grounds, so he wiped them as best he could on his already dirty apron and stepped up the wide stairs leading to the pillars.

The day was brilliant and crisp, but it was always shadowed within the church. Father Patrion had entirely forgotten the felt hat still perched atop his head as he passed between the columns and into the chill sanctuary of the church proper.

A woman stood at the altar.

Father Patrion let out a long sigh. Here was another patron come into the church that seemed to have no god in particular. He hated this part—approaching the new petitioner at the altar and not knowing which particular form of deity he would have to address or whether his first words uttered would be a complete offense to the person before him. It had become a game that he did not care to play, always starting in the most general terms and trying as quickly as possible to figure out the specifics of the person's faith.

"May I help you?" Father Patrion offered.

The woman wore a long, hooded cape of ultramarine hue. She knelt at the altar.

Patrion cleared his throat, speaking a little louder. "May I help you?"

The woman lifted her head and turned around. Seeing the priest, she smiled and stood up. Her face was a pretty oval, framed pleasantly in the hood. Her eyes were an unusual cobalt blue. "You're . . . Father Pantheon, aren't you?"

Father Patrion drew in a patient breath. "Yes, my child; that is what the townsfolk call me."

"It's a good name," she said, laughter wrinkling the corners of her eyes. "I like it. I think it suits you very well."

"I'm . . . sorry," the priest said, walking toward the woman. "Have we met before?"

"Oh, I know you well," she said fondly. "However, our meeting is too long overdue. You've a beautiful church here, Father Pantheon."

"Well, thank you," Patrion answered. "The town built it."

The woman cocked her head slightly as though listening, then said quietly, "Then blessed is the town of Eventide."

"Yes," the priest said, looking at the ground. "I pray that it is."

The woman looked back at the priest. "I have come on a mission of forgiveness, Father Pantheon. Can you help me with that?"

"I . . . I don't know, my child. I . . ."

"You seem troubled, Father," the woman said, reaching out and touching his arm.

He looked into her eyes. They looked back at him with such sympathy that he could not lie to her.

"It . . . it is a foolish thing," he said. "I shouldn't trouble you . . ."

"Come, Father, it is just the two of us here," the woman said with a shrug as she leaned back against the altar. "What weighs on your thoughts?"

"Well, some months ago, back when Spring Revels were being held—do you know about Spring Revels?"

"I do indeed!" the woman replied. "A great festival and a marvelous Couples' Dance, I understand."

The priest winced. "Yes. Well, I was supposed to arrange meetings between two young couples. I wrote down the instructions that same night—I was so careful about it. But when the day of the Revels came, I knew, I just knew I had the instructions wrong. I couldn't shake the feeling that I had somehow mixed everything up. I don't know what was wrong with me. I went out into the town, found the two young men involved, and switched their instructions."

"Switched them, you say?"

"Yes!" he said angrily. "Those young men ended up with the wrong women, and nothing has been right with any of them ever since. How inspired a man can I be if I can't even follow my own written instructions?"

The woman shook her head. "You did it perfectly, Patric."

Father Patrion looked up. "What did you say?"

She took both his hands in hers. "I need to tell you something."

"What?" the priest asked, his heart quickening.

She leaned forward and spoke quietly in his ear. "You wrote it down correctly . . . just not right."

Father Patrion pulled back. "Who . . . what does that mean?"

The woman smiled quietly. "It means that I told you to mix up the instructions . . . and you heard me and did as I asked."

"But . . . why?"

"Because a young man needed to learn what lasting love required," the woman said, "and that it doesn't come in a Treasure Box."

Father Patrion stared in wonder at the woman.

"More than that," she laughed. "So that you, my faithful friend, would learn after all that I know how well and forever remembered you are for serving this blessed town on my behalf . . . my own, dear Father Pantheon."

She reached up and pulled back her hood, and the radiance of the sun filled the church. When it faded, the Lady of the Sky was gone.

And Father Pantheon never again wrote to the Masterpriests in Mordale—but happily served all the people of Eventide all the days of his life.

"This is the worst plan I have heard yet!" shouted Aren, his voice nearly shaking the rafters of his own home. "He's going to bring a *dragon* . . . here to Eventide?"

Abel could only shrug.

"That's what the note said," Beulandreus huffed. "And the whole town knows about it."

"You mean he told them he was bringing a dragon to the town?" Aren looked down at the dwarf in astonishment.

"No, not at all!" the blacksmith replied. "He told them that the dragon was coming to ravage the countryside and burn down the town. He suggested that the town fathers form some sort of a defense and that the only logical one to handle it was the bravest man in all Eventide . . ."

"Jarod Klum," they both said at the same time.

"Aye, that's what he told them," the dwarf continued. "And pretty much what that Gossip Fairy and that whole group of hens on Cobblestone Street have been spreading about the town all day."

The centaur folded his arms across his wide chest and shook his head. "He cannot seriously think this is going to end in anything but a disaster, can he?"

Abel tried to look anywhere but at Farmer Bennis.

"The note here says," Beulandreus pointed at the parchment in his hand, "that he will ask the great dragon Khrag to fly over the town a time or two after Sobrina and Lucius get wedded, spout a bit of flame, and then fly off. Jarod will be the hero of the day and Caprice will be his the next day."

"So, he's left us with a pretty story and run off," Aren said, seething.

"Says here," Beulandreus continued reading the note, "that you'd say that and that he is leaving his scribe here as his assurance of his return."

The centaur scowled at the scribe, who feebly waved his hand in reply.

"If that's our assurance, then we've seen the last of the fabled Dragon's Bard," Aren said in a husky voice. "The only thing to do is take that note to the town fathers and let them know they've been tricked."

"Unless they ain't," Beulandreus said, folding up the note.

"What are you talking about, blacksmith?"

"I mean, what if he *has* gone off to get a dragon?" the blacksmith replied. "We go to the town fathers with this note, they don't do anything about defending the town, and then a dragon shows up? That don't do anyone any good."

"So then Jarod spends all his nights watching the skies for a dragon that is never going to show up?" Aren threw his hands up in the air. "How does that help him win the heart of his woman?"

"Well, I've been thinking about that on the road out here, you might say . . ."

"Please, I'm not sure I want to hear—"

"What we need is a contingency dragon," the dwarf pronounced.

"A . . . what?" Aren thought perhaps the world was going mad. "Where would we get *another* dragon?"

"Well," said the smith, "I could *build* one."

It is a curious thing about humans that they like to scare themselves. The dire news of the approaching dragon galvanized the town and set them on a determined course to provide for their own defense. The ladies of Cobblestone Street spoke of being murdered in their beds by the dragon while Jep Walters and Squire Melthalion argued endlessly over the preparations being made for the defense of the town.

This, of course, was all being done to counter the rumored approach of a dragon that no one had ever seen. Prior to this, the fact that no one in Eventide had seen a dragon had been attributed to the Dragon's Bard having done his job so well in collecting stories that the dragon had withheld its wrath. Now the Dragon's Bard had disappeared, and rumors of impending doom ran rampant in the town. No effort was being spared to save Eventide from this unseen menace.

So the Dragonwatch was formed the next day. Made up of a volunteer militia, this muster of valiant, stalwart men and (thanks to Deniva Kolyan's insistence) valiant, stalwart women as well were to defend the town against any attack by this newly perceived threat. Nearly everyone in town insisted on being listed in the ranks, except for Lord Gallivant, who said that he had seen too much of that sort of thing and would just wait in the inn until it was over. Aren

Bennis, the dwarf blacksmith, and Abel were all conspicuously absent but excused as they seemed to be working on a project of their own out in the barn behind Bolly's Mill.

Jarod the Fearless (as he had become universally known in the town) was by unanimous acclaim put in charge of the watch—his bravery after his induction into the Black Guild Brotherhood now the talk of all Eventide—and though he had never served in the King's Army, the village put their faith in his planning for their defense.

Jarod took the news of his posting well. It came with regular pay for his services, straight from the parish council, which would slowly allow him to build up his bride price offering. Those coins he started putting in his Treasure Box, counting them each day. Yet he knew that the very survival of the town had been entrusted to him, and he took his duties most seriously.

He sat down at his desk in the countinghouse and drew out a few sheets of parchment, having decided to come up with a plan.

Jarod had heard a number of tales about dragons and used these stories as a basis for his deliberations. His father always told him to take his time and reason through things step by step in his mind before he did anything. Jarod approached the defense of the town with serious thought.

Dragons, he reasoned, flew through the air; therefore, it would be in the air that they would need to mount their defense. People, he then reasoned, do not fly, and he considered possible ways of changing that condition but could come up with no workable solution. Pixies flew, he thought, as did fairies, but he hardly thought they could do enough damage to a dragon to be of use. Then he remembered the dwarf showing him some tapestries he had made depicting some of the epic sieges of the past against castles and dragons. Those had large devices that looked like enormous crossbows hurling bolts the size of tree trunks high into the sky—ballistae, the dwarf called them.

At the time, Jarod's mind had leaped at once to the possibilities of using these machines to launch the men and women of the Dragonwatch into the sky to fight the dragon . . . but the dwarf said the boy was missing the point. When Jarod calmed down a bit, he realized that the dwarf meant to hurl the enormous bolts into the sky to pierce the dragon, but Jarod wanted something more dramatic . . . what if the huge bolts carried *fire* with them?

Now, *that* would look wonderful in a tapestry!

At Jarod's insistence, the town built two huge ballistae—all they could afford—and stationed one of them in Trader's Square just in front of the Guild Hall and mill while the other was placed across the river in Charter Square next to the sundial. Each of them stood pointing skyward in anticipation, the tips of their huge bolts covered in oil-soaked peat from the southern bogs. Burning torches in braziers were placed near at hand, ready to ignite the bolts with flame in an instant. Extra bolts were laid up against the sides of the inn and the mill. Open kegs of oil were also stored in the mill, should the first bolts fail to hit their mark.

At last all was set. Jarod took the first watch. The crews for the ballistae stood at the ready.

All that night . . .

And the next . . . and the next . . .

Night after night passed, and though the skies remained as free of dragons as ever before, the tales of the dragon's potential terror rose with each passing sunset. The latest rumor said that the dragon was magical and could actually make itself invisible so that the power of its terrible breath could rain down on the village homes before it was ever even seen. The Muster of the Dragonwatch redoubled its efforts now to see the dragon even if it was invisible.

Jarod, however, began to despair. He really did not care about killing the dragon—the prospect of killing anything frightened him—and he hoped the dragon would simply not show up. Each night on watch he sat quietly by the Charter Square ballista until the early hours of the morning before dawn, staring at the sundial, turning his wooden Treasure Box over and over in his hands. He pondered the curse that had broken the wishing well. He wondered how it could be ended by a sunset and sunrise being heralded at the same time and if there were any way to put a sunset inside his wooden box.

"Hail, my old friends! It is I, the Dragon's . . ."

The centaur clasped his enormous hand over the mouth of Edvard and dragged him into the back of the blacksmith shop.

"What are you doing here?" Aren demanded.

"I've returned, as I said I would," Edvard said. "Surely you knew that of all minstrels, a Dragon's Bard is a man of his word!"

"I'll let that alone," said Beulandreus. "Did you bring that dragon after all?"

The Dragon's Bard was suddenly crestfallen.

"Alas! Dragons are fickle and difficult things," the Bard replied. "Though I pressed my case to him in most earnest terms, I fear he will not be able to assist us as I have hoped. He did give me every assurance that he would make an attempt, barring further conflicts and previous commitments, of course . . ."

"So you mean 'no,'" the centaur grumbled.

"Not exactly," Edvard replied. "There is most definitely and positively something of a chance that he will attend."

"Then Friday night it is, dwarf," Aren said. "The night of the wedding."

"The wedding is this Friday?" Edvard exclaimed. "What an excellent opportunity. I shall delight the assembly with my rendition of 'My Love Lies Softly There' and perhaps a ballad or two . . ."

"No, you'll be with us, since this was largely your doing," Aren said, gripping the Bard's shoulder in his enormous hand.

"And what are *we* doing that night?" the Bard asked.

"Flying a dragon," the centaur replied.

"We are?" Edvard gulped.

"Yes," said the dwarf. "We've our own fine plan."

Had they asked, even Edvard could have told them that of all the fine plans ever devised, *none* have ever gone according to plan.

# CHAPTER 21

# The Siege of Eventide

With the everlasting Lady of the Sky smiling down upon you . . . and the blessing of gods you honor in your thoughts and deeds . . . and before the good citizens of Eventide . . . I wed you, Sobrina Morgan, and you, Lucius Tanner, one to another as wife and husband and unite you as one before the gods and our community."

The couple turned toward each other. Lucius drew Sobrina into his arms and kissed her passionately.

The Pantheon Church was overflowing with guests, all cheering wildly.

Sobrina and Lucius turned to face their friends. Sobrina was resplendent in her wedding gown, its yellow color still as vibrant as on the day her mother had worn it. The lightly fit bodice of the dress came to a point in front, accentuating her narrow waist. The skirt was of heavy satin that flowed in princess lines over her hips and flared wide to the floor. Her light hair fell in waves down her back, crowned with a circlet of delicate dried flowers that Aren Bennis had brought over the night before and, in a quiet and somber voice, begged Sobrina to wear. It was a remarkable gift that Sobrina was inclined to refuse, but Caprice interceded, seeing how the centaur was so heartbroken and sincere in his offering. The wreath crowned her head in glorious display.

Lucius had cleaned up remarkably well and stood before the altar in his long coat and a high button shirt. His boots were polished to a shine brighter than still waters under a clear sky.

But all the splendor of their dress and careful grooming was nothing compared to the radiance of their smiles and the joy they felt in their union. Sobrina, standing before the roaring approval and applause of her neighbors, was transformed. The Frost Queen had somehow melted in the chill of the changing late autumn wind. Now her eyes shone with a startling warmth and there emerged a smile that warmed the soul just to look upon it.

Lucius and Sobrina both raised their hands, showing the assembled townsfolk the two halves of their marriage coin. The crowd cheered again all the louder. Sobrina laughed out loud, then stepped away from her newly minted husband toward the dwarf standing nearby.

Beulandreus Dudgeon stood in the front near the altar. He was dressed in his best leather coat, and he stood still holding the red velvet cushion on which he had presented the "broken" marriage coin to Father Pantheon. The smith had carefully cut the coin himself and had felt terribly honored when Lucius and Sobrina had come to him and asked him to be part of their wedding ceremony.

Sobrina stood before the dwarf, still gripping her half of the coin, and joyfully bent over, kissing Beulandreus on the forehead.

The dwarf never moved, but a tear escaped from one eye and fell onto the velvet pillow.

Meryl Morgan and his younger daughters stood to the side, beaming with joy. Caprice and Melodi both held small nosegays that were threatening to come apart under their excited applause. Abel stood as near to Melodi as custom and decorum allowed, one of the Dragon's Bard's more interesting volumes in his hand as he searched for a proper moment to present it to the youngest of the Morgans with his appreciation for her interest in such tales.

The centaurs from north of town, standing just beyond the columns outside the church, bellowed their husky approval with a loud, hooting sound. Aren Bennis was there among them, leading them in their peculiar cheer.

Yet not everyone in the congregation was happy.

Jarod Klum stood trapped uncomfortably close to Vestia Walters inside the church. She was standing next to her father and mother on the other side of half a dozen dwarf-dwarves and the Widow Merryweather, who looked rather discomfited among the diminutive tannery workers. Ariela Soliandrus hovered nearby, trying to keep a discreet distance between herself and the dwarf-dwarves while still remaining close enough to the ear of the widow. Vestia kept smiling at Jarod and waving her gloved fingers in his direction. Standing behind her was Percival Taylor, whose carefully affected steely gaze and menacing frown were also fixed on him.

Jarod pulled at his tight collar and thought how ridiculous a spectacle he must look in his uniform.

The fervor of the town regarding its defense against the rumored impending dragon attack had quickly carried down to include the ladies of the town. The ladies of Cobblestone Street reacted quickly and decisively: several committees were formed and bandages were rolled out of old bedding as quickly as possible in order to tend the inevitable horrible casualties of the coming conflict. The saying even got about that they might be cooked and eaten in their beds—the first change in horrible fates among the Cobblestone ladies in years.

Among those carried away in the fervor was Winifred Taylor, who, upon hearing of Jarod's appointment as Captain of the Muster of the Dragonwatch, decided that her best contribution to the effort would be a proper uniform for its commander. She felt that such a position would require a gloriously dignified ensemble so as to command the respect and attention of his subordinates in the Muster. She enlisted an equally enthusiastic Merinda Oakman to construct an equally impressive and matching hat.

The result was an outrageous red tunic embroidered in yellow with matching hose. Over this was fitted a black jacket closed in the front with yellow toggles and cords. Then, knowing the long, uncomfortable hours the Captain would have to spend out of doors, all of this was topped by a thick woolen grey watch coat and a red-lined cape that almost covered up the epaulet boards on both shoulders— each ornately decorated with small dragon tapestries. The entire affair was extraordinarily hot even at night and caused Jarod to break into a sweat whenever he wore it. The hat, unfortunately, was the worst part, for it sported a metallic band around the plush red velvet of the beret with small ornamental dragon wings fixed to both sides. Merinda had, no doubt, gotten them forged at Beulandreus's shop, and Jarod could only imagine the hours of amusement that had given—and probably was *still* giving—the dwarf. All this was topped off by an old sword Aren had given him that was too long and too heavy for him to wear without having to constantly pull up his belt.

Jarod was suddenly aware that the crowd was moving. Each person had a handful of grain, and they were positioning themselves outside the southern end of the church. With the crowds thinning before the altar, Jarod moved quickly forward.

"Caprice?" he called to her. "Please, wait."

Caprice stopped, turned, and spoke to him in a brusque voice. "What is it, Jarod . . . what do you want?"

*You,* he thought at once.

"I need to talk to you . . ."

"I've no time now," she said. "I've got to go."

"Later, then," he said, reaching for her arm.

She pulled away from him. "It is a busy day, Jarod. I've a great deal to do . . ."

"Tonight, then," he asked quickly. "I'm on the Dragonwatch . . . I'll be in Charter Square manning the ballista there. Please, Caprice, it's important."

"If I can," she replied as she walked toward the front of the church. The wind was picking up, blowing through the columns. "No promises, Jarod."

"Please . . . if you can . . ."

Everyone afterward remembered the terrible wind that shook the trees, windows, and rooftops of the town that night, and all agreed that it must have been from the beating of the wings of the dragon Khrag as he flew over the town. That the wind had started earlier in the evening with the gathering of the clouds made some people comment that the dragon must have had magical powers over the weather as well.

The exact sequence of events was long debated after the fact, but of its terrible consequences, no one was in doubt.

Jarod leaned against the ballista near the center of Charter Square, his arms folded across his chest. There was a damp chill in the air that somehow was made only worse by the wind whipping at his watch coat. Percival Taylor and Constable Lamplighter—no longer Pro Tempore after his official appointment as town constable—were both manning the ballista across the bridge in Trader's Square. Damper Muffe, at his father's insistence, had joined Jarod along with Jep Walters at the Charter Square ballista. It was the second hour of their watch, and the valiant Muster were talked out and well settled into their places, huddled against the cold.

Jarod again considered the Cursed Sundial, as he had done for many nights of the watch. It stood near the enormous weapon, a dark shape in the cold, oppressive night, and had become a symbol to him of the terrible times in which he found himself.

*If only I had been born in a time when the wishes weren't broken,* he thought to himself again. *If only there were no curse and I could have the wish of my heart. If only . . .*

"Did you hear something?" Jep asked, suddenly awake.

"No, I don't think . . ."

A loud banging sound came from across the river.

"That sounded like it was—"

"Yes, behind Bolly's Mill!" Jarod said, walking around to the front of the ballista, peering into the darkness. The siege weapon in Charter Square was situated east of the Cursed Sundial and aimed across the river toward the west in the general direction of Trader's Square, while its opposite across the river was aimed more in their direction toward the east. Jarod thought this arrangement would allow them to protect each other when the dragon attacked. "There's that old barn back there, but I don't think anyone's used it since—"

"*By the Lady of the Sky!*" Jep shouted in the first proximity of a religious utterance Jarod had ever heard from the man. "*Look!*"

Rising up over the mill across the river was the enormous shape of a dragon. Its fixed wings rippled in the strong wind as it rose majestically skyward, its long tail curling and writhing.

"Khrag!" Damper shouted and bolted at once east down King's Road toward his home off Hammer Court. No one later blamed him for abandoning his post in the face of the flying terror, and it was agreed afterward that his noble desire had been to warn the village. His shrill, panic-filled voice certainly woke up anyone who had been sleeping between Charter Square and the east side of town. "Mom! It's Khrag! It's the dragon! The DRAGON!!! Mama!"

"Captain!" Jep Walters shouted at Jarod, his eyes wide. "What do we *do?*"

Jarod stood frozen for a moment, the world slowing around him while he seemed unable to move.

Across the river in Trader's Square, he could hear the shouts and cries of Percival and Xander as they tried desperately to prepare the weapon to fire. More than anything, the ballista resembled a gigantic crossbow capable of throwing oversized bolts with tremendous force through the air. This required that Xander and Percival crank back the launching cable, bending the bow and then inserting the bolt into the slot.

The dragon pitched to the left with a rushing sound in the wind, its tail smacking against the roof of the Guild Hall. It suddenly righted itself and soared straight up before stopping, seeming to hang in the sky.

Jep was working the arming crank of the ballista behind Jarod with a fury. "Jarod! We haven't any time! We've got to kill the beast before it eats us all in our beds!"

"Wait a minute," Jarod said. "There's something wrong with that dragon."

Jarod caught a glimpse of a black cable in the air above the river. It ran from the heavy bushes and trees of Boar's Island just where the Wanderwine River split in two and up across the river directly to where the dragon was now pitching to the right and then soaring up into the sky again.

Jarod rolled his eyes. He was not sure which of his friends was behind this latest nonsense, but he had a pretty good idea. He stepped back to the ballista and began calmly to help crank back the cable and bow. "All right, Master Walters, let's kill this terrible dragon."

"I've set the bolt!" the cooper shouted back. "Shouldn't we light it on fire?"

Jarod's original plan had included flaming bolts, but now that seemed like not nearly as good an idea as it had before. A glance across the river confirmed his suspicions, as Percival and Xander had not only managed to light their bolt on fire but somehow the entire oil-soaked ballista had been most cooperative in catching fire as well. Percival and Xander could be seen silhouetted against the small bonfire opposite the river, dancing about the flames and un-sure as to how to extinguish the blaze. If anything, the light from the fire was giving dramatic illumination to the gigantic dragon rushing back and forth above the mill.

"I think perhaps we won't need to light the flaming bolt," Jarod said to Jep Walters. "Let's just shoot the dragon and be done with it."

Jarod calmly stepped back and, with both hands, shifted the ballista's base so that it would fire over the mill.

Caprice Morgan came around the corner of the Griffon's Tale Inn and screamed. She ran at once across the square to Jarod's side.

"Jarod!" she cried with panic and fear in her voice, "what are you going to do!"

The Captain of the Muster shrugged in disgust as he adjusted the aim of the ballista to center it better above the mill. "I guess I'll just have to kill a dragon."

Caprice grabbed Jarod's arm.

She pleaded, *"Which one?"*

Khrag had come out of his lair for the first time in uncounted years and was, for a time, lost. It was partly the fault of the weather, which had obscured the ground beneath him, and it was partly the fault of the Dragon's Bard, whose directions were simply not that good. But he had felt like it was time to feel the open sky again, and terrorizing a village always satisfied his ego. He was a carnivore, but his tastes ran more in the direction of mutton and cattle. Still, it was always good to keep up appearances and instill a healthy panic in those who lived upon what he considered to be his land.

The real problem, however, was that his eyesight simply was not nearly as good as he thought it was.

So, having finally found the Wanderwine River and followed it up its course more by smell than by sight, the ancient dragon Khrag, who loved stories more than anything else, found himself unwittingly in the center of a tale being forged. He circled the east edge of the town, and as he was approaching the central courtyard he thought he saw something that was a personal affront to his honor and his pride.

Another dragon was terrorizing his village.

*That* he could not permit.

The wings of Khrag were so wide that their tips disappeared behind the gables of the Griffon's Tale Inn and stretched all the way past the cooperage. With a terrible cry, the ancient dragon reached downward with its hind talons, gripping the roof of Harv and Merinda's shop for its perch. It craned its long neck skyward, trumpeting its challenge. The tail flicked and slammed into King's Road, shattering the cobblestones and gouging a deep gash across the street.

Jarod turned, appalled. "Jep! Help me turn this around! Now!"

The dragon craned its neck down, eyeing the dragon across the way. Its angry roar shook the square as its head bobbed, following every motion of its false counterpart flying back and forth above the mill.

Jarod was terrified! The ballista that had once seemed so powerful now looked small and insignificant before the frightening enormity of the dragon rising above him in the square. He could turn the weapon, but even if he managed to fire it and hit the monstrous creature, he was sure he could only wound it at best, calling attention to himself away from the dragon-kite that seemed to hold the dragon's fascination . . .

Out of Jarod's panic rose a desperate idea.

"Caprice!" he shouted. "Get away from here! Run!"

"Come with me!" she called, but Jarod was already running toward the bridge, pulling Aren's sword from its scabbard.

Jarod saw where the blackened rope hung low across the river, crossing the low wall around Trader's Square. Without thinking, he jumped up onto the wall and then leaped for the cable, grasping it with his free hand and wrapping his legs around it. Only one thought screamed in his mind: if the dragon-kite flew away . . . maybe the real dragon would follow it. He started desperately sawing on the cable with the blade of the sword, its edge surprisingly keen as the cords began to separate and unravel.

Jarod glanced back across the bridge. The dragon took a step into the square, its gigantic claw slamming down close to the ballista. Jep Walters was fumbling in his pockets, pulling out his ancient and never-fired wand.

Caprice was trying to hide behind the ballista, the dragon's head stretching toward the mill over her.

"Caprice!" Jarod shouted. "Run!"

The dragon drew in a great breath.

The cable separated.

Jarod crashed down on his side near the west end of the bridge.

An enormous spout of flame surged from the dragon's mouth, roaring overhead with a terrible heat. But the false dragon, cut from its mooring, suddenly shifted, and the full impact of the rush of incandescent fire streamed directly into Bolly's Mill.

The flour dust within the mill exploded, mixing at once with the oil left at the ready inside its doors. The ensuing fireball lit up the night, engulfing the structure immediately in searing, raging flame.

The paper dragon, caught in the heat of the blast, rose upward, itself catching fire. Tipping forward, it rushed on its false wings directly toward the dragon in Charter Square.

Jarod got to his feet and started running across the bridge. He was too slow, he thought desperately, trying to outrun the downward rushing false dragon.

Suddenly, he felt himself leave the ground. An enormous fist had gathered up the collar of his watch coat and lifted him off the ground, rushing him across the bridge and into the square.

"I'd like my sword back now," Aren said as they galloped forward. "You go save Caprice."

The centaur tossed Jarod toward the ballista. He lost his footing in the rush, tumbled, and fell at Caprice's feet. Jep Walters was shaking, gripping his wand, and trying to point it toward the dragon directly overhead.

Jarod looked up. The flaming dragon-kite was rushing directly toward them from over the Cursed Sundial.

A new column of fire roared over their heads, catching the paper dragon and tossing it high into the air.

"Now!" Jarod yelled, grabbing Jep and Caprice by the arms and rushing toward the Griffon's Tale Inn on the north side of the square. Behind him, he felt the heat and heard the roar as the enormous kite crashed down on top of the ballista and ignited the oil sitting around it.

The mill was burning furiously on the far side of the river. Townspeople were pouring from their homes, shouting. In the best of times a single fire could threaten an entire village, and now they had roaring blazes on both sides of the town.

On both sides, Jarod thought. Both sides at once.

Tomas Melthalion stood in the open door of his inn, risking his own life as he beckoned them in his direction.

"Go to the Squire," Jarod said to Caprice, pushing both her and Jep Walters toward Tomas and his open door. "Go now!"

Jarod turned at once toward the Cursed Sundial.

He glanced to his left. Through the towering flames of his own ballista he imagined he could see Aren Bennis, sword in both hands, speaking with the dragon. The dragon's head was bent over attentively.

Jarod glanced to his right. The mill was ablaze, its flames threatening the Guild Hall and soon all the homes on Cobblestone Street.

He came to the Cursed Sundial.

The flames of the mill cast a faint shadow across the face of the sundial as though it were sunset.

The flames of the dragon-kite and the burning ballista cast their own shadow across the face of the sundial as though it were sunrise.

Jarod reached inside his watch coat, undid the top buttons on his shirt, and pulled out his amulet from Caprice.

"I wish the curse were broken," he said, pressing the amulet against the center of the sundial's face.

He waited.

There was a cracking sound.

Suddenly, the pedestal crumbled into shattered fragments of granite as a column of light rushed skyward, pierced the clouds, and then slowly faded.

The dragon trumpeted once more and then spread its great wings. The air rushing beneath its downward stroke nearly pushed Jarod to the ground, but in a moment the dragon was high above the rooftops and turning east before disappearing in the low clouds.

Jarod felt a drop fall on his cheek. Then another.

In moments, a torrential downpour engulfed the town. The sky poured out a sea of water, dampening the fires more effectively than all the buckets in Eventide could have ever hoped to achieve. The townspeople still had to deal with the oil fires, but those were far more manageable than the general conflagration they had been faced with minutes before. Bolly's Mill was a complete loss and was going to burn for some time, but the men in the village were already working to contain that blaze, and the kite fire was already nearly out.

Caprice Morgan rushed out of the inn. Her beautiful auburn hair was soaked at once as she ran across the flooding square toward where Jarod stood. She gazed in wonder at the shattered sundial, then, with a smile, turned toward the wrecked wood and canvas dragon smoldering behind him.

"I guess now they'll call you Jarod the Dragon Slayer?" Caprice said lightly.

"More likely Jarod the Mill Slayer," he sighed. He took off his watch coat and put it around her shoulders. "I don't suppose there's much call for mill slaying, is there?"

"I've had a call for one," Caprice said. "It took a Mill Slayer to break the curse. Now that you've fixed my wishes, I suppose your bill will be terribly expensive, won't it?"

"You'd be surprised at what I work for," Jarod smiled at her.

The clomping sound of Aren Bennis was approaching. Jarod turned, "Aren, whose idea was it to . . . Aren? Are you all right?"

The centaur had a pained look on his face as he spoke. "Khrag was just a little confused, is all. I knew him from . . . when was that? I can't seem to . . ."

The centaur's sword fell, clanging loudly to the ground. Aren grabbed his left arm, wincing with pain.

"Aren?" Jarod stepped toward the centaur.

Farmer Bennis dropped down to his front knees. "You're a good lad, Jarod. Don't waste a minute . . . not a single minute . . ."

Aren fell heavily on his side, his face a mask of peaceful sleep.

Jarod fell to his knees next to his fallen friend, trying desperately to rouse him, but Aren never awoke again.

The old centaur was gone.

The torrential rains wept around Jarod.

The young man had no more wishes left.

## · CHAPTER 22 ·

# The Wake

Farmer Bennis had lived a quiet life on his farm north of Eventide. There were those who knew that the elderly centaur had fought in the Epic War many years ago, but none of them knew anything of his service—whether he had been present at any of the mythic battles whose songs everyone knew or if he had had occasion to see any of the heroes of that age. He was just a farmer who had seen some service, a good neighbor and a quiet, gentle soul.

No one ever made much fuss about a funeral for a farmer. Dying in Eventide was as much a part of their lives as the seasons. After some debate, they brought his massive body to Beulandreus Dudgeon, who was beside himself with grief. Nevertheless, the smith built a sound iron frame for the centaur's coffin and called on Harv Oakman to come carve the wooden panels that were to fit it on every side. Beulandreus offered Harv any amount for his best work, but the carpenter refused any pay, crafting the ornate carvings specifically to the rather astonishing details directed by the dwarf. It was an extraordinarily long coffin as such things go, designed by the dwarven smith to allow the centaur's body to be laid out at length, his torso leaning forward, his arms under his head, laid facing to the right as though he were asleep after the manner of the centaurs. Then his sword was set in the coffin next to him and his buckler, retrieved from his home, laid across his back.

With the centaur seemingly at rest, the coffin lid was set into place and Beulandreus himself secured it, tears streaming from his eyes the whole time. It took sixteen men to lift the funeral box and carry it to the Pantheon Church. There they set him in front of the altar, the coffin's bulk too large to properly set on the altar itself. Thus they left Father Patrion to determine to which of the gods they should commend his soul and the proper manner of his burial—the prospect of interring the plough-horse-sized farmer leaving the priest at a complete loss.

In all the concern of the town over the burned mill and the raid by no fewer than two dragons at the same time, no one noticed Ward Klum speaking quietly to Meryl Morgan, who left at once on horseback with a message to Mordale.

However, everyone quickly learned of the reply.

The greatest heroes of the age—the very men and women of legend who had fought in the Epic War and saved all the land from terrible darkness—all began to arrive in the village. Princess Aerthia took several rooms for herself and her ladies. Teron, hero of the Mordale Siege, and his companion Karmados, the warrior-dwarf, both arrived, along with their families. Each of them quietly took lodgings in the inn. However, when Lord Pompeanus arrived at the inn door with an entire cadre of his knights—all in their finest livery—the Squire himself inexplicably disappeared, leaving his wife, Daphne, to deal with the unexpected and impossibly honorable lodgers.

Each of them had answered the call—because a centaur farmer had died in Eventide.

Jarod stood as close as he could come to the Pantheon Church. His father and his mother stood with him at his side.

The mourners overflowed the church, packed shoulder to shoulder down the steps and out onto the green. It was a sea of people, the likes of which had never been seen in Eventide. Ranks of centaurs stood on either side of the coffin, kneeling down on one fore-knee with their heads bowed in honor. Lord Pompeanus's knights stood at attention in their ceremonial armor. Lords and ladies, heroes of legend, and, arriving earlier that same morning, King Reinard and Queen Nance themselves. The Queen wept quietly before the coffin as King Reinard knelt before it, stretched out his hand to rest upon it, and bowed his head.

The Dragon's Bard and his scribe pushed their way carefully through the crowd until they stood next to Jarod. Edvard took off his ornate, impossible hat and gripped it with one hand as he folded his arms and considered the scene.

"Why, Father?" Jarod asked quietly, afraid to disturb the respectful quiet. "Why have they come?"

"I can tell you," the Dragon's Bard sighed, more thoughtful than anyone, even his scribe, had ever seen him before.

"Then tell me," Jarod said.

"It's a very old story—one that I could not tell before now," the Bard continued softly. "It was a story *he* never told and preferred that others not tell either."

The Bard looked up into the late autumn sun and paused, considering.

"Go on," Jarod urged.

"During the Epic War there was a dark time when the king— then but a prince—was a young and inexperienced commander," Edvard began, though his telling of the tale was now, for the first time, simple and unembellished by his typical histrionics. "He led the armies of the Eastern Glory against Urchik and the Shadow-soul Thieves."

"Everyone knows that story," Jarod said, turning back to contemplate the farmer's demise.

"Do you?" Ward Klum asked.

Jarod turned an astonished look toward his father.

"It's a good story," his father said. "You should listen to the Bard."

"The prince was surrounded, captured, and imprisoned in the mountain fortress of Urchik, who had vowed to torture the prince to death for the wrongs his father had supposedly done to Urchik's followers. Lord Pompeanus vowed to lay siege to Urchik's fortress, but Teron and Karmados argued for a rescue instead—a rescue that would have failed if a common centaur warrior had not volunteered to go with them."

"Yes, I know this one, too," Jarod nodded. "Bentarius Magnus, who charged the gates of Urchik Keep and held it against the hordes of the Soul-thieves until Teron freed the prince and—"

Jarod froze in shocked realization.

"But . . ." Jarod stammered. "He was a farmer!"

"He was many things," the Dragon's Bard said, considering the multitude that overwhelmed the green around the church.

"But you must be mistaken," Jarod said. "Bentarius Magnus

was rewarded with vast treasures by the king! And he had a companion—a knight errant who was with him at those gates who was driven mad by Urchik's visions-horde and whom the centaur warrior refused to leave behind. Bentarius vowed never to be parted from him."

"Interesting calling to be a knight errant," the Dragon's Bard smiled. "How they *gallivant* around the countryside and all."

"He was rich," Ward Klum interjected.

Jarod turned back to his father. "He was? You *knew* who he was?"

"Yes, Son, I knew," Ward said. "Both Meryl Morgan and I knew, though Meryl would never speak of it. You see, Master Bard, there is more to the story than even you know."

The Bard frowned. "No, I think I've got the complete epic—"

"It's not always about the epic," Ward smiled a gentle smile. "Many years ago there was a young centaur who was in love with a beautiful centaur filly. But he was a poor and unaccomplished farmer and he didn't feel he had enough to offer her. So he took up the king's call and joined his army for the Epic War. But the war was long—far longer than anyone feared in their darkest nightmares. And while this young centaur grew older on the endless fields of battle, his beloved filly fell in love with someone else—a handsome young human man."

Ward turned to look Jarod in the eye. "And because this filly centaur happened to be a wish-woman of the well, she made a great wish—perhaps too great a wish—and forsook her centaur form to become a woman. All she kept was her name—Brenna."

"No," Jarod breathed.

Ward nodded. "By the time Aren returned, the woman he had left to impress was no longer waiting for him—in fact, had changed completely. All the riches he had acquired, all the praise and the stories and the legends became as worthless as dust. He went back to his farm and lived his life as best he could. He never loved another—but he helped others quietly and without their knowledge when he could. He kept his wealth a secret. His life was his treasure—how he lived it and what he did with it."

"I never knew what he was trying to tell me," Jarod said, letting out a long breath. "I never understood."

"Abel!" Edvard said in a stage whisper behind his hand. "Did you get all that?"

The scribe poked the Bard with his stylus.

Jarod turned suddenly and started pushing his way out of the throng.

"Jarod!" his father called in an urgent, low voice. "Where are you going?"

"To assemble a treasure!" Jarod replied as quietly as he could and then disappeared in the sea of people.

"So *now* he knows where to find one," the Bard sniffed. "Which reminds me, what ever happened to the farmer's treasures, Master Klum?"

Ward adjusted his hat more squarely on his head. "He left them to the town, Master Bard."

"Ah, so I suppose the mill will be rebuilt after all," Edvard observed in flat tones. "I don't suppose he mentioned me in his will at all, did he?"

The sun was setting beyond the trees of the Norest Forest. The autumn sky was brilliant with orange and salmon hues as the spent storm clouds gave way to brighter skies. They cast a rosy glow down on the glade atop a small rise and the figure of Caprice Morgan as she made her way from Wishing Lane up the ancient path toward the well.

"Caprice! Please, wait!"

The young woman stopped and turned to see Jarod Klum running up the path behind her. He had somehow lost his awkward gait. There was something about him that was sure and, to the eye of the young woman, straighter than he had been before.

"Master Klum, it is getting late," Caprice said.

"But not too late," Jarod answered, slightly out of breath. "May I accompany you to the well?"

She smiled slightly and nodded. He fell into step beside her as they walked side by side silently up the path. As the wishing well came into view, Jarod, too, smiled.

The wishing well was magnificent in the deepening sunset. The wooden latticework was completely healed, its white finish now a shiny polish glistening beneath the brilliant sky. The stones about the well were clean. The well itself emanated a cheerful, amber glow. All round the now restored gazebo that sheltered the well, a wide circle of grass had awakened and become green again while flowers were budding and blooming all around the base of the well.

"It's miraculous!" Jarod breathed as they approached the well.

"That's the way it is supposed to be with wishes," Caprice said, stepping up to the well. "A perpetual spring even in the depths of winter."

"Really?" Jarod said, stepping into the gazebo to join her next to the well. "So how is it supposed to work?"

"It's simple enough," Caprice said, leaning against the low wall surrounding the well itself. The glow from the well shone in her auburn hair, giving it a wondrous radiance. "You put something of value in the metal box over there—giving up something to the wishes in the well—and then come over here and make your wish. The more you put into the box, the more the wishes in the well will give you back."

Jarod nodded. "I've been thinking about what to put in a box for quite some time. And I've finally brought it—the right gift for you."

"A gift?" Caprice asked skeptically.

"A treasure," Jarod corrected.

He handed her the marvelous Treasure Box.

"It's beautiful," Caprice said, turning the small box in her hands and examining it closely.

"I've been searching all year for something to put in it for you," Jarod said, his eyes shining in the fading light. "I first thought of a hat . . ."

"Don't mention hats," Caprice said with a warning smile.

"I thought maybe gold or status or reputation might be good enough . . ."

"How were you going to put a reputation in a box?" Caprice chided.

"I wanted to find something . . . *something* I could bring to you," he said. "And I think today I finally found it. Open it!"

She laughed. "I don't know how! Show me?"

"Press the diamond shapes on either side," he said.

Caprice pressed the sides of the box. Its sides unfolded in her hands, growing larger as she held it. It unfolded again . . . then again . . . and again . . .

Caprice set down the box quickly in the greening grass at the side of the wishing well and stepped back.

It stopped when it reached the size of a large traveling trunk.

Caprice waited a moment, the evening breeze rustling the tall grasses and bringing a scent of violets around them.

"Now what?"

"Now we open it," Jarod said.

Together they lifted the lid of the trunk and peered inside.

The inside of the Treasure Box was larger than the outside. Within she saw the interior of a one-room cottage. A fireplace stood to one side with a pair of chairs next to it. There were two more chairs up against a small, clean table. A bed stood pushed against one corner. Cupboards and a few chests completed the room.

"This is my life," Jarod said to her in a quiet voice. "That's what I put in the box, and I'm giving it to you. It's all I have—all that I am—and it's yours if you'll take it."

Caprice smiled wistfully as she looked in the box. "It's not enough."

"It's not?"

"No," she said turning toward him and putting her arms around his neck. "Not until I put my life in it, too."

Caprice and Jarod continued down Wishing Lane hand in hand. The sky had deepened in color with the coming night. As they crested the hill, Jarod could see the unfinished mansion of the Morgan household below. Lucius Tanner was sawing some timbers. The once-abandoned work to complete the house was begun anew and, with the well no longer cursed, the future of the Morgans looked bright once more.

Caprice tugged at Jarod's hand, leading him toward the bright and warm light of the kitchen door, where her father was no doubt waiting for them both.

Within the county of Windriftshire, north and east from the Blackshore anchorage and up the northern road two leagues beyond where the Butterfield road branches off to the east, is the village of Eventide. You know the village well . . . for you or someone you know has been in or from one of uncounted similar townships that struggle everywhere to survive. It's a quiet place that people often come from but seldom are going to. The villagers there are stronger, kinder, happier, and gentler than those of more recent acquaintance—a place that grows in its longing proportionate to its distance in memory. The greatest heroes of legend always come from Eventide or places so similar as to be interchangeable in any tale of our age, though these same heroes seldom return to these humble, quiet places that they claim as the home of their origin.

Eventide lies on both sides of the Wanderwine River, the main waterway through Windriftshire County and, as such, an ancient trade route between the sea and the plains cities to the north. Here the Wanderwine splits into the West Wanderwine and the East Wanderwine Rivers; the West Wanderwine is six feet longer than the East Wanderwine, as measured twice by Jep Walters after losing a bet with Squire Tomas Melthalion. The river runs exactly one thousand forty-four feet and five or seven inches from the tip of Prow Rock where the river splits to the end of the sand spit at the river's confluence just south of the newly renamed Dwarf-dwarf Tannery. The rivers diverge in the north and converge in the south, surrounding a piece of land known locally as Boar's Island—although no one remembers ever seeing a boar there. It is a matter of local pride that the courses of both the West Wanderwine and the East Wanderwine lie entirely within the charter limits of their town.

Eventide is also blessed to be at what everyone in the town considers to be an important crossroads of trade. Not only does it lie squarely on the route between the deep, if somewhat narrow, harbor of Blackshore and the city of Mordale to the north, but at the junction of the roads to Butterfield to the southeast, Welston to the northeast, and Meade to the west—thereby making Eventide the place where cheese, grain, and ale all meet in commerce. This happy fact led to the early establishment of the market in Trader's Square and the increased prosperity permitted the local fathers to finance the construction of the Pantheon Church—which elevated Eventide from the status of hamlet to a full village by Royal Charter.

As for the village itself, its greatest claim to fame is the wishing well that lies north of town on the eastern slopes of Mount Dervin, a grandly named hill that barely crests nine hundred and eighty feet above sea level. The wishing well of Eventide grew in fame during the years before the Epic War, bringing an increasing number of pilgrims until the tragic curse that broke the well and rendered its wishes somewhat unpredictable in their results. Since then, the broken well has been tended and kept supplied with wishes by the Fate Sisters, who live in the home—on which construction has recently been renewed—near the wishing well, where they also tend to their widowed father, Meryl Morgan. Sobrina is the eldest: stern, thin, and austere, although far less so after her marriage to Lucius Tanner—a man made wealthy by the sale of his business to dwarf-dwarves. Melodi is the youngest: forgiving, plump, and prone to giggle—and a lover of fine books as well as of those who write them.

Which, of course, leaves Caprice Morgan and Jarod Klum very much in the middle of just about everything as the dragon-slaying hero from Eventide and his princess who both brought their wishes to the well.

### Tales of the Dragon's Bard

**BOOK TWO**

# Blackshore

The Dragon's Bard travels on,
collecting more exciting stories to entertain
his followers and save his neck!

COMING SUMMER 2013